Praise for the Emily Cabot Mysteries

"McNamara has a keen eye for zeroing in on how a metropolis can fuel and deplete the human spirit."
Chicago Sun-Times

"[*Death at Pullman*] convincingly recreates a pivotal moment in American labor history…Besides plausibly depicting such historical figures as Eugene Debs and Nellie Bly, McNamara throws in some surprising twists at the end. Laurie King and Rhys Bowen fans will be delighted."
Publishers Weekly

"McNamara…proves, if anyone was asking, that librarians make great historical mystery writers…[In *Death at Woods Hole*] so accurately portrayed is that small-town-in-summer feeling, when towns are overtaken by visitors, who coexist uneasily with locals… I'd follow Emily to any location."
Historical Novels Review

In [*Death at Pullman*] a "little romance [and] a lot of labor history are artfully combined…Creating a believable mix of historical and fictional characters…is another of the author's prime strengths as a writer…[she] clearly knows, and loves, her setting."
Julie Eakin, *Foreword Reviews*

"The combination of labor unrest, rivalries among local families, and past romantic intrigues is a combustible mix, an edgy scenario that is laid out convincingly….A suspenseful recreation of a critical moment in American social history, as seen from the viewpoint of a strong-willed, engaging fictional heroine."
Reading the Past

D1447330

Also by Frances McNamara

The Emily Cabot Mysteries

Death at the Fair

Death at Hull House

Death at Pullman

Death at Woods Hole

Death at Chinatown

Death at the Paris Exposition

DEATH
at the
SELIG
STUDIOS

Frances McNamara

ALLIUM PRESS OF CHICAGO

Allium Press of Chicago
Forest Park, IL
www.alliumpress.com

This is a work of fiction. Descriptions and portrayals of real people, events, organizations, or establishments are intended to provide background for the story and are used fictitiously. Other characters and situations are drawn from the author's imagination and are not intended to be real.

Book and cover design by E. C. Victorson

Front cover image: adapted from a poster for
"The Flaming Tower" episode of the 1920 serial
The Lost City of the African Jungles starring Juanita Hansen

ISBN: 978-0-9967558-9-4

Library of Congress Cataloging-in-Publication Data

Names: McNamara, Frances, author.
Title: Death at the Selig Studios / Frances McNamara.
Description: Forest Park, IL : Allium Press of Chicago, 2018. | Series: An Emily Cabot mystery ; 7 | Includes bibliographical references.
Identifiers: LCCN 2018008154 (print) | LCCN 2018008318 (ebook) | ISBN 9780999698204 (Epub) | ISBN 9780996755894
Subjects: LCSH: Women detectives--Fiction. | Murder--Investigation--Fiction. | Selig Polyscope Company--Fiction. | Motion picture industry--History--Fiction. | Chicago (Ill.)--Fiction. | GSAFD: Mystery fiction. | Historical fiction.
Classification: LCC PS3613.C58583 (ebook) | LCC PS3613.C58583 D434 2018 (print) | DDC 813/.6--dc23
LC record available at https://lccn.loc.gov/2018008154

in memory of my brother Ned McNamara

The Selig Polyscope Studios, Chicago

One

Chicago

June 1909

I dropped two boxes onto Detective Whitbread's desk and handed him a neatly bound typescript. "Those are the last of the identity cards we were working on, and here is a compilation of the results. It includes an analysis of offenses by children who were later committed to juvenile reformatories."

"Very well. I expect you'll be off to Woods Hole now?"

"Next week." I was eager to get home to my family and complete our packing. We'd been spending our summers on Cape Cod for years, and I was yearning to taste the salt of summer breezes there. It was very hot in Chicago that June. "I hope you and your family manage to get away, too." Whitbread was married to my friend Gracie. I knew she had a hard time getting him to leave the city, he was so devoted to his work. He just nodded absentmindedly and flipped through the pages of our report.

Before I had a chance to make my way out of the detective's office, a knock came on the door. A uniformed officer stood waiting to speak.

"Sir, there's been a shooting death on the north side." He consulted the paper in his hand. "At the Selig Polyscope Company.

It's a place where they make films for the nickelodeons. A Mr. Alden Cabot was found standing over the corpse. Will you be going up there, sir?"

I gasped. Alden Cabot! That was my brother's name. Surely the police officer was mistaken. Alden was a reporter for the *Tribune*. He wouldn't have any reason to be at such a place and certainly wouldn't have killed someone. As far as I knew, he didn't even own a gun. Detective Whitbread and I looked at each other, equally shocked by the news.

"I'll handle this myself," he said, then stopped to frown at me. "Emily, I know if I don't take you with me, you'll just make your way up there yourself. Come on, let's get going. The faster we get up there, the sooner we can get this sorted out. I'll arrange for a motorcar to take us." He turned to his telephone to order transportation.

Whitbread was an earnest policeman. Some might think him pompous, but I knew he was both honest and competent. His integrity was one reason I wanted my students to work with him. Tall and skeletal, with wiry sideburns and a flourishing mustache, he spent much more time out on the streets of Chicago than in his office, where my students and I compiled statistics from boxes of identity cards collected from all over the city. Yet he had a sincere appreciation for the academic study of criminology and kept up to date on the latest theories. Time was that he would have excluded me from a murder investigation, but I had so often managed to get myself included, by hook or by crook, that he knew trying to keep me from a case involving my own brother would be hopeless.

"Alden was supposed to go to Cape Cod with you, wasn't he?" the detective asked me.

"Yes, we were all due to leave soon. But I want to go with you," I replied. In the back of my mind a little minx was pulling at me, reminding me that I was expected home. My husband, Stephen, and Alden's wife, Clara, both did research at the Marine

Biological Laboratory in Woods Hole in the summers. Every year, we all eagerly anticipated the trip, but I wouldn't be able to concentrate on that with Alden in trouble. I was more annoyed than alarmed at that point. I thought it was typical of my brother to get into some kind of a scrape just when we were all preparing to move our households to the Cape for the summer. A busy newspaper reporter, Alden was not known for being solicitous of other people. Our nursemaid, Delia, would have to manage the packing without me.

When we descended to the first floor, I discovered that we'd be transported via the coroner's van. It was disconcerting to think the same vehicle would carry the victim's body back to the morgue, but I accepted a hand from Whitbread to climb up to the high seat between him and the driver. It was a new sensation to sit above the crowds we traveled through, and we were jostled a bit as we moved through the city streets.

The throngs of people reminded me how the city had grown in the years since I'd arrived from Boston to become one of the first women graduate students in sociology at the new university. Our plan was to use the city as our laboratory. More than a decade had passed since then. The city had grown and changed, and so had I.

There were still horse-drawn carriages on the streets but more and more motorcars were taking their place. The streetcars had been electrified and there were many more women riding them, as young women came to the city for jobs. Every day, Chicago became more crowded. I usually felt invigorated by the energy of the city but, by this time of year, I was worn out. The summer was for wading in saltwater pools with my children, eating clams and lobsters, and having adventures on boats. I took a deep breath, feeling a tickle of anticipation for the cool sea breezes of Woods Hole. I was ready to get away from all this…just for a while. This business with Alden had to be a misunderstanding. I couldn't imagine any circumstance in which he'd shoot someone.

Soon, we were out of the crowded Loop and traveling to more sparsely populated areas. What could have brought my brother so far from the center of the city? Finally, we reached the corner of Western Avenue and Irving Park Boulevard where we stopped in front of a three-story building. It looked like an office building that had a greenhouse dropped on top of it. The top floor was constructed entirely of big rectangular windows. As we climbed down I saw the logo of a white diamond with a large "S" inside in stonework above the doorway. A man who stood nearby, smoking, confirmed to Whitbread that this was the Selig Polyscope Company and, when we entered, we were directed up to the third floor. Two men with a stretcher followed us.

The stairs led to an enormous open room. Despite the sunlight that streamed in through the huge windows, it was unexpectedly cool. Two beleaguered-looking uniformed police officers were trying to hold off a small crowd of men and women in the middle of the room. As I glanced around the immense space, I saw a number of completely different scenes. To the right appeared a whole street, complete with a saloon and fences and wooden walkways before the buildings. But they were only the fronts of buildings propped up with wood from behind. To the left was a parlor or drawing room, furnished with a desk, a lamp, a fireplace, and paintings on the wall. Beside it was an old-fashioned kitchen, complete with a wood stove and a large wooden table. Stores of flour and sugar, and cans of beans, were on the shelves. Beyond the crowd of people in the middle, there was a space that looked like a woman's bedroom with a four-poster bed and frilly curtains hanging from open windows. Farther away, in a corner, I could see what looked like trees and vines, with a tent set up on an area of sand made to look like a desert. There were even more scenes arranged throughout the huge space, but my attention returned to the crowd of people grouped around the bed chamber. I followed Whitbread as he elbowed his way through.

"Police, make way, please. Police."

When we got to one of the uniformed officers he seemed relieved. He and Whitbread conferred, while I looked at the spectacle on the bed. Against the gauzy white counterpane, a small man lay back, eyes staring upward. I noticed his shoes were shined and his gray pants had a sharp crease. He wore a crisp white shirt with a well-starched collar under a black top coat. A gold watch chain was draped across the waistcoat on his plump little stomach, and small gold cuff links could be seen in his stiff white cuffs. He had a square face with jowls, clean shaven except for sharply cut sideburns, and his thin black hair was neatly parted in the middle and slicked down. He looked like a very unpretentious little man who'd gotten dressed up in his finest clothes. There was no expression of panic or fear on his face. He looked quite peaceful...except for the ugly hole in his forehead. He'd fallen onto his back and blood dripped down the sides of his head. It was a large, black, crusty hole. His hands were inexplicably folded in his lap, with one wrapped around a tiny little gun with a pearl handle. I forced myself to look at his face again, trying to ignore the gore. I thought he looked mildly surprised.

He certainly didn't belong in that frilly bedroom. It was a stomach-churning sight, that man lying dead on the white gauze with the pink roses of the wallpaper and the lacy flounces of the window curtains surrounding him. While Detective Whitbread continued to examine the body, I turned to the left and saw my brother seated in a cushioned wing chair that seemed to have been dragged over from some other set. His hands were in metal cuffs.

"It's all a mistake," Alden said. "I didn't shoot him. He shot himself, can't you see?" Alden was an attractive man, with curly dark hair and vivid blue eyes. He was unconscious of his good looks and had an easy manner that captivated people as soon as they met him. His instinct for reaching out to touch something in people as soon as they met had served him well in his profession.

"Alden, what is this about? Are you working on a story? I thought you'd already started your leave from work." Despite the charm that worked on everyone else, I always had difficulty understanding my brother. Now that he was a fully grown man, a newspaper reporter, father of two, and husband of my best friend, I expected him to be responsible. That was my mistake. Seeing him sitting there with narrowed eyes and wrinkled forehead, his slight build still boyish, I could tell he was going to turn this around to make it seem like I was in the wrong somehow. He always did that to me and it was annoying.

"I'm working on something, but that's irrelevant. They're holding me because I was here when we found the man who was shot. They're saying I did it, but they're wrong. He shot himself. I could tell by the way I found him. He was lying on the bed with the gun in his hand. They've stopped all the work and they won't listen to anybody. The man killed himself, that's all there is to it." He started to rise, then fell back when a uniformed officer stepped toward him. Looking over at Whitbread, he called to him. "Detective Whitbread, it's a mistake. You've got to let us get back to work or it'll ruin the shooting schedule."

"The shooting *schedule*?" I was horrified. "You mean, in addition to the death of this man, they plan more shooting? Alden, what have you gotten yourself into?"

"No, no, no. Honestly, Emily, for someone who's a lecturer at a university you're so ignorant sometimes. This is a studio where they film motion pictures…we shoot *film*…you see?" He looked at my blank face and clenched his fists, raising his eyes as if imploring heaven to keep him from expiring at my stupidity. "Moving pictures, like they show at a nickelodeon. You're such a snob, Emily."

Of course, I'd heard of nickelodeons. I'd seen a moving picture shown as part of a lecture by Professor Frederick Starr about his journey to the Congo, but I had no idea they created such things here in Chicago. Nickelodeons were patronized by working people. They showed mindless comedies about clowns slipping and falling, or melodramas about young women being oppressed by bad men. Simplistic and extremely short, with no words, only popular music in the background, they were not considered theater. They were more like the dubious vaudeville shows that attracted working-class families to spend their hard-earned money. As an entertainment, they were better than saloons, but not by much.

Whitbread joined me, facing Alden. He looked around, then shook his head. "This place is a madhouse."

"No, it's not," Alden said. "It's a motion picture studio. This is where we film the interior scenes. We do some exterior shots in here as well. And we do others out there." He gestured to the view through the windows. I could see a large plot of land with a sort of lake in the middle and a few buildings and even streets laid out. In another area, a tangle of bushes might have been a jungle. "It's one of the largest and most important studios in the country."

"We?" I asked. "What do you mean by 'we'? Are you involved in this? Aren't you here as a reporter?"

"Yes, Mr. Cabot, what *is* the nature of your relationship to this establishment?" Whitbread asked, waving a hand to indicate the expanse of the enterprise.

A portly man with a flourishing mustache turned from a nearby conversation and took a few steps toward us. "Mr. Cabot writes scenarios for our local producers, Mr. Otis Turner and Mr. Arnold Leeder," he contributed, pointing to two men who were consulting with cameramen at the other end of the studio.

"This is Col. Selig, the owner of the Selig Polyscope Company," Alden said. "Colonel, this is Detective Whitbread and my sister, Mrs. Chapman."

"Pleased to meet you." The colonel made a gracious bow. He wore a gray wool suit and vest with a small red bowtie. He looked like he ought to be jolly all the time, not like someone who'd just viewed a corpse. It was as if he had to work to maintain a serious composure that was unnatural to him.

So, this was Col. Selig. But that still didn't explain what Alden was doing here. "Alden, what does this mean? You're not here as a reporter for the *Tribune*?"

My brother frowned and I could see a hint of red on the edges of his face. "Emily, I'll explain all that later. Right now, you need to help me convince the police I had nothing to do with this, then we need to get the studio back on track. I know it's a terrible thing that's happened, but it has nothing to do with us...with the studio. I have no idea why he came here to kill himself. You don't understand the pressure. There are three films that need to be shooting right here...in this space."

A dead man lay not twenty feet from us, but Alden was only concerned with getting rid of the police. I was confused. I'd expected him to be working on a newspaper story with a deadline but, apparently, that was not the case. I knew his experiences had made him somewhat callous in the face of tragedy, but this seemed excessive. Especially if he wasn't even here as a reporter.

"Yes, Detective Whitbread, we would be most grateful if you could allow us to resume," Col. Selig said. "We're all very sorry for this most tragic occurrence, I assure you." He turned back toward the bedroom, biting his lip. "We're terribly shocked this could happen here. But you must understand that few of these people knew Mr. Hyde, and they're all very anxious to resume their work. We're committed to releasing three films per week from this studio and an additional two from our California studio. The film exchanges are expecting those stories, you see. Today is Wednesday and we have a lot of work to do to get those films completed, processed, and in their cans for distribution by this time next week."

Whitbread put his hands on his hips. "Now, look here, a man's been shot. A murder investigation takes precedence. I don't care how many films you've promised to release, a man is dead." He turned to my brother. "Mr. Cabot, tell me what you saw."

I glared at Alden as if that would force him to be truthful. It had worked when he was a child.

With a big sigh, my brother told his story. "I came in this morning to make sure all the props were set up for this scene. It's one I wrote. Kathlyn Williams plays Missy Snow, and yesterday she caught her foot on a corner of the rug so I wanted to make sure it was fixed before the start of shooting this morning. That's when I found him, lying on the bed, with the gun in his hand. At first I thought it was Charles Clooney, who plays the evil St. John, rehearsing or something. But when he didn't answer me, I realized it was a dead man. When I saw it was Mr. Hyde, I was shocked."

"And how did you know this Mr. Hyde?"

Alden glanced at Col. Selig. "He's a censor, with the Chicago Film Board."

"Mr. Cabot, according to my officers, Mr. Leeder over there said he saw you place the gun in the hand of the dead man," Whitbread said.

"Oh, surely not," Col. Selig protested.

"He's mistaken," Alden said. "I was just bending over Hyde when Leeder came in. He misinterpreted what he saw, that's all."

I stared at my brother. No wonder he was in handcuffs. Someone claimed to have seen him putting the gun in the hand of the dead man. Why would anyone say that? What had Alden done? He was denying it, but I didn't trust him. I shocked myself with my doubt. How had it gotten to the point that I could believe he would lie about something like this? My own brother. But I could, and I wondered what he was up to. At that moment, there was a commotion at the door.

"Good lord, not him," Whitbread muttered.

I looked across and saw a tall, stout man with a florid face waving away a uniformed policeman at the door, and I recognized Mr. Peter Francis Fitzgibbons. Fitz, my sometime friend and the irrepressible political operative, had arrived.

Two

Fitzgibbons was framed in the doorway, where he'd stopped to catch his breath after the climb. Tall and broad shouldered, his girth was beginning to reflect the food from the wakes and weddings he tirelessly attended in whichever ward he needed votes. Middle aged now, there were streaks of white in his muttonchops, mustache, and the reddish hair that brushed his collar. His hazel eyes were slightly rheumy under the rim of his bowler hat. As always, he wore a three-piece woolen suit and an open overcoat, despite the warmth. His big hands were planted in his pants pockets and he rocked a bit on his heels as he took a measure of the room before entering.

When he saw me, he perked up and strode over. "Mrs. Chapman, how delightful to see you here." He gave me a spiffy bow, then he turned to the others. "Colonel, good to see you. We hear there's been a terrible accident and the mayor now, he sent me over to be sure it's all taken care of. I see you're in the best of hands with Whitey here." He started to swing an arm to clap Detective Whitbread on the back but thought better of it when he saw the look on Whitbread's face. "Now, what can I do to help?" Fitz spoke with a mild brogue, although I knew for certain he'd been born in the city.

I nodded stiffly in response to his recognition of me. His arrival only made the situation more complicated, as far as I was concerned. "Mr. Fitzgibbons, I see you're still employed by our reprehensible mayor," I said. Not polite but, really, the current mayor was a disgrace. He let the saloons, gambling hells, and houses of ill repute operate openly. For as long as I'd known Fitz, he'd been a political operative who bent with the winds of political change, barely surviving one regime or administration so he could creep back in at the edges of the next. I would be forever grateful to him for rescuing my young son during a harrowing adventure in Chinatown some years earlier, but I was completely disgusted by his current affiliation. I'd been avoiding him as a result. Finally meeting here, he looked shocked at my vehemence, and I saw a flush of color seeping over his pale, freckled face.

"Cut it out, Emily," Alden said. "Just because you and your Hull House cronies lost another election, that's no reason to insult Fitz." Then he turned to the big Irishman. "Besides, as it happens, Mayor Busse's wife also writes scenarios for Col. Selig. So, you see, not everyone's a snob like you."

I wasn't even aware that our scandalous mayor had gotten married, although I could see why he would keep that a secret since he had given a brothel in the Levee district as his voting address.

"Yes, yes." Fitz had regained his jocular composure. "Mrs. Busse is a noted contributor to the films here." He nodded at Col. Selig, who was smiling benevolently. No doubt he contributed money to the mayor's campaign chest.

"We would be working on one of Mrs. Busse's scenarios right now if we weren't prevented from resuming. Detective Whitbread, can you predict when we'll be able to get back to work?" Col. Selig asked politely.

I could see Whitbread simmering up for an explosion. There was no chance he was going to allow them to ignore a death in their midst in order to continue making their films. Having known him a long time, I could tell that he was outraged by the callous attitude of the film people.

Before Whitbread could reply, Fitz chimed in with, "Whitey, you're to check in with your captain before this goes any further."

I wasn't surprised. If City Hall had sent Fitz, it was likely that they would also have called Whitbread's superiors to insist he cooperate. That was how "pull" worked in the city. Col. Selig quickly led Whitbread away to use the telephone in his office on the floor below.

"Is it true it's Mr. Hyde who's the victim of this regrettable accident?" Fitz asked. "He's a censor for the film board and a cousin to Mrs. Busse. When the mayor heard, he wanted to be sure everything's done to explain this sorry happening." He shook his leonine head.

Explain it away, more likely, I thought. I had an uneasy feeling that was Fitz's real task here and I didn't like it that Whitbread was called away as soon as the politician arrived. Was this interference from City Hall?

"I assume Mr. Hyde was here to review some films?" Fitz asked, with a glance at me. "Is it perhaps possible he was inspecting one of the scenes and unwittingly fired a gun he thought was a prop?"

"Oh, really," I said. Fitz was already manufacturing a story to smooth things over. Clearly, he wanted people to think the man had been shot by accident. Of course, that was also exactly what Alden wanted people to believe. If the man had shot himself—on purpose, or not—my brother would not be arrested. But I knew Whitbread. If he thought it was murder, it probably was, and Alden was found with the man *and* the gun. What had he done? Not murder, surely.

"No, the censors don't normally come here to the studio." The man who spoke was Mr. Leeder, the producer who'd seen Alden bending over the body. He'd been standing at the outskirts of our group for a few minutes. He was thin with a very thick thatch of curly brown hair. His shirtsleeves were rolled up to his elbows and he was smoking a cigarette he swung wildly as he talked. "Selig has a room for the censors in the office downtown on Randolph. Hyde was there yesterday, looking at the films we made last week, but he rushed out before they were finished." He pulled the fingers of his left hand through his thick curls. "And then we found him here this morning...dead. I saw Cabot there putting the gun in his hand when I came in."

"That's not true," Alden said. Ignoring the officer guarding him, he rose from his seat. "I just found him that way. I wasn't doing anything with the gun. You don't know what you're talking about. You misinterpreted the whole thing."

Leeder shrugged. "I know what I saw."

"You didn't see anything," Alden said. "You made that up. Your imagination is getting the better of you, that's what it is. This isn't a scenario, man. Hyde shot himself. Why he came here to do it is a question, but that he did it himself is not. So shut up with your stupid accusations, will you?" He grabbed the other man's arm.

I thought Leeder looked a little guilty and I wondered if he'd dramatized what he'd seen for effect.

"In any case, there's another problem," Leeder said, pulling his arm away from Alden. "Hyde left before he signed off on those films yesterday. It was just a reel of three shorts. Maybe you can do something about that, Fitzgibbons. Who's going to approve last week's work so we can get it out?"

I was shocked by such concern for the film studio's work while a man lay dead across the room, but Fitz appeared sympathetic to the producer.

"Now, now, the mayor has thought of that, and he's gone ahead and appointed me as temporary chief censor."

"Thank God," Leeder said. "But we've got to get going here. You have no idea the kind of pressure we're under. We've got to get the shots, then develop the negatives, and they have to be reviewed before we can let anyone go, in case a shot didn't come out and we have to do it again." He shook his head and stomped away.

"I'm sure it will all—" Fitz had directed his attempt at soothing words toward the man's back but suddenly he stopped talking. His mouth hung open.

I turned to see what he was looking at and saw our former president, Theodore Roosevelt, standing in the doorway between two rather confused-looking uniformed policemen.

Three

The effect was spoiled when the man opened his mouth. He squeaked. His voice squealed in such a whiny and irritating way that it was clear this was not the man who'd mesmerized followers with his political speeches. I, myself, had heard him speak when he visited the University of Chicago in 1903. This man *looked* like Teddy Roosevelt—with his jodhpurs, high boots, many-pocketed jacket, and the pince-nez hanging from a black ribbon—but he was definitely an imposter.

I'd turned toward the door, feeling my heart race. But, as soon as I realized the truth, I saw that Alden was grinning at my reaction. "Pretty good, huh?"

"What?" My confusion might have been funny if not for the sight of the dead man, who was being lifted from the bed onto a stretcher at that very moment.

Alden seemed to realize how inappropriate the joke was when he glanced over to the men preparing to take the body away. He shrugged guiltily. "Roosevelt promised Col. Selig that he'd take one of the studio's cameramen with him when he went on safari. But then he backed out, claiming the Smithsonian objected—they were funding the expedition and wouldn't approve a commercial film being made of it. But then Selig found out that Roosevelt took another photographer, so we decided to film *Hunting Big Game in Africa* right here." Alden smirked. "Wait till you see it. We're using live animals. There's a real lion and it'll actually get shot. It's going to be fantastic."

ated, alas, for nothing. Before I could chide
Alden for his lack of concern for the dead man, an angry-looking
Detective Whitbread returned, following Col. Selig.

"Well, this is just wonderful," Selig said. Whitbread did not
appear to agree. His hands were clenched at his sides and his jaw
was set like a stone statue. Noticing the ill will he was radiating,
Selig took two steps away from him. "The police have agreed we
can open up and get working again."

Everyone paid attention to that. Fitz nodded as if it was what
he'd expected.

"What about Alden?" I asked. "Is he free to go?" That was
what had brought me to this madhouse and I was anxious to leave.

Whitbread frowned. I could almost hear him grinding his
teeth. "The investigation will continue, but we will not be charging
anyone until there is further evidence. Mr. Cabot, you are free to
go, but do not leave the city and I will expect you to be available
for further interviews, as necessary." He nodded to the officer
who proceeded to unlock Alden's handcuffs.

Col. Selig gave him a little bow. "We're really grateful to you,
Detective Whitbread, and to the Chicago Police Department.
Now, people, let's get to work."

"Thank the mayor," Whitbread said with an angry glance at
Fitz. The big Irishman looked away.

At a wave from Col. Selig, people began pouring into the
room, and the producers started yelling. I saw Alden sigh with
relief then race across the room to a blonde woman, without even
stopping to explain to me what had happened. I looked at the
young woman he was greeting.

"That's Kathlyn Williams," Fitz said in my ear. "She's their
main dramatic star. And the little one following her is Babe Greer.
She's new. She does all the ingénue parts and a lot of the comedies."

15

Col. Selig came over. "Fitzgibbons, they say you can sign off for the film board. Is that true? Oh, thank goodness. Can you come down to my office now? And, Mrs. Chapman, have Alden give you a tour before you leave." He took Fitz by the elbow and led him to the doorway. Looking at my brother's back across the room, I doubted he wanted to give me a tour, nor was I at all interested. The sooner I got back to Hyde Park the better, as far as I was concerned.

Detective Whitbread was not happy. I could tell he was fuming. Two red spots were spreading on his gaunt cheeks. He spoke quietly, barely moving his lips. "Headquarters insisted we release the premises back to them. Look at this, it's bedlam."

It was. They were making moving pictures that would be silent, with music played in the theaters for background, but the actual production was anything but silent. As soon as the stretcher with the covered body was carried out, there were yells and screeches that echoed across the room. In one corner, a cowboy was swinging a lasso in front of a saloon while two Indians in elaborate headdresses chatted nearby. In another corner, the fake Teddy Roosevelt was crouched in front of a cluster of tents and an animal was being led into the scene, accompanied by instructions shouted to his handler. Over at the open parlor, near where the dead man had lain some minutes before, they were rehearsing a scene of tender farewells. The body on its stretcher had been removed in the midst of all that commotion and a woman had moved in and stripped the bed of its bloody covering, replacing it with another. Death had come and gone without leaving an impression on these people. Perhaps they thought it was a fake body, like all the fake scenery around them. Perhaps they couldn't distinguish the real from the false.

Watching Alden, I wondered how Kathlyn Williams could concentrate, with all the talking and movement of the cameraman and producer right in front of her, only a few feet away. As Whitbread had said, it was bedlam. How could he conduct an investigation in this madhouse? I very much wanted to leave but I was uneasy. I didn't think Whitbread believed the man had killed himself and, no matter what City Hall did, I knew the detective would worry the case until he got to the truth of it. I looked at my brother.

Alden was planted in front of the parlor scene watching every move with a strange intensity. He seemed to be almost imitating the actions of the characters in the scene. It looked somewhat demented. I left Whitbread and walked over to him. Alden attempted to wave me away but I grabbed his arm and pulled him to the side. "That's enough," I whispered, not wanting to air our family argument in public. "They're back in business, now you need to come home with me. You heard Whitbread, you won't be able to leave town until he lets you. You'll need to tell Clara. You've got the summer off from the *Tribune*, haven't you? Or did you only get a month?"

He pulled his arm away from me and straightened his jacket. "I resigned," he said without looking at me.

"What?"

"I resigned. I'm not employed by the *Tribune* anymore."

Four

Despite the chaos around us, I finally got the truth out of him. He hadn't resigned, he'd been fired. I should have known. He missed a deadline, arriving late after a night of drinking. It was not the first time, and then he had a fight with his editor about the story he was working on. He claimed he was being forced into yellow journalism and he hated it. He refused to go along.

I took a huge breath. The problem was that it wasn't really a surprise. It was just another example of Alden's irresponsibility. How often had he done this? He'd started at Harvard and left. Then he had a job at a bank in Boston, but he left that to come to Chicago and became a reporter. During the Pullman strike, he grew disillusioned. He began reporting on the struggle of the striking workmen but, when the strike spread to the major rail lines, the proprietors of the newspapers all sided with the railroad managers. When Alden continued to write articles about the plight of the strikers, the papers refused to publish them. He quit and returned to our uncle's bank in Boston but that didn't last. When he married, he returned to Chicago and to reporting but jumped from one paper to another. How his wife could put up with it was beyond me. He'd nearly broken our mother's heart with his antics. Now, once again, he'd disappointed us all.

"Oh, Alden, how could you?"

He pulled his sleeve from my grasp and stalked away, yelling something to Mr. Leeder. Soon, they were in a loud argument. From the bits I could hear, it was about the scene they were filming, though. They seemed to have forgotten all about the death of Mr. Hyde.

Meanwhile, Detective Whitbread tapped me on the shoulder. "Mrs. Chapman, a word, if you please."

He led me downstairs to an empty office and shut the door. "It wasn't suicide. We've learned through examination of the body that Mr. Hyde was left handed. Had he shot himself, it would have been through the left temple. The entry wound was on the right side. It would have been impossible for him to reach around to shoot himself that way. So, it appears that someone got close enough to him to shoot him before he could move, and then they placed the gun in his right hand to make it appear that he shot himself."

"And Mr. Leeder claims that he saw Alden putting the gun in the dead man's hand?"

"Yes. That's what he says, although your brother denies it." Whitbread paused, as if deciding how much to tell me. "In the course of my interrogations, I uncovered some information implicating your brother. It seems that last week when Mr. Hyde reviewed films from the Selig studios, he rejected two in which a Miss Kathlyn Williams was shown in tattered clothing. The rejection was fully in accord with his duty, although Col. Selig tells me this kind of rejection is not very common. They're careful to arrange their scenes to pass the censor. When it does happen, they withdraw the film and redo it, then resubmit it the next week.

"Your brother was not happy with the criticism, and he sought out Mr. Hyde at the downtown office when he was there yesterday to view the new version of the film. They had words. Alden left in a rage. Afterward, when Hyde was reviewing the film, he suddenly ran from the office...before the ending. He was not seen again by anyone from the Selig studios until he was found this morning by Mr. Leeder, with your brother standing over him. You can see that Alden must be considered a suspect."

Alden. What was he doing? "I see. He argued with the dead man, I can believe that. But, surely, that was only about some film work. It's no reason to shoot a man."

Whitbread cleared his throat, an unusual action for him. He never hesitated to speak, whether it was good or bad news he was delivering. "There is something else, of an unfortunate nature that I must convey to you. It is the opinion of a number of their co-workers that your brother and Miss Williams have developed an intimate relationship. It is also believed that Mr. Hyde had demonstrated some sort of bias against Miss Williams. Apparently, this was not the first time he censored her work. In fact, it was becoming so much of a problem that the producer, Mr. Leeder, and Col. Selig were considering using another actress in order to meet their schedules. It has been suggested that your brother might have acted to protect Miss Williams's career, which was in jeopardy."

I couldn't speak. Alden and Kathlyn Williams? No, that couldn't be. I was furious. I felt my heart skip a beat then jump, and blood pounded in my ears. *Alden, how could you? What about Clara? And Oliver and Penelope?* Alden had always been contrary. He'd always sought out dangers and thrills. I thought his job as a newspaper reporter satisfied that craving, but this? No, I couldn't accept it. He would never purposefully do anything to hurt his wife and children. In any case, murdering the man seemed like an extreme measure to take.

"I don't believe it. Alden wouldn't do that to his family."

"Unfortunately, it does happen. Apparently, for the past month their co-workers have been aware of numerous secret meetings between them. They would leave together in the evening and spend time in Miss Williams's rooms."

The past month? Alden said he left the paper, but he hadn't said when. I assumed it just happened. A month? Had he really been fired from the *Tribune* a whole month ago and then spent all of that time at the Selig studios?

"I'm sorry to be the one to give you this news. I assume you may want to communicate these matters to Mrs. Cabot, or not, as you see fit. But you can see that Mr. Cabot will not be allowed to leave the city while the investigation continues." I could see he regretted having to detain Alden, but he would never compromise. "You can see it looks rather bad for your brother at this point. It is somewhat irregular but, since I've known you and your brother for so many years, I believe the best, and fastest, way to get to the truth is for you to assist me in this investigation. Only the truth will dispel these very grave suspicions."

"Oh, yes. It looks very bad for Alden, my fool of a brother. I *will* get to the bottom of this, Detective, I promise you. Even if I have to stay here, instead of going to Woods Hole. This is an impossible situation but I *will* get the truth out of Alden, even if I have to thrash him for it." Not that I could have, but it would have given me some satisfaction. I thought of our poor gentle mother and was glad she was not here to see what Alden had gotten into this time.

Five

When I was unable to persuade my brother to return to Hyde Park with me, Fitz insisted on giving me a ride back to the city in his motorcar. From there I got a train home. Although it was nearly suppertime when I arrived, I went directly to Clara and Alden's town house on University Avenue. Like me, Clara was a lecturer at the university, but her subject was chemistry. My best friend, she'd turned thirty-nine in April, as I would do in September. Alden was five years younger, and sometimes I thought he'd never grown out of his childhood. He was spoiled, plain and simple. Here he was the father of two children, Penelope, an eleven-year-old, and Oliver, ten. Yet, too often, Alden was like the third child of the family with an age of perhaps twelve, like my youngest son, Tommy. I knew not everyone felt that way about my brother, but it was how I saw him.

I found Clara in the washing room that was behind the kitchen in her house. It had walls faced in white glazed brick and was where she had a laundress come in to do the wash twice a week. Two young maids were helping her fold and pack linens for the trip to Woods Hole. The Marine Biological Laboratory in Woods Hole was where Clara and Alden became engaged, years ago, after a tumultuous summer when Clara was betrayed by a young scholar and accused of academic sabotage and murder. When it happened, Alden staunchly defended her. Despite those associations, we'd spent pleasant summer days there with our children ever since.

"Clara, do you know where Alden is?"

She didn't look at me as she folded a tablecloth. "I believe he was planning to be at the Selig studios this week," she said. I wondered if she knew he'd left his job at the *Tribune* and started working at the studios a whole month before. Would I have to tell her?

"A man was killed there this morning, and Alden was found standing over the body. One of the film people claims that Alden did the shooting then put the gun in the dead man's hand to make it look like suicide. I was with Detective Whitbread when he was called to the scene." The three women stopped their work to stare at me and I regretted blurting it all out. But Clara had to know what was happening.

"Has Alden been arrested?" Clara asked, her normally creamy complexion looking gray.

"No, no. I'm sorry to alarm you. Whitbread's still investigating. He hasn't arrested anyone and he let Alden go, but he told him not to leave the city. But, Clara, Alden had a fight with the dead man yesterday. He was a film censor. That type of disagreement is no reason to shoot a man, of course, but I had no idea he quit his job with the *Tribune*. Did you know?"

She bent to choose another piece of cloth to fold and gestured to the maids to continue their work. "No, I didn't know that he left his job. It doesn't surprise me, however. He wants to move to California." Clara was from Kentucky and there was always a soft twang in her voice that reminded me of that fact. When that twang became more pronounced it was a signal that she was angry. Her back was straight in her chair and she held her head high but I thought her teeth were clenched as if waiting for a blow.

"What?" I couldn't believe it. "California? Has he ever even been there? He's mad, Clara. You mustn't let him get away with this."

"Oh, he went out there last year to cover a boxing match, but that was to San Francisco. He wants to move to southern

California, Los Angeles. It's for the motion picture company. Apparently, the weather is better there, so they can make pictures outdoors all year round. He said Col. Selig's already opened a studio there and that's where he wants to go."

"So, he never intended to go to Woods Hole with us this year, at all?" With so many good memories of our summers on the Cape, we were always eager to leave the dirty city behind for the beaches swept clean by its brisk sea breezes. Why he would want to give that up for an unknown life in California was beyond my comprehension. "He's mad, Clara. You've got to stop him. If he wants to work for Selig, they already have a massive studio here. I saw it. It's huge." I found I couldn't tell her what Whitbread had said about Kathlyn Williams. I couldn't really believe it myself. How could I be the one to tell Clara of such suspicions? My mouth wouldn't form the words.

Clara bit her lip as she smoothed the linen sheet she'd folded, then she handed it to one of the maids to put into a big trunk that lay open on the tile floor. We were sitting in straight-backed wooden chairs from the kitchen. "He's been seduced by the film business," she said. She was staring off at a blank wall. She shook her head as if shaking away flies. "But, even so, he would never shoot a man unless it was in self-defense, Emily. You know that."

After that, she asked the maids to continue packing upstairs and waited until they left the room. Then she said, "Alden's never been happy about the wealth I brought to our marriage." Clara's grandmother had supported her studies and then left her a large inheritance. For the first time, I noticed some fine lines around Clara's mouth that reminded me we were getting older. She'd always been a stunning beauty, a tall woman with glossy black hair and a fine bone structure to her face. I could see a few gray strands now. As with my own reflection in the mirror, those gray hairs took me by surprise.

"He feels undervalued," she said. "And it's been worse the past few years. They keep having newspaper wars and demand ever more exciting stories to compete with the other papers. Alden says if he's going to write fiction, he'd rather have it *labeled* fiction. I know he tried to write a novel. He hid it from me, but I came across it one day. When I asked him about it he got very angry." Folding her arms, she sat back looking at me. "I think he really wants to write stories like Ring Lardner, but he hasn't been successful yet."

"Well, if that's what he wants to do, why doesn't he just do it?" I asked, flapping a towel I was supposed to be folding. It was true that, with Clara's money, he could afford to do whatever he wanted. I didn't like the idea, as I thought he really should be supporting his family, but I knew it was possible.

She shook her head. "He won't. He thinks it's wrong to live off my money. I don't know what to do, Emily. I can see he's so unhappy, but he won't let me help him. He just gets furious when I suggest anything."

"That's so like Alden," I said. "How is going to California supposed to help? Not that you can expect Alden to have a rational explanation, I know. That would be too much to ask." I was tempted to go on in that vein, expressing my frustration with my exasperating brother, but I noticed how sad Clara seemed, and I was worried.

"I don't know," she said. "I don't know what he thinks moving to California would do to improve the situation. Perhaps he's saying it in an attempt to be free of all this." She waved her hand to encompass their house and the home she'd created for them. "Or to be free of me."

She looked so forlorn. It made me doubly angry with my brother. I just couldn't tell her about Whitbread's suspicions that he was in a relationship with a film actress. Telling her that he'd nearly been arrested, and was still under suspicion, was bad enough. So, instead, I promised her that I'd work with Detective Whitbread to clear Alden's name by uncovering the actual murderer. As Clara was well aware, I'd participated in many of

Whitbread's investigations over the years by chance, or invitation, or pure stubbornness on my part. I pointed out that there was no sense worrying about Alden's plans to move to California as long as the threat of arrest hung over him.

○

When I returned home, I found my husband, Stephen, seated at the kitchen table with two of our children, eating omelets. "Where's Tommy?" I asked, as I removed my straw hat and tight jacket. Delia, our nursemaid, smiled as she cracked eggs into the pan to make another omelet for me. I worried about my youngest son. At twelve years old, Tommy was a hellion. Smiling at Delia, I brought a plate and utensils to the table in time for her to serve me from the pan. "Jack?" My fourteen-year-old was the quiet, responsible one and I could usually depend on him to curb his younger brother.

Jack gulped down his latest mouthful and glanced at his father. Stephen was trying to look innocent as he carefully cut a piece of bread. At fifty-one, his hair was a little grayer and a bit sparse. His left arm—which had been damaged by a shotgun blast so many years before—ached more than ever when it rained, and there were deep lines that scored his face, although some of them were from laughter. I could tell that he and Jack were both reluctant to face me.

"Tommy threw rocks and broke Mrs. Chalmers's window so she's making him weed her flower bed and she won't let him go, 'Till every single weed is gone, young man,'" my daughter, Lizzie, said, imitating our widowed neighbor. She squinted her eyes, pursed her lips, and wagged one finger up and down with each word, and I had to cough to keep from laughing. At thirteen, Lizzie was nearly as incorrigible as Tommy, but she was quicker to escape the consequences of her actions. Still, I tried not to encourage her impertinence.

I planned to wait until we were alone to tell Stephen about Alden's predicament and his strange plans to move to California, but I mentioned that I'd visited the Selig Polyscope Company. Both children looked up with interest and Lizzie shouted, "Oh, can we go? Uncle Alden promised to take us. Ollie says they've got cowboys who ride and shoot, and I heard they're building Oz there. I want to go. Can we?"

"Sounds like an exciting place," Stephen said. I frowned at him. I didn't want him to encourage them.

"Sit down, Lizzie, and eat your omelet. You know we're getting ready to go to Woods Hole next week. Aren't you excited about that? There's no time for visiting motion picture studios. You can do that when we come back. It's way up on the north side and, besides, there's nothing to see. It's just a lot of fake scenery."

"Did you see Tom Mix?" Jack asked. When I looked puzzled, he said, "The cowboy. He's making a movie there. Don't you know, Mother? Uncle Alden says he does all his own stunts."

I stared at him. "Who? How do you know about that, anyway?"

Jack grimaced and looked down at his food.

"Jack?" I asked. I could see my husband was trying not to grin. Jack mumbled something. "What did you say?"

"The nickelodeon. Ollie and I went...to see the moving pictures."

Ollie was Alden and Clara's son, and was younger than Jack. His sister, Penny, was almost Lizzie's age. The children all attended the university's laboratory school together.

"Jack, shame on you. You know that nickelodeons are just cheap amusements for people who have no education." Most of them were in the Levee district of the Loop. I wondered when Jack and Ollie had managed to go there without supervision. It was a challenging thing, this raising of children. I didn't want them to be afraid of the world but, at the same time, there were plenty of places I didn't want them to go.

"Perhaps Alden took them?" Stephen suggested as he reached for another piece of bread.

"It only costs a nickel," Lizzie said. "And they're good. Besides, Uncle Alden promised to take us to see the studios. He said they're building Oz. I want to go." Lizzie was a big fan of the Wizard of Oz books by L. Frank Baum. I'd read them with her over the years.

I rolled my eyes. It was typical of Alden to get the children all excited like this. I'd discuss it with Stephen later, but I feared that now we would never get them safely on the train to the East Coast without a visit to the place where they manufactured dreams, up there on the north side. Perhaps a glimpse of the tawdry behind-the-scenes of the motion picture company might even disillusion the young people, and that might not be a bad thing. However, a man had been shot there and, if it wasn't suicide, that meant a murderer was loose in the studio. So, I was not happy with the prospect of having my children exposed to the place. And I couldn't help wondering myself, was it really murder? And was Alden involved? It couldn't be, but I couldn't be sure he was innocent, either. I ought to be able to be sure, but I wasn't. When had we grown so far apart that I could have such doubts about my own brother?

Six

The full force of the danger to my brother and his family hit me when I was alone with Stephen at the end of the evening. Delia had chased the children off to bed and we were sitting in the study. Unlike Clara and Alden, who had a whole town house, we rented a single floor and a basement kitchen on a side street in Hyde Park.

"You didn't tell Clara about Kathlyn Williams?" Stephen asked.

"I couldn't, I can't believe it myself. How could I tell her? You don't believe it, do you?"

"I don't know," he said. "I haven't seen Alden much this past year."

"He couldn't be that cruel to Clara. And what about Penny and Ollie?"

Stephen frowned. "It certainly is unfortunate, if it's true."

"Unfortunate? It's a catastrophe. If he's done this, Clara should throw him out. I'm just glad our mother's not here to see this. Stephen, what are we going to do? What if he really did this?"

"What, became involved with an actress, or shot a man?"

"Why would he murder that man?"

"If you don't believe he'd do such a thing, do you believe he'd betray his wife?"

"I don't know what to believe. He's always been unpredictable, even unreliable, but this?"

"Emily, what will Whitbread do?"

I looked at Stephen sitting back in the worn armchair where he usually spent late evenings reading. His eyes were in shadow and I thought he looked tired. Even more than me, he needed the refreshing summer breezes of Cape Cod. I felt a knot tightening in my throat. "Whitbread won't stop until he gets at the truth of what happened," I said.

"What if he finds out that Alden *did* shoot the man?"

"In a fit of rage? In a careless act of anger?" I asked. I remembered Alden as a child grabbing a doll from our sister, Rose. As he ran away, he swung it carelessly, smashing it against a door and breaking off a chunk of its porcelain head. Rose was devastated. He did it to retaliate when she told a lie about him, but he never meant to destroy her doll. He only wanted some kind of revenge. Sorry and ashamed, he came to me, desperate for help in making it right with her. I don't think she ever forgave him. It was his recklessness that I found myself afraid of.

"What if Whitbread proves he did it?" Stephen asked, again. "What if it *was* self-defense? Or to protect someone else? I could see Alden doing that."

"Whitbread wouldn't let it go," I said, shaking my head. "No matter the excuse, he wouldn't let it go."

"I thought that. But what will you do then?"

I hated to admit that Alden might be guilty and that Whitbread would find a way to prove it. I bit my lip.

Stephen looked sad. "He's your brother, Emily. No matter how angry you may be with him, he's still your brother. I know you. I know you'll try to defend him. But what if he *is* guilty? He's not your child, Emily. He's your brother, but he's not your child."

What if it was Jack? Or, more likely, Tommy? I was staring into space, thinking hard about this. Alden was not my child that I needed to protect. He was my brother, but he was a grown man. He had to be responsible for his own actions. I knew if our mother was still alive, she'd want to defend him. I felt as if I were at the edge of a sand dune watching the earth swirling away at my feet, each second moving closer to the moment when I would be caught and pulled down. I couldn't act but I had to.

I felt Stephen's hand on my shoulder. It slid to my neck and he gently raised my chin so that I would look in his eyes. He looked sorry. "Emily, maybe it would be best if we left for Woods Hole and let Whitbread deal with this."

Tears blurred my eyes. I took a big breath and straightened my shoulders. "No. I can't leave him. You and Clara should go. Take the children. I have to see this through, however it ends."

Seven

Alden had argued with the dead censor and he'd been spending time with Kathlyn Williams, when we all thought he was working for the *Chicago Tribune*—these were undeniable facts. And Whitbread suspected that he shot Mr. Hyde to protect Kathlyn Williams. I felt as if I'd been socked in the pit of my stomach and needed to gasp for air as I fought my way through the morning crowds to the detective's office in the Harrison Street police station. The sergeant at the desk nodded to me as I turned up the worn stone stairs to the second floor. I found Whitbread seated at his desk.

"Detective, I'd like to assist in the investigation into the death of Mr. Hyde. You suggested it yesterday, and I think you're right. I can help you find the truth of the matter." I said all of this while still standing in the doorway.

I was usually very comfortable in that narrow office, for I'd spent many hours there, first alone, then later directing my students. We would go to the closet where Whitbread stored the boxes of identity cards describing criminals arrested in the various precincts throughout the city. Name, address, age, and Bertillon measurements were all listed, along with the crime they were accused of. We'd transcribed and used the information in many research studies.

Whitbread was an unusual policeman who read criminology texts by Lombroso and others, and who believed in the latest scientific advances in criminology. To me, he was a mentor, a colleague, and a friend. But that day, knowing my brother's freedom was in jeopardy, I felt cold.

"Emily, come in." He rose, tall and gangly, to shut the wooden door behind me, then pulled out a chair. "I value your assistance. While it may be slightly irregular—since your brother must be considered a suspect—I have every confidence that you will do all in your power to uncover the truth behind Mr. Hyde's death."

I sighed. "Yes, I will." I was uneasy with the knowledge that he believed I would do anything for the truth, while my husband was sure I would do anything to protect my brother. "You're sure it couldn't have been suicide?" I asked.

"It is unlikely, but we will consider all possibilities, of course. Now, the first thing to do is to return to the Selig studios to pursue further inquiries. I'll be talking to Col. Selig again. While I'm doing that, I want you to see if you can interview Miss Williams and anyone else who'll talk to you. As Mr. Cabot's sister, you may be able to get information they're reluctant to share with me."

I knew he thought that I could approach Kathlyn Williams about the rumored relationship with Alden. I certainly planned to confront my brother on the matter. I was sure Whitbread planned to ask Alden plainly about it, but I wanted to get to my brother first, if I could.

I agreed to the plan, and we left the building to force our way through the crowds to the streetcar that would take us north. It was easier to make way with Whitbread there to plunge into the throngs, taking my arm and dispersing people with his commanding manner. He hadn't yet been assigned an official motorcar. Political operatives like Fitz were always first in line for such conveniences; working police detectives were much further down the list. On the streetcar, Whitbread glared at a man until he gave up his seat to me.

When we got out of town, the trees were still decked with blossoms but looked like their time was over and they were about to wilt. I knew it was my own sour disposition that made it seem so. Still, I couldn't shake the impression. I longed to leave for Woods Hole.

When we arrived at the Selig studios, Whitbread headed for the colonel's second-floor office, while I was directed to the outside area they called the "backlot" to find my brother. It was a sizable yard and, in the middle, I saw a saloon that looked exactly like the one on the third floor that I'd seen the previous day. But there were more buildings, a whole street of them. A group of men hollered and whistled as a cowboy tried to maintain his seat on a wild horse. The animal jumped and bucked, straining at the reins in his mouth. It looked like an extremely dangerous occupation as the horse tried to rid himself of his rider. The man's hat fell off, and then his body followed as the horse jumped, then turned, leaving the man hanging in the air behind him. As the flailing cowboy struck the ground with a loud thump, the horse dashed off around the corner. It was closely followed by two other cowboys on horses. I rushed to the fallen man, fearing the worst.

"Hey, get out of there." I heard someone yell. "Oh, never mind. Stop for now, Sam. Lady, what do ya think you're doin'?"

When I looked around, I saw a man with a megaphone standing beside a large camera on a three-legged stand, and I realized I was the "lady" he was yelling at. The cameraman continued cranking a handle until the producer waved him to a stop.

The man who'd fallen was sitting up by that point, checking himself for damage and looking around for his hat, which a young boy brought over to him. The boy was my son Jack.

"Are you all right?" I asked the cowboy. The fall had looked catastrophic to me.

"Oh, yes, ma'am," he said with a big toothy smile. Then he stood up, dusting himself off with the tall-crowned hat.

I turned to my son. "Jack, what are you doing here?" I thought I'd made it clear that any tours of the studio would have to wait until after we returned from Woods Hole at the end of the summer.

My son looked as shocked to see me as I was to see him. The cowboy stepped across, holding out his hand. "Tom Mix, ma'am. Glad to meet you." I shook his hand, feeling a warm, strong grip.

Meanwhile, the producer—who I guessed must be the Mr. Otis Turner who'd been pointed out to me on my first visit to the studio—stalked up to us, yelling commands in several directions as he did so. "Here, what do you think you're doing? You've just about ruined the shot, although maybe we can use it up to the fall. And you, kid, I see you and your buddies in those bushes. Get out of there or you'll be showing up in the negatives and we'll have to re-shoot the whole thing. Get out!"

Tom Mix continued smiling while Turner ignored my attempts to apologize and Alden came up behind me, grabbing my arm to lead me away. When we were at a safe distance, he turned and beckoned to Jack and some other children who were hiding in the sparse bushes beside the saloon.

"Come on," he said. "Over here."

I was dumbfounded to see not only Jack, but Lizzie, Tommy, Ollie, and Penny. Alden had brought them all.

"Wasn't that great?" Jack asked me. He was starry eyed with admiration for the cowboy who, I saw, was matter-of-factly mounting another horse that immediately began to try to unseat him. Soon, that horse was bucking all around the square in front of the saloon while the other men hooted and Turner boomed suggestions through his megaphone. Pandemonium, as far as I could tell.

"I promised them," Alden said when he saw the look I gave him. "I promised I'd bring them before they had to leave for Woods Hole. Didn't I, kids?"

There was a resounding affirmation from the five of them with pleas for more. Before I could protest, Alden herded them toward another part of the lot where he said they'd see lions and tigers. Lions and tigers? Was this a zoo?

"It's for the *Hunting Big Game in Africa* film with the Teddy Roosevelt impersonator," Alden explained, as the children skipped ahead of us. "Wait till you see it. It's fantastic. Selig bought a whole circus and Big Otto's the trainer. I'll introduce you to Olga the Leopard Lady."

Alden wanted to hurry after the children, but I grabbed his arm and anchored him in place. He looked annoyed. "Alden, why didn't you tell us you lost your job at the newspaper more than a month ago? Did you even tell Clara? What have you been doing since then? Have you been lying about where you were at night?"

I thought I might not want to know the answers to my questions but I had to confirm my suspicions. I had to hear it from his own mouth. "Alden, answer me."

He forcibly removed my fingers from his arm. "You and Clara, and Stephen, all you know or care about is what goes on at the university. Why should you care if I'm no longer at the *Tribune*? What's it to you? You hardly read the papers. You're more interested in the solemn tracts of your reformer friends than my articles. You didn't even notice that my byline's been missing from the *Tribune*."

"So, instead, you're writing melodramas for the nickelodeon? Alden, Clara said you wanted to write novels or stories. Can't you do that and get them published in the papers? Do you have to sink to this?" When I looked around, all I saw were half-finished rooms or buildings. None of it was real.

"*This* is the future," he said, waving his arm at the dusty lot. "I don't want to write stories, Emily. I want to make pictures."

"But it's a sham, Alden. It's all fake." My eyes followed the children, who'd reached what looked like an attempt to imitate a jungle. I thought I heard the roar of an animal and it made me jerk my head in that direction. I was a little frightened. "What was that?"

"*That* was a very real lion," Alden said. He sneered at me and started to move away.

"Wait. Stop. Alden, Whitbread says you had an argument with Mr. Hyde the day before he died. What was that about?"

He stopped, then shrugged. "It was just a disagreement. There was a scene where Kathlyn Williams was grabbed by the villain and he kissed her. Hyde objected. I merely pointed out to him that the scene exactly duplicated the actions in a comedy we released last week with Babe Greer in it and he hadn't objected to that one. He was just a little tin-pot dictator throwing his weight around."

"What exactly is your relationship with Kathlyn Williams?" I asked. "Why are you spending so much time with her?"

He stared at me.

"Alden, answer me. What's going on?"

"Going on? Nothing's going on. You're so small minded, Emily. Just because I work with a woman, you want to accuse me of being unfaithful."

"I never said that. I just asked why you're spending so much time with her."

"How dare you? Do I ask you why you spend so much time at Hull House? Or what about Whitbread? How much time have you spent with him, away from your husband and children?"

"It's not the same."

"Sure it's not, because it's me, and you always think the worst about me. Leave me alone, Emily. I'm working at what I want to do. If you want to find someone who would do anything to ruin the Selig studios, you should look at Essanay." When I looked confused, he continued. "The Essanay Film Manufacturing Company is the colonel's competition in town. They got started when Selig's star Broncho Billy quit and started his own studio because he was mad. He broke with the colonel when Selig wouldn't make him a partner, and he'd do anything to spite Selig. Why don't you ask what relationship he had with Hyde? Tom Mix is set to become the next cowboy star, and old Broncho Billy would do anything to cramp Selig's style. Why don't you go bother him? Let go of me, I need to catch up with the kids." He pulled away and hurried after the children.

I was grinding my teeth with frustration when I heard Col. Selig call my name. "Mrs. Chapman, Detective Whitbread, here, was telling me that you've worked with him in the past and will be helping to resolve the issues around the tragic passing of Mr. Hyde." Whitbread was watching Alden disappear into the fake jungle. "We'll all be very grateful if we can close the book on that unfortunate incident. As you can see, we're very busy trying to meet our schedule for our exhibitors. They expect new films each week and we advertise several weeks ahead, so we're anxious to fulfill our promises to them. Can't keep the public waiting, you know."

"I've explained to Col. Selig that we're doing the best we can to find out the truth about Mr. Hyde's death," Whitbread said. "To that end, it is necessary that we establish the backgrounds of the principals involved. I was asking the colonel how he came by his title." Whitbread's wiry eyebrows were raised as he attempted to look curious. I suspected he already knew the answer to his question.

"Yes, yes, well it's an honorific, if you know what I mean." Selig hemmed and hawed a bit. "It's common in the world of vaudeville, don't you know, when you organize a troupe. I had a minstrel troupe. I had a magic act before that, 'Selig the Conjurer.' But, yes, it was with the minstrel troupe that I was called 'Colonel' and it stuck. We traveled up and down California then. Those were the days. We were in Dallas when I saw an early version of the motion picture, very crude. But, back here in Chicago, we were able to develop our own mechanical version that's far better than others and so the Selig Polyscope Company was born."

"Thomas Edison insists he owns the patents for those things, though, doesn't he?" Whitbread asked. Clearly, he'd already done some research.

"Hmm. Yes, yes. There have been some legal proceedings. All very costly. But, luckily, we were able to do some commercial films for the Armour Company in return for their assistance with legal issues. That freed us up considerably, yes it did."

"Yes," Whitbread said. "I was made aware of Mr. Armour's interest in your company."

I imagined he must have gotten an earful. Armour was an important businessman who had a large interest in the Chicago stockyards. His enterprises had come under attack after the book *The Jungle* was published. It described many horrid practices of the meatpacking industry. The meatpacker's interest in Selig's company, combined with the mayor's wife's involvement, would be a distraction for Whitbread. Armour was one more powerful man advocating for Selig. But I knew from experience that Whitbread never caved to that kind of influence, no matter what it cost him personally.

"But what about Edison...are you still having a dispute with him? I've heard he hires strongmen to try to maintain his rights," Whitbread said.

"Yes, that's been an issue. But it's the exhibitors who suffer, I fear. Edison's bullies have been known to go in and destroy equipment and films they claim violate his patents. But our contact with him has always been through lawyers. And, anyways, we believe there's relief on the horizon."

"Really? You anticipate Edison will give up some of his claims?"

"Not exactly, but I'm not at liberty to discuss the matter at this point. In any case, there would be no reason for Edison's men to harm a film board censor. That's really not their concern."

"Yet the actions of the censor were costing you money when he failed to approve some of your films."

"Yes, that's true. But you can ask anyone and they'll tell you that I've been very supportive of the Chicago Film Board. We want to increase the number and type of people who enjoy our films and, to do that, we need the seal of approval of the censors. I tell you, very soon everyone—families, grandparents, everyone—will find great enjoyment in the moving pictures. That's our goal, and the censors will help us reach it."

That sounded very conciliatory on the part of the colonel, but I wasn't sure if I believed it.

"This must be a very costly enterprise," Whitbread said.

Col. Selig made an expansive gesture to include the whole outdoor area. "Our studios and stables extend over five acres. We believe in giving the public the most realistic picture we can get. We have another five acres in Los Angeles where we get some of our best scenic effects. We're spending a lot of money, but we'll get it back."

I stared across at the cowboys, who were once more watching Tom Mix get thrown from a bucking stallion. "How long does it take to photograph that scene?" I asked.

"We always do it at least three times. Then they have to develop the negative and we look at it. If it's OK we send it to the print room to make prints. If it's not, then we throw it away and do it again. The staff members can't leave for the day till we've reviewed what we've got and made sure we can print it," Selig said.

I wondered if my children would show up in the negatives for the cowboy scene and if that would force them to do it all over again. I hoped not, but it was on Alden's shoulders if it happened.

"Col. Selig, my brother mentioned the actor Broncho Billy as someone who might have a grudge against you. Do you think he would have known Mr. Hyde?"

Detective Whitbread looked up at that. It was news to him.

Col. Selig considered it. "Well, Gil—Broncho Billy's his stage name, Gil Anderson's his real name—did some films for us but then he left and started his own studio with George Spoor. They call it Essanay. 'S' for Spoor, don't you know, and 'A' for Anderson. They're on West Argyle Street now. They also have their films reviewed by Mr. Hyde and the other censors, just like us. But I don't know if he knew the man personally."

Just at that moment, an innocent-looking young woman with large blue eyes and amber ringlets came up to us. I thought she looked like she was about sixteen and terribly out of place.

Col. Selig nodded to her. "You can wait until the negative for your scene is developed but, meanwhile, go up and tell Tom Nash we need to fix some of the posts over at the saloon. They're falling down. He's upstairs. Oh, sorry, this is Miss Babe Greer. She plays ingénues in our comedies. Mrs. Chapman, Detective Whitbread."

"Colonel, is Miss Kathlyn Williams here? Mrs. Chapman is anxious to meet her," Whitbread said, giving me a hard stare that challenged me to contradict him. I understood. In return for my participation in the investigation he wanted me to question Kathlyn Williams about her relationship with my brother. Distasteful as it might be, it had to be done and I was the one to do it.

"Why, yes. She's shooting inside, next door to the set where Hyde was found, as a matter of fact. Miss Greer can take you up, Mrs. Chapman. I'm sure Kathlyn will be happy to talk to you, when she's done with her scene, of course. We have a lot of time to make up after the hiatus yesterday."

With a worried look in the direction of the jungle, hoping that the children would be safe in Alden's care, I followed the young actress to the main building. As we entered, she pointed down a corridor on the first floor. "Down there they make the camera and projector machines," she said. Then she led me to a large door and we peeked in. There were rows of desks where women in smocks sat peering into machines. Stacks of round canisters sat on each desk. "That's where they inspect and finish the prints before they're shipped out, and there are other rooms where there are no lights, only red bulbs, where they develop the films and punch holes in the sides so they'll move on the reels. It's like a magic factory."

We climbed the stairs to the second floor, where Miss Greer told me there were offices for the writers and producers, individual dressing rooms for the main contract players, and shared dressing rooms for the minor players. There was a huge room full of costumes and another for props.

On the third floor, the young actress pointed to a whole wall of windows, against which a long line of people in all sorts of outfits sat or leaned. "They're waiting to be called," she said. "That's how I started. I came to be an extra…in the background, you know. And Mr. Leeder saw me and he put me right into a scene with Alonzo Swift. I was so thrilled I couldn't say a word." She laughed. "But that was all right because they're silent pictures. Alonzo Swift's a thespian," she said, clearly relishing the word. "He was in the theater in New York and around the country. He's so well known. All the women just love him. See, he's in the scene they're filming with Kathlyn Williams."

She led me across to the open-ended parlor, where they were playing the scene. It was only yards from the four-poster bed where Hyde's body had been found. It seemed a bit sickening to think of, but the actors appeared insensible to it. The fact that they could forget the man found dead the day before made me uneasy. How could they block such a horrid scene from their minds so completely as to go about their business without any thought?

Kathlyn Williams was at the center of the tableau. She was a very beautiful blonde woman with expressive features. In the scene, she was being threatened by an evil-looking man who held a knife to her throat. Suddenly, the door burst open and a tall man with broad shoulders and smooth black hair entered. Babe Greer grabbed my arm. "That's Alonzo Swift," she said in a whisper. I wasn't sure why she was being quiet, as no one else was. The producer, Mr. Leeder, yelled through a megaphone, as the cameraman cranked away at the handle on the camera. Others rushed around, just out of the camera's eye, commenting on the action, and yelling to each other across the set. How the actors could concentrate in such chaos was beyond me, yet I was drawn to the woman at the center of it all, who was swooning in the arms of her rescuer. Could this woman be the "work" that was drawing Alden further and further away from his family? Poor Clara.

Eight

When the cameraman stopped cranking, I noticed a very strange thing happen. Alonzo Swift abruptly released his grasp on Kathlyn Williams then casually straightened and smoothed his hair, looking around for someone to bring him water. She righted herself and dropped into a chair, where she started a lively conversation with the villain of the piece, who was stroking the curl of his mustache. We were close enough that I could hear him begin to tell her a story about a turtle in a barn. How strange to see them switch so abruptly out of their pretend world.

"That's Kathlyn Williams," Babe Greer told me. "But we have to wait until Mr. Leeder tells them it's all right to break. So just stay here." She clutched my sleeve to keep me in place. The producers certainly held everyone in thrall during the process of making the moving pictures. I was content to watch as the tearful heroine relaxed into a very ordinary-looking woman in front of my eyes.

"Kathlyn Williams is quite an important actress here, as I understand it," I said.

"Oh, they call us 'pantomimists,' not actors or actresses," Babe Greer said. "She's just like me. I mean, I think she *was* a minor actress, in stock theater in New York, and she got work with Biograph, that's another film company back East. That's how she started. She gets all the melodramas. I only do the comedies…

for now." She turned to look at me. "They say Col. Selig wants her to go out to the studio in Los Angeles. But there's a bit of a scandal. She sued her husband for divorce and tried to get a lot of money from him. A lot. She's very attractive to men." Babe raised her eyebrows in a suggestive manner. "Oh, good. He's released them. Come on, I'll introduce you."

She led me to the blonde woman who looked just a bit tired as she slumped in her chair. When Babe said Col. Selig had sent me, Kathlyn Williams perked up.

"Oh, look," Babe said. "The mail. Excuse me, I'll just go tell Mr. Nash he's needed." She headed across to a table by the door where a man was emptying some mail bags. I saw Alonzo Swift look up and follow her.

"It's letters from people who've seen the pictures," Kathlyn Williams told me. "Very nice of them, of course. But sometimes they seem to think we *are* the people we play in the pictures. Babe is impressed, though. She's new to this. I let her read my mail when she has none." She turned her crystal blue eyes on me and asked, "So, what can I do for you, Mrs. Chapman? Did I hear that you're working with the police?"

She was as self-contained as my friend the famous Bertha Palmer at one of her soirees. Suddenly, I realized that I'd stepped into the film world, where Kathlyn Williams was queen. I tried to picture my elegant friend Clara beside her, and I could feel the animal magnetism that Kathlyn Williams projected so naturally. The force of it reached out to you. It was what made her touch people from the screen. I resented it when I thought of Clara and her children.

"Actually, I came here yesterday in answer to a call about my brother, Mr. Alden Cabot. You know him, don't you?" I wanted to see how she'd react.

She looked down at the papers spread on the table and straightened them as she spoke. "Of course. Mr. Cabot's been providing scenarios for Mr. Leeder." She looked up, straight into my eyes. "He wrote the story for this one." When she gestured toward the parlor around us, I couldn't help staring beyond the parlor to the bedroom. The actress followed my gaze.

"Oh. That's where Mr. Hyde was found shot yesterday morning, isn't it?" I said.

"Yes. I suppose it shocks you that we can just clean it up and get on with it. It should shock me, but I'm so used to it—the pressure to meet the schedule, you know, not the death, of course. These stories need to be turned out every day just to keep the beast fed…the public. They demand new stories every week and it's our job to provide them. It's what we do here."

"I understand Mr. Hyde was a censor and he refused to pass quite a few of your pictures during the past month. Do you have any idea why he would do that?"

She looked troubled and drew a hand across her brow. I wondered if it was genuine distress or a gesture borrowed from one of her films. I knew I was not necessarily being fair to her, but I wanted badly to chide her for her actions with Alden. I found it impossible to approach the subject directly, though. I couldn't do it.

"It's true, Mr. Hyde rejected some of my work but, when we looked at those scenes, there didn't seem to be any reason for it. I didn't even know the man. Someone told me he was married when he lived in Indiana, but his wife left him to run away with a salesman, so he sold his place and moved to Chicago. I wonder if I reminded him of his wife or something." She shrugged. "It was a bother but, luckily for me, I'm popular enough with the public that Col. Selig has supported me. So far, at least."

"Is it true that you've been involved in a very public divorce? Could your husband have anything to do with Mr. Hyde's death?"

She sat up, offended. "He's my *ex*-husband and he's in New York. I sued him for money he owed me. He disapproved of my acting. I refused to give it up. I support myself now, and we're completely done. There would be no reason for him to pursue me. We owe each other nothing. That is over. Whatever led to the death of Mr. Hyde, it cannot have anything to do with me. Now, if you'll excuse me, I have another scene to prepare for. And I believe there's someone looking for you." As she stood up, she nodded to a figure across the room and I saw Mr. Fitzgibbons waving to me.

"Miss Williams, where were you the night before last?" I asked her, before she could move away.

"When Mr. Hyde was shot?" She shook her head. "I was at home in bed, Mrs. Chapman. In case you haven't realized it, this is a very tiring profession, and we often work into the evening. That was true Tuesday night. I left at seven and retired immediately when I got home." She started to turn away but thought better of it and faced me directly. "One thing you should know, Mrs. Chapman, your brother has some great ideas for motion pictures. He could do a lot of really good work. I hope you and other members of his family will support him in that."

Before I could form a retort, she hurried away.

Nine

M rs. Chapman, I see you've met Kathlyn Williams. Isn't she a miracle?" Mr. Fitzgibbons asked when he reached me. We were shooed away from the parlor, so we moved to a hitching post outside the saloon set. Turning, I looked up at Fitz with some skepticism. Was he aware of the rumors concerning Alden and Miss Williams? He avoided my eyes and nodded in the direction of another stage set. "And there's the newest heart throb, Miss Babe Greer, the embodiment of innocence, and Mr. Alonzo Swift, the handsomest man in the country. I've no doubt that the pile over there is for him." He pointed at a heap of letters on the table near the door. "Women from all over the world write to him with propositions."

In the scene they were filming, several courting couples strolled by on what appeared to be a path through a city park. They passed a forlorn-looking Alonzo Swift sitting on a bench. Then, when Babe Greer trotted along, alone, he rose and accosted her. With much yelling from the sidelines, the girl modestly looked at the ground while the man clung to her hand entreating her. She finally pulled away and trotted down the path again, leaving him to mope on the bench.

"It's an exciting industry, Mrs. Chapman," Fitz said, as the scene broke up and they prepared to repeat it with changes. "This administration intends to make Chicago the capital of the motion picture industry. Just think what fame it'll bring the city."

There were so many much worthier causes that would benefit from attention by City Hall that I felt an urge to burst his bubble. "So why are they moving to Los Angeles?"

"Rumors, mere rumors. They take their cameras to many different places to get realistic backgrounds. Selig is especially proud of the real scenery in his films. He's sent groups to Florida and Colorado, and the actor and cameraman from his Monte Cristo film out to the California coast to get real pictures of the ocean. His operation is huge and his vision is just as large. Why, he's negotiating to buy the boats that were built for the Columbian Exposition to represent Christopher Columbus's journey. He wants to make a film about Columbus. I'm telling you, Selig has big ideas and he's doing a lot for the city."

Personally, I couldn't see how the making of the little scenes, like the one we'd just observed, could in any way help the jobless and indigent who lived in the tenements of the West Side, but I knew Fitz and his boss were thinking of newspaper headlines and society gatherings. I could also bet that increased income for the nickelodeons in the Levee district would add to their campaign coffers. That was how things worked in Chicago.

Before I could debunk his high-flying claims, Detective Whitbread joined us. He asked Fitz what he could tell us about the dead censor.

"Hyde was the second cousin of Mrs. Busse," he said.

Whitbread grunted. "The mayor's wife."

"Yes, well, he had a grocery store in a small town in Indiana, where she grew up. It seems his wife left him and he was quite distraught. Couldn't bear the small-town gossip, so some of the relatives got the idea to ask Mrs. Busse to help him get settled up here, in the city. They got him to sell the business and, because he'd been spending all his time at the nickelodeon...since his wife's betrayal, don't you know...he seemed a good candidate for censor. They're required to spend a considerable amount of time watching films. Anyhow, it was arranged and he moved here six months ago."

"I assume he was grateful enough to contribute some of his profits from the sale of his business to the mayor's campaign?" I asked.

Fitz frowned at me. "Now, now, it's only to be expected that he'd be grateful. And he's been extremely faithful to his job. He's prompt in his reports and has kept the motion picture people happy by not holding up their production schedules."

"Except for refusing to pass pictures with Kathlyn Williams in them," I pointed out.

"Now, that's a very recent thing." He looked across to the blonde actress, who was sitting near the parlor set.

I'd known Fitz since the Columbian Exposition. He'd never married. I wondered if, like my brother, he was susceptible to the beautiful blonde screen star. Maybe Alden wasn't the only one. At least I knew that Whitbread was incorruptible in this, as in all things.

Whitbread asked about other Selig studios staff, but Fitz knew no more than what had been reported in the papers and Whitbread was already aware of those facts. I could see that Fitz had been assigned by the mayor's office to keep an eye on the investigation and I knew he would stick to Whitbread like a leech. Whitbread knew that as well. In fact, he was used to avoiding Fitz. I knew it was why he hadn't asked me to report on my conversation with Kathlyn Williams yet. We would discuss it later, in private.

"I've established that the premises are woefully insecure," Whitbread said. "Keys appear to be handed out like candy and, while the main activities must be conducted with the aid of sunlight, the evenings are by no means quiet. Any number of people are liable to be around preparing for the next day. Of course, none of them admit to seeing Mr. Hyde or going near the set where he was found. And Selig assures me that the duties of a censor should never involve a visit here, in any case, as the viewings are all done at the downtown offices. He claims to be at a loss to explain Mr. Hyde's presence."

"Perhaps some local hoodlums broke in?" Fitz asked hopefully.

"Mr. Fitzgibbons, as you are well aware, we are far from the stomping grounds of the usual ruffians here. As far as our city gangs go, we're beyond the boundaries of their territories. No, it's unlikely they'd be lured here. The scarcity of people or businesses for them to prey on is obvious. They would be sorely tried to maintain a living. No, we must look to one of the current or past employees of Selig as the most likely perpetrator, I'm afraid."

Fitz sighed. I was glad to see that Whitbread maintained his usual independence from the suggestions of the mayor's representative.

"What about Broncho Billy Anderson?" I asked. "Alden suggested we look at him. Alden said Anderson quit when Selig wouldn't make him a partner."

Fitz didn't like that suggestion. "Oh, you're talking about Gil Anderson. He's a partner in another wonderful enterprise up here—the Essanay studios on Argyle. I'm sure he had nothing to do with this. His problem was with Selig, not Hyde."

Whitbread, however, was interested. He already knew of the connection. "Perhaps there is more to the situation than we know. Fitz, you have a motorcar, don't you? Why don't you take us to Argyle Street and introduce us to the famous cowboy?"

"I suppose I could do that."

"Then what are we waiting for? Let's go and see Mr. Anderson, and then Mrs. Chapman and I can meet Col. Selig downtown to view the particular reel of film to which Mr. Hyde had such a negative reaction yesterday. Come, sir, let's go."

Cowed, Fitz led us out to a large touring vehicle and I was glad to see he had a driver, as he had the night before. I checked in quickly with Alden before we left to see how my children were faring, and asked him to get them home in one piece, once they were done with their visit. I knew Detective Whitbread was including me in the investigation because he would prefer not to have to detain my brother. But, if we didn't find other viable suspects, Alden would be at risk. The possibility of his arrest hung like a cloud on the horizon. I really would have preferred to return home with my children and continued packing for the summer, but I knew that I wouldn't be able to bear leaving the city until Alden was cleared. Once that was accomplished, I also hoped to persuade him to give up his idea of heading out to California. I intended to remind him firmly of his commitment to Clara and their children.

Ten

Because Fitz had a driver, I sat between him and Detective Whitbread in the enclosed back of the vehicle. The driver cranked the engine, then hopped back into his seat. It was quite noisy, and occasionally we jerked forward, but it was faster than taking a streetcar.

Our journey took us farther north, through some empty land to another set of buildings that looked as if they were still under construction. Fitz explained that film people always lived in temporary settings, everything brought together then dissolved in an instant. Change was incessant for them.

Our automobile coughed to a stop and Fitz helped me to climb down. I still felt a little motion when my feet were on the ground. We followed Detective Whitbread through a door in the fence into a yard. After walking by a group of men who were busy with carpentry, we were directed to the dressing rooms where we found Gil Anderson. He was a good-looking man with a square jaw and dark hair. He wore a red kerchief knotted around his neck, large leather gloves, and leather chaps that looked like flaps attached to his pants—the very image of a cowboy. He greeted Fitz who then introduced us. Whitbread told him about Mr. Hyde's demise and asked if he'd known the man.

Anderson looked at Fitz. "We'd met, of course. We submit our films for review and he was one of the censors. Sometimes we even rent space from Selig downtown, so the censors can look at our pictures without coming up here. It's important to get it done as efficiently as possible to keep up with the schedule." He admitted he'd previously worked for Selig but denied that he'd been to that studio lately or even that there was any enmity involved. "Selig's good enough," he said. "But he lacks vision. And he didn't want to make Westerns any more, not like we are. He's content to just churn out the same type of pictures, but we want to do more, something more important, more substantial." He crossed his arms and leaned back. "Wait till you see what we have planned. We're developing a lighting system that's going to be better than anything the other guys have, including Selig. So don't be surprised if some of his cameramen get interested and come over to us. This is the future, right here."

Fitz sighted a couple of figures walking across the yard. "Say, is that Ring Lardner I see?"

Anderson grinned. "Right, and George Ade, too. Both are newspapermen but we've got them working on scenarios for us. 'Photoplays,' we call them. We'll stop at nothing to get the best for our pictures."

I recognized the two writers as men my brother admired. Newspapermen, they both also published stories that were quite popular. The fact that they were drawn to work on films gave me pause. At least Alden wasn't the only one. But I wondered if it would prove to be false gold for all of them.

"Mr. Anderson," I said, "is it true that your Western films will compete with the ones Selig is making with Tom Mix? And didn't Selig refuse to make you a partner? I heard that was why you left."

He frowned at me, and Fitz put a hand on my elbow, but I pulled away. Alden insisted that Gil Anderson had a grudge against Selig and I wanted to make sure we asked him about it. Fitz's need to placate the people in this industry was not shared by me. I wanted to clear Alden and get my family away from all of this. Whitbread merely raised an eyebrow.

"I have bigger ideas," Anderson said. "Too big for Selig. I'd say *he* has a grudge against *me* for leaving." Seeing how Tom Mix had bowled over my oldest son, I doubted that. But Anderson continued, "If you're looking for a feud, you should look into Selig's relationship with Thomas Edison. Now that's a long-term rivalry. Edison nearly put him out of business with lawsuits not so long ago."

"Col. Selig claims a détente is in the offing there," Whitbread said.

Anderson looked startled. "What do you mean? That's not possible. Edison's got patents he uses to try to force a monopoly. He's not giving that up."

"Surely that must apply to Essanay as well as Selig," I said.

"Yes, but the feud between Selig and Edison has been going on for a while. It's bitter. We're relative newcomers, so we've been sidestepping it. Selig's the one who's had lawsuits thrown at him and Edison's thugs raiding his exhibitors. We're small fish, too small to worry Edison. Maybe Edison got that censor to come down harder than usual on Selig. You should look into that." He appeared to be gratified by his strategy. "If there's nothing else, I really need to get back to work."

We followed him outside and saw him helped up onto a horse by a couple of lackeys. He didn't look anywhere near as comfortable as Tom Mix had. I thought I was seeing things when another man, dressed precisely alike on a similar horse, arrived on the scene. Fitz saw me staring. "That's a double," he told me. He was happy to show off his familiarity with the strange world of moving pictures. "Unlike Tom Mix, who really was a cowhand at one time, Broncho Billy never got on a horse till his first Western, so they hire a horseman who looks like him to do some of the action."

"I see," I said, wondering what my son Jack would think of that.

"I think we have heard enough here," Whitbread said, looking at a large pocket-watch he pulled from his vest. "We are to meet Col. Selig at his offices to view the films that Hyde saw the day of his death."

"I suppose Anderson's in the clear," Fitz said.

Whitbread grunted. "By no means. He knew how to get into Selig's building and he had reason to want to harm a rival. Why he'd kill *Hyde* to get at *Selig* I can't figure out, but he's not clear of suspicion yet. Come."

"Why does Anderson say you should look into Edison?" I asked.

Whitbread had apparently already researched this. "It would seem this film business is cutthroat. Mr. Edison is trying to establish a monopoly, so he sues all the other companies, claiming patents on the machinery used."

"When that doesn't work," Fitz added, as we walked toward the motorcar, "he sends in bully boys to beat up exhibitors who show films from other companies."

I realized that Edison's company was not in Chicago, so Fitz would naturally ally himself with the local businessmen who brought money and jobs to the city.

"So it is alleged," Whitbread corrected him. "In any case, Mr. Anderson wants to throw suspicion on Mr. Edison and his employees to draw it away from himself. He's suggesting that Edison might have had the film censor killed in order to make trouble for Col. Selig."

"Enough trouble to drive him out of the business," Fitz said, nodding his head.

"But why would a man of Mr. Edison's stature have a man killed just to cause trouble for a competitor?" I asked.

I saw Whitbread and Fitz exchange a glance.

"It's becoming *very* big business," Fitz said. "It's going to be very big indeed, you wait and see."

But, if that was the case, I wondered why Col. Selig would deny any possible involvement of Edison and his cronies. Why didn't he take advantage of the suggestion from Detective Whitbread that Edison might be responsible, at least to divert him from scrutinizing the staff of the Selig studios, so they could get on with their filming? It didn't make sense to me.

Eleven

Fitz was kind enough to drive us to Selig's Randolph Street offices. I was glad to step down and find myself back in the city. The hustle and bustle of the crowds was at least real. Here the buildings were solid, not just painted fronts. Here the problems were real, the dramas and tragedies were very real, and it was all a sharp contrast to the half-built, half-felt staged scenes we'd left behind at the two film studios.

When we reached the third-floor offices, we were greeted by Col. Selig. He bowed us into a room where the windows were blacked out by heavy drapes. Introducing a young man as the projectionist, he ushered us to padded seats in front of a large screen. "So, I've asked Jeff to show you the reel Mr. Hyde was reviewing on Tuesday. That was the last time he was here. This is a reel of three shorts—a comic cowboy scene, a melodrama, and a romantic comedy. Of course, in the nickelodeon, there would be music, but we leave it to the exhibitors to provide that, with some suggestions, you see."

The single light was turned off and we heard the clickety-clack of the projector as the screen flickered with the white Diamond "S" for Selig Polyscope Company. Then we saw, in quick succession, a cowboy tricked into mounting a horse that threw him immediately; a beautiful, young Kathlyn Williams being harassed by an evil little man, then saved by the entrance of the handsome Alonzo Swift; and, finally, a bashful Babe Greer being proposed to by a kneeling suitor who was also played by Alonzo Swift. In the final scene, acceptance was followed by a vigorous embrace and long kiss. It was all over very quickly, then Col. Selig turned the light back on.

"Were you present when he watched the film?" Whitbread asked him.

"No, actually, I was out of town. That's why I asked Mr. Cabot and Mr. Leeder to be here. You see, we'd re-done the scene with Kathlyn Williams so the villain never touches her. Mr. Hyde objected to an earlier version where the landlord grabbed her." He cleared his throat. "Mr. Cabot suggested we put the scene on a reel with the romantic comedy of Babe Greer for contrast. He rightly pointed out that Mr. Hyde had never objected to any of Miss Greer's scenes. I told him it's not worth arguing with the censor, he has the power, but he had a point. It's true that Kathlyn Williams is always in more tragic melodramas. Still, you must see that nothing unacceptable is happening in the scene."

"Could we see that once more?" I asked. There was something that bothered me about the scene, but I couldn't say what it was.

They turned out the lights and showed the reel again. This time I realized what I'd seen.

"That man, the villain in the scene with Kathlyn Williams," I said, when the lights went on again. "Doesn't he look a lot like Mr. Hyde?" I could see in my mind, the little man fallen back on the white gauze of the frilly bedspread. "He was short and squat with sideburns, just like that man, wasn't he?" I bit my lip as I remembered the scene. It was impossible not to feel the taboo of a body bereft of its spirit. You naturally turned away from it. I didn't know anyone who would look at a corpse by choice. How strange to see someone you know is gone appear on a screen as if he were still alive. Mr. Hyde had seemed to be on the screen. I was sure the resemblance was real.

Col. Selig looked uncomfortable and fiddled with his large hands, which hung from his lap.

"Colonel Selig," Whitbread said.

"It was another idea of Mr. Cabot's. Last week we used a different actor. This one is our Teddy Roosevelt impersonator without the false teeth and pince-nez. Mr. Cabot recognized a similarity with Hyde and suggested we use him for the part when we re-did the scenario. It was mischievous of him, of course. I didn't realize until we saw the negatives. By then it seemed better to go ahead and print it."

"I suppose Mr. Hyde took offense at being portrayed as the villain assaulting Kathlyn Williams and that's what caused him to storm out?" Whitbread asked.

"No, he stayed for the whole reel," the projectionist said. "He saw the whole thing and then he rushed off. Mr. Cabot tried to stop him, to make him admit the middle scene was less scandalous than the last, but he kept going."

"Mr. Hyde was very conscientious," Fitz said.

"Unfortunately, he wasn't conscientious enough to sign off on that reel of film," Col. Selig said. "And, as a result, we've been unable to release it."

"Well, I think we can take care of that," Fitz said. "As temporary chief censor, I can see nothing wrong with it."

Col. Selig sighed. "Please, come to my office so we can deal with the paperwork. This is what I told you about back at the studio. The rest of the forms are here."

They left Detective Whitbread and myself with the projectionist who ran the short films one more time so Whitbread could confirm my impression about the man who looked like Hyde. Really, the scene with the landlord appeared quite chaste. And, when rescued by her leading man, the heroine portrayed by Kathlyn Williams barely held hands with her rescuer, looking away and down. He appeared to burn with admiration for her but there was no suggestion of intimacy.

Alden had been clever to follow that with the Babe Greer scene, especially since the same leading man was embracing the innocent young girl in the end. Yet, in the comedy, it was all done in good faith and with obvious intentions for a happily married future for the couple.

"These censors certainly have a lot of power," I said to Whitbread when the lights were on again. The machine clicked in the background as the projectionist rewound the film.

"All the more so, with the scandals in the Levee this year and the crusaders down there every night, serenading the houses of ill repute with psalms," he said. "After the arrest of one of our police captains for taking money from brothel owners, the mayor can't take any more bad press on morals issues. The Film Board is a way for the mayor to demonstrate he's serious about enforcing morality. And I understand Selig really has been cooperative. He's anxious for the audience to be expanded beyond those who go to the Levee for entertainment. He wants to appeal to the wives and children, not just the men out for cheap entertainment."

"So you wouldn't expect him to murder a censor, then?"

"No, I could see some of the hotheads down in the Levee getting worked up and taking a shot at one of the reverends who go parading down there trying to reform the harlots, but not Selig. I think he'd just do whatever the censor asked." Whitbread walked to a side table and picked up a couple of printed newspapers. They were tabloids devoted to the film business. "See this? That's the type of publicity Selig wants."

He handed me the paper and I saw a prominent article about a romance between Babe Greer and Alonzo Swift. There was a picture of them both in a motorcar, waving. It was all very sweet and chaste. My eye was caught by a smaller headline further down. I read the article then passed it back to Whitbread. "I assume this is the type of publicity he doesn't want." It was about how Kathlyn Williams was in the midst of a rancorous divorce. There were rumors of unfaithfulness on her part and accusations of miserly behavior on her former husband's. "Perhaps that's what Hyde had against Kathlyn Williams. She left her husband, as his wife left him. The man seems to have taken rather irrationally against her. Comparison of those scenes clearly shows that bias," I said.

"And your brother appears to be Miss Williams's defender."

The projectionist was placing the reel of film into a tin container. "Is Mr. Cabot your brother then, ma'am? He sure was upset with that Mr. Hyde. He ran after the man, yelling at him, and Mr. Leeder had to grab his collar to pull him back."

"But arguing with the man is one thing. That's something Alden would do," I said to Whitbread. "He wouldn't shoot the man, though. Besides, he didn't follow him in the end, did he?" I asked the projectionist. "You said Mr. Leeder pulled him back?"

"That's right. Him and Mr. Leeder went back to the studios up on Western Avenue. They had a big shoot in the morning and they said they had some things to fix there."

Well, that wasn't helpful, either, because they'd gone back to the studio where Mr. Hyde was shot later that night. Alden was definitely not in the clear and I could tell, by the way Whitbread looked at me, that he knew it, too.

Alden, however did you get yourself into this mess?

Twelve

P erhaps we should postpone our departure," Stephen said when I returned home that night. "If Alden's still under suspicion by Monday, perhaps we could put off our trip for another week."

"No, no, no," I protested. We were standing in the kitchen, where the children had just finished a supper of soup, bread, and cheese. Alden had returned them home, full of stories about their trip to the film studios. I was annoyed that he was their hero of the moment, when all he was doing was wrecking everyone else's life. "No. You and Clara must get there in time to claim your laboratories or you know they'll be taken by someone else."

At the Marine Biological Laboratory in Woods Hole there was always a competition for the best laboratory space in the buildings. The summer session was so popular with scientists from all over the country that there was never enough space. Stephen and Clara both had ongoing studies and, over time, they'd managed to secure prime space for their equipment. If we arrived late, there was no way to guarantee their spots. Why should they suffer because my selfish brother was detained for a police investigation? No, that wouldn't be fair at all.

"We should just pack up and leave him behind," I said. "No, really, Stephen, this is the last time I'm going to change all my plans to accommodate Alden. You know the past two years he came with us, then left to go back to the city anyway. When it's

Christmas, he says he'll entertain at his house, then he flies out after some news story and leaves Clara to do it all by herself. It's shameful."

"Clara has plenty of help," Stephen said.

"I know that. Clara has plenty of help because Clara has plenty of money. But that's no excuse for Alden not doing his part. He can't even be home for a Christmas party but he can show up unannounced and spirit the children away to a film studio, without seeking my permission, and get them all excited when they need to be getting ready for the trip east."

Stephen turned to our three children, who still sat around the rough kitchen table. "How was your trip with Uncle Alden?" he asked them. He gave me a look and I knew he didn't take my complaint seriously. I knew I was just jealous that Alden was such a hero for them when all he did was cause trouble for the grown-ups. "Would you rather have been at the laboratory with me?"

"Oh, no, it was great, Father," Jack said. "I met Tom Mix. And we saw him riding ponies. Tommy almost got run over by one, only Uncle Alden pulled him back."

"Tigers," Tommy said. His eyes were wide. "We saw tigers and even a baby elephant. They said tomorrow there'll be leopards and lions."

"Tommy was bad," Lizzie said. "He tried to grab the elephant by the trunk, and the elephant yelled, and Uncle Alden pulled him off."

"He didn't yell, he roared," Jack corrected her. "Anyway, you kept trying to go back inside when Uncle Alden told you to stop it. You and Penny."

"We wanted to see Oz," Lizzie said. She was standing with her arms akimbo, frowning. "Uncle Alden said we would see Oz. But it wasn't there. I told him he *has* to take us back for that. He asked somebody and they said most of Oz will be next week so he said he'd take us back."

"Lizzie, we're going to Woods Hole next week, on the train," I said. "You're not going back to the Selig studios no matter what your uncle promised."

She was outraged. I should have known better. At thirteen, my daughter was one of the most opinionated young women I'd ever met. What I didn't understand was why her opinions so seldom coincided with my own. Where did she get these ideas? Now she was intent on seeing Oz at the Selig studios, and she stood up straight, hands by her side like a little soldier glaring at me. "Yes, we are. We're going to see Oz. Uncle Alden *promised!* He *promised!* We're not going to Woods Hole until *after* we see Oz. He *promised.*"

I glared back at her but, before I could compose a reply, I felt Stephen's hand on my arm. "We'll see, Lizzie. Now, didn't you say you were going to find your copies of the Oz books to take with you this summer? Did you pack them yet?"

Lizzie was gratified that he, at least, understood her pre-occupation with Oz. "No, they're in the study somewhere. I'll go find them." She took a step, then pulled back. "May I leave the table now?" she asked, as she'd been trained to do. At least that was something I'd taught her.

"Yes," Stephen said. "Go and look for them. And you boys can go as well. Make sure you've put out any books you want to take on the trip. We'll be there all summer and we need to send the trunks of books separately. Go ahead."

I rolled my eyes as they scurried away. Lizzie and her Oz. She was quite capable of throwing a complete tantrum in the train station if she didn't get what she wanted. I set my jaw grimly. At some point, I would need to have a serious discussion with my daughter about her temper, but I was tired from the day and I wasn't willing to face her down that evening.

Delia was clearing off the dishes and I noticed she was staring at me as she did so. It seemed like she couldn't take her eyes off me. My husband noticed it as well and gave me a quizzical look.

"Delia," I said. "What's the matter?"

She looked down guiltily as she stacked the plates. "Oh, nothing, it's nothing. Only, is it true that you were at the Selig studios today? Like the children?"

"Yes, I had some business there." I didn't want to explain that there'd been a murder and that my brother was a suspect.

"Mrs. Chapman, ma'am, did you happen to see Mr. Alonzo Swift while you were there? I asked the children, but they were all looking at the cowboys on the horses and the animals in the zoo jungle there. They didn't seem to know about the actors. Did you see him? He's the most handsome man in the world, they say. And they say every girl would do just about anything to give her heart to him."

I sensed my husband suppressing a chuckle. He *would* think it was funny that poor Delia was taken by a matinee idol, while I was merely annoyed at my brother for introducing my family to the film world. "Yes, Delia, as a matter of fact, I saw Mr. Swift performing in a scenario written by Mr. Cabot, and afterwards we were introduced."

That was too much for her. She dropped the pile of plates back on the table with a rattle of silverware and she clasped her hands to her bosom, like a heroine in one of the motion pictures. "Oh, ma'am, that must have been wonderful for you."

"I managed to survive it without fainting, I'm happy to report," I told her, and Stephen restrained himself from laughing at that. "Do you need help with the dishes, Delia?" We had more help during the academic year but we'd dismissed the others in preparation for our trip to Woods Hole.

"No, ma'am, I'm fine. I just think it's very lucky for you to have met a star like Alonzo Swift."

She returned to her work and I shook my head. Delia was an adult and I had no call to comment on what she did with her days off, but I was disappointed that she was spending time and money at nickelodeons. What was the world coming to when young people spent their time at such amusements? When we returned from our summer holiday I would need to consult with Detective Whitbread's wife, who was Delia's aunt, about finding some more appropriate activities for her. I wondered if I took her for granted too much. She was a sweet girl and I couldn't imagine how my family could get along without her.

Stephen steered me into the parlor where several trunks lay open, waiting for more of the linens and utensils we would need for the summer. "Are you quite sure we shouldn't postpone our departure?" he asked.

"No. Alden's caused enough grief. I'll do what I can with Whitbread to clear him so that he can join us, but I have to tell you that I'm not at all sure he'll come, even if he's allowed to. He's talking about going to California, and I'm not sure what Clara will do. It's a big mess, and it's all Alden's fault."

"What will you do tomorrow?"

"I agreed to return to Selig's studio with Whitbread. Can you help Delia with the packing? I know you have your laboratory things to ship. I wired the rent to Mrs. Townsend, so all should be ready for us. I don't know who shot that poor man but, even at his wildest, Alden wouldn't do that. Would he?"

Thirteen

The next morning found me tucked into Mr. Fitzgibbons's motorcar again, on my way up to the Selig studios with Fitz and Detective Whitbread. I'd escaped a tearful Lizzie, who was furious that I was going to the studio and she was not. All she thought about was Oz. I reluctantly promised to find out when they would be filming scenes in the fairyland. Jack was content to help his father, still luxuriating in the memories of meeting Tom Mix. And Tommy was already out climbing the neighbor's trees when I left. Delia seemed merely sorrowful at the thought that her idol was many miles to the north and beyond her reach. Honestly, the effort expended on thoughts about these fantastic characters known only from a flickering screen was beyond my comprehension.

"Oh, yes," Fitz told me on the ride over, "people can be quite enamored of the beautiful girls and handsome men. They get declarations of undying love and proposals of marriage in every mail sack. I've even heard of one handsome leading man being attacked by the husband of one of his admirers. It's amazing how serious some of these people can be about the characters they see on the screen. When they go into the dark of the nickelodeon, they escape their dreary lives and there they are, close up to all those beautiful, handsome people living in circumstances ordinary people could never aspire to."

Detective Whitbread moved restively beside me. He was angry with City Hall for interfering with his investigation. Even though he'd accepted a ride from Fitz, he was still in a huff at the big Irishman and didn't say much. As we rode through some of the unhealthy-looking tenements, to get to the sparser territory northwest of the city, I could imagine the need for such an escape, but books had always been my portal to larger worlds. With books, you made the pictures in your own mind and they could be of any shape or hue. The images I'd seen in the darkened room at the Selig offices were somewhat dreamlike, but they were also someone else's images, not mine. They looked like rooms and streets where I'd been, but I knew they were not, because I'd seen how those moving pictures were made. Beyond the edges of the screen were other unrelated rooms and people yelling instructions. It was a strange silly business.

At the studios, we began by interviewing Mr. Leeder. He was the producer of the melodrama starring Kathlyn Williams and Alonzo Swift, and he was the one who claimed to have seen Alden putting the gun in the dead man's hand. We found him in an office he shared with others on the second floor of the main building and Whitbread asked him about Alden's argument with Mr. Hyde. Fitz stayed quietly in the background.

"Yes, well, Cabot was pretty pissed off, you know. The way Hyde kept giving them trouble about any scene Kathlyn was in. It was like he had something against her, you know?" He was waving around a cigarette as he spoke. "So, Cabot was fed up. I can't say as I blame him. I mean it really slows things down to have to redo scenes all the time. Selig asked us to be there. He had some big hush-hush meeting out of town so we were supposed to babysit Hyde, cozy up to him, you know? But Cabot got mad. I thought it was pretty good the way he got them to put the Babe Greer scene on the same reel. It clearly showed there was a bias. But Hyde wasn't having any of it. Instead of arguing, he just got up and left, without a word. Cabot was furious and started to go after the guy, but I pulled him back. We don't need the bad press that would come if he attacked the man. I calmed him down and brought him back up here."

"What happened after you returned to the studio?" Whitbread asked.

"We did some work, then we both left, Cabot and me. A few other people were still here—Alonzo Swift, I think, and maybe Mix and some of his pals."

"Did you see Mr. Hyde again?"

"Up here, you mean? No, not till the next morning. I came in and there he was dripping blood all over the bed and Cabot was putting the gun in his hand. It was pretty frightening, believe me."

I felt an icy finger down my spine. He'd seen Alden putting the gun in the hand of the dead man. "You didn't see Alden actually shoot the man, did you?" I asked.

"No."

I gritted my teeth, trying to think of a way out for my brother. Why would Leeder lie about seeing him putting the gun in the dead man's hand? Unless Leeder had done it himself, of course. But why would *he* kill the censor?

"Did you hear the shot?" Whitbread asked.

"No. I don't think so."

"Think. How did you enter? Did you hear anything on the way up?" Whitbread asked.

Leeder frowned. "I came in the door. I used my key. Mix and some of the wranglers were outside getting the horses ready. I saw some of the workers downstairs, just coming in. I came up the stairs. No, I don't recall hearing a shot, but perhaps I didn't notice. Cabot and I had talked about checking the set before the shoot." He looked up. "But he was standing over the dead man and he was putting the gun in his hand. I saw that all right."

"Mr. Leeder, they're ready for you to do the next scene." It was Babe Greer, looking demure in a blue and white polka dot dress. She looked a little anxious about interrupting.

"Babe, honey, you're here early, aren't you?" Leeder said, as he snuffed out his cigarette.

"Aren't you glad to see me?" She looked nervous. "Did I interrupt something important?"

"We were just talking about you, darling. About how smart it was of Cabot to put that scene between you and Alonzo right beside Kathlyn's, for Hyde to look at. She looked like a nun in comparison."

The auburn-haired beauty blushed. "I just did what you told me. Anyhow, they're ready."

"Fine. You'll have to excuse me, folks. Duty calls. In any case, I have nothing else to say that might be of interest to you." He hovered over Babe Greer. "And you be ready when I call, darling."

She stepped away from him. "Of course."

Leeder frowned and looked up at Whitbread. "If I think of anything else, I'll get back to you."

He stomped away and Babe turned back to us. "They're shooting a scene with real animals outside. It's for *Hunting Big Game in Africa*. Want to watch?"

Fitz was enthusiastic about the chance to watch, but Whitbread had other ideas. "We need to ask if anyone saw Broncho Billy here recently."

I was going to volunteer to help him when Babe spoke up. "I did. You mean Gil Anderson, right? I saw him the other night talking to Emmet O'Neill. He's a cameraman. I didn't expect to see Gil here after the big blowout he had with the colonel, so I was surprised."

It was the night of the murder that she'd seen him. She convinced Whitbread the easiest way to find O'Neill was to watch them shoot the jungle scenes, as he was one of the cameramen.

She led us to the backlot and over to a corner where they'd planted a jungle. Ferns and plants with hanging vines were draped around a large area.

"Where's this cameraman?" Whitbread asked.

Babe looked around helplessly.

"What are you doing here?" Alden asked. He'd come up

behind me. When he heard that we were looking for O'Neill, he pointed to a safety cage, inside of which there was a platform raised about twelve feet above the ground and camouflaged by vines. On the platform, a man stood behind a large camera on a tripod. "That's one of the cameras, to get shots from above. There'll be another one down on the ground. They always have multiple cameras for these shots with the live animals, in case one of them misses something."

"The animals don't always cooperate when you have to reshoot a scene?" Fitz asked. He seemed to quite enjoy learning about the filming. I, on the other hand, was anxious to get on with the investigation. Alden didn't realize the danger he faced. He assumed Whitbread and I would be able to clear him. I had no such confidence, but I didn't want to argue with him in front of the others.

"Where's this O'Neill?" Whitbread asked.

"On the platform. You'll have to wait till they finish shooting," Alden said, but Whitbread was impatient. He insisted on talking to O'Neill immediately, so I trailed him as he stomped into the security cage and up onto the twelve-foot-high platform. I took a deep breath to hoist myself up and climb the narrow ladder behind him.

A small man in rolled-up shirt sleeves and suspenders, and with a bowler hat perched on his head, was fussing around the mounted camera. Whitbread introduced himself and asked O'Neill when he'd last seen Broncho Billy at the studios.

"Anderson? Oh, yeah, he's been around lately. Not just for me. He's looking to steal away a couple of cameramen. But I told him, 'No, thanks.' The colonel's been pretty good to me."

As he stood, scratching his head under the hat, trying to remember the dates when he'd seen Broncho Billy and where they'd met, I teetered to the edge of the platform and watched the preparations going on below us. The previous shoot had finished and they were setting up for *Hunting Big Game in Africa*.

An experienced-looking hunter in khaki clothes held a rifle as he directed some local Negroes who were made up to look like African natives. They dug a hole, then brought in a goat and tied it to a stake.

Looking down at the fake African scene, I remembered the Dahomey Village exhibit at the Columbian Exposition so many years before. The natives there were confused, and cold, and they couldn't speak or understand English. It was the French who'd colonized that country and shipped over the exhibit, which consisted of people, as well as huts and artifacts. Like the Eskimos in another exhibit on the Midway, the Africans had suffered from the Chicago climate.

By comparison, the pretend Africans in the pretend jungle yelled to each other in English. They moved uncomfortably in skimpy outfits, made with prickly feathers, and rattling bone necklaces. Lines of white paint obscured their faces. They were used to the weather but unused to the outfits and the tangled vines. As they did their best to set up the goat as bait, O'Neill told us they'd been recruited from south State Street, while the animals had come from a bankrupt circus in Milwaukee.

"Hush," he said suddenly. "They're gonna start."

There was much yelling below, and I could see another camera on a tripod just outside the safety cage but with its lens directed through a big hole in the fence. After another round of yelling, an elderly lion was released from a smaller cage. His mane made a scruffy halo around his face and his mouth was open as he panted a bit. Loose skin hung from his narrow ribs and, when he moved, he ducked his head as if each step was an effort. I felt sorry for the old boy. His black-rimmed, triangular eyes looked sad.

The platform was a little unsteady, without any railing, but I leaned out to see the men outside poking at the lion with sticks to get him moving toward the pit with the goat. He gave a deep-throated growl, took a few steps then lay down.

"Where is he?" I heard Mr. Leeder scream. "Come on, come on. Roosevelt, get in there." Leeder was safely outside with the second cameraman.

At the other side of the cage, the Teddy Roosevelt impersonator looked around cautiously, then stepped through a gate followed by a group of men, all dressed up in pith helmets and puttees. When the cameras turned on him, "Roosevelt" planted his pince-nez firmly on his nose and stuck out his hand to one of the others. "De-lighted, de-lighted," he said, in a fair imitation of the former president. I had to remind myself that the audience would not actually hear those words, just see the actor's lips move.

The "natives" were still trying to get the old lion on the other side of the cage to cooperate. One man crawled up behind him and forced him to his legs and forward. Others stood farther off but kept poking him with bamboo poles or jabbing him with sticks. The lion snarled and retreated.

"Come on, get him going," Leeder shouted. When they finally managed to get behind the beast and drove him forward at a slow walk, Leeder yelled, "OK, ready everybody. Ready, aim, fire!"

Roosevelt raised his rifle but the real shot came from the hunter outside the cage. At the deafening noise the lion shrieked, then roared. But he didn't fall down, and now there was panic in the cage. People screamed as the old lion roared and leapt at the fake natives. They quickly escaped through a gate. So did Roosevelt and his men, followed closely by the stalking lion who roared and roared. He was anything but dead. We were still inside the cage but perched twelve feet above it all on the platform. There was more yelling and I noticed O'Neill kept cranking his camera. I thought it served the film folks right that the lion had turned on them after such goading. I was rooting for the lion.

Still issuing roars that came from the pit of his stomach, the lion turned in a circle looking for something to attack. He came to a stop facing in our direction and I realized we were the only ones left inside. Even though we were on the platform above it all, suddenly I was no longer rooting for him.

The lion bounded toward us and leapt at the platform. He roared and the structure rattled as he slid down it. He leapt again and I saw his staring eyes and bloody mouth. He'd been hit in the jaw and was enraged by the pain. I felt a spring of the platform floor and, looking behind me, saw O'Neill climb over the top of the cage then drop to the ground outside. He ran away without a backward glance.

The platform shook as the enraged animal kept leaping at it, slamming his body into the supporting framework as he fell. It shook so much I feared it would collapse. Whitbread pushed in front of me and I clutched him around the waist, my face on his jacket as I peered over his shoulder. The roars of the wounded animal filled my ears.

Suddenly, Whitbread thrust me back. As I stumbled and grabbed the side of the cage I saw him pull out his long-barreled pistol. Steadying himself on one bent knee, he used two hands to point the gun and fire. The platform shuddered, so I reached out one hand to grab him. But he straightened and there was silence as a cloud of smoke rose in the air. The lion was dead.

Fourteen

M rs. Chapman, are you hurt?" Whitbread asked. My knees gave out and I dropped to the floor of the platform. He leaned over me, a hand on my shoulder.

"I'm all right," I said. I felt foolish but it was a physical reaction. All energy had just drained from me when the danger was over. "I'll be all right in a moment," I corrected myself. I watched as, below us, the film people poured back into the cage. The Roosevelt impersonator tiptoed forward, reaching out with his rifle to test that the lion was dead.

The real hunter brushed past him and bent to check the body. "He's dead." He looked up at Whitbread. "I was having a hard time getting a second shot off. Good thing you had a pistol."

I don't know what I expected—some concern, some apology, perhaps, for the fright we'd endured. But that was not how things worked in this off-kilter world. On the contrary, we were ignored as Emmet O'Neill was chastised and boosted back up to the platform.

"Why did you run?" Col. Selig asked O'Neill. "He couldn't reach you at that height." He twisted his neck to look up and, noticing me, gave a polite nod as if we were at a tea party.

When O'Neill reached the top of the ladder he shrugged. "It didn't look that way." He glanced at me guiltily but continued over to his camera to prepare for the next scene. Whitbread just shook his head and sat down beside me, his arm around my shoulders.

It was wildly incorrect and inappropriate. We'd just been attacked by a wounded lion that lay dead and bloody below us, yet the only reaction was to get on with the new scene. I felt like Alice when she stepped through the looking glass. I spotted my brother in the crowd below and, once he saw I was unharmed, he avoided my eyes. Surely he must be as shocked as me but apparently not. The way Whitbread continued to shake his head and narrow his eyes, I could tell he shared my amazement. We could have demanded to be let down and out of the cage, but we were too dumbfounded to speak. We just continued to watch the spectacle as we recovered our senses.

With the assurance of the real hunter that the animal was dead, Mr. Leeder started yelling through his megaphone and soon the cameramen were cranking again as one of the "natives" emerged from the jungle and gave an excited yell at the sight of the poor old lion collapsed on his side. The king of the jungle looked at rest, as if he had finally escaped the prods and noise. A nervous-looking Roosevelt stepped up, followed by the rest of his party, and the hunter took the lion's tail in his hands and pulled the corpse out into the open under the loud directives of Leeder. Suppressing an obvious distaste, Roosevelt acknowledged Leeder's commands and lifted the head to count the bullet holes. Still under direction, he let the head fall, put his right foot on the lion's prone body and waved his hat with his left hand to signal victory. Suddenly, his party of hunters and all the "natives" were shaking hands and smiling for the cameras while Leeder screamed at them. Just as suddenly, the cameras stopped cranking and everyone dispersed.

Whitbread patted my shoulder. "Shall we descend?" He helped me to the ladder and my brother had the grace to assist me at the bottom, before turning away.

Col. Selig smiled broadly. "I believe we've come as near to the real thing as could be done," he said, and I realized he expected us to be as thrilled with the result of the action as he was.

I was dumbfounded for a moment as I got my legs steady on the firm ground again. Behind me I could hear Leeder and his crew discussing how they would tie the lion to a pole and parade him around before setting up for the hunter to skin the animal in front of the cameras. I had no wish at all to see any of that.

Col. Selig noticed my discomfort so he tucked my hand in his arm to escort me out of the safety cage. "It's all quite safe, my dear," he reassured me. "The animals are all kept in line by Mr. Breitkreutz. We call him Big Otto." He pointed to a broad-shouldered bald man wearing only an undershirt and short pants of a shiny material who stood beside a series of cages that held more animals. He moved from cage to cage with a bucket, shoveling slops into feeding mangers. "Big Otto had a circus in Milwaukee and it was great luck that I ran into him. We have an arrangement—he gets to keep and feed his animals, and we use them to get very real effects in our films." Col. Selig was proud of himself. "The lion was old. I bought him outright with the intention of having him shot before the camera. It'll be a fantastic effect unlike anything people have seen before."

I shivered. I couldn't help it. He noticed. "Now, my dear, you mustn't worry. If we'd sent a cameraman on the real hunt, you would have seen real animals killed, you know. Many more than this. That's what a hunt is. But it would have been much harder to get really good film of the animals and been much more dangerous." He steered me around to look back at the jungle set. "This way we can get close to the animals without getting mauled."

"It didn't *feel* safe," I said. Whitbread, who was following close behind us, agreed.

"No, no, you don't understand," Selig said. "Compared to wild animals, these ones are domesticated. As a matter of fact, that lion was bred in captivity and never stepped into a jungle before today. Come, I want to introduce you to someone." He led us to a long, wide cage where I was appalled to see a tall woman lying on a chaise lounge surrounded by three leopards. Two of them stalked lightly, muscles rippling across their shoulders. Another lay with his head in the woman's lap.

"Olga, this is Mrs. Chapman and Detective Whitbread. They're here about poor Mr. Hyde's death. This is Miss Olga Celeste, our Leopard Lady," Selig said.

Fifteen

Olga Celeste stood up, gently pushing away the leopard on her lap. When she turned to walk over to the door of the cage, it seemed to me her walk imitated the animals. She rolled her shoulders back and bent her knees slightly as she moved. Her dark hair was cut short, a rather shocking fashion for the time. She had large dark eyes, very pronounced cheek bones, and wore a print silk dress with a pattern in yellow and brown. The small capped sleeves showed powerful arms well tanned by the sun. She murmured a greeting in a deep voice and slipped through the gate without paying any attention to the prowling leopards. They ignored her as well.

"You see, my dear lady," Col. Selig said. "It's all a matter of expertise. Olga is here to teach our staff how to act with the animals, so we can make the most realistic films ever made. Kathlyn, dear, you're learning from Olga today, aren't you?"

Kathlyn Williams had come up behind me. Her attitude toward me was still a bit formal. I looked back at the animals with considerable doubt. Would she really be expected to enter the cage and sit with the leopards as Olga had done? I wondered how she felt about that.

"It's all part of the job," she said.

Col. Selig beamed with approval.

"But isn't it dangerous?" I asked. I noticed Alden behind

us and fully expected him to raise objections on behalf of Kathlyn if he had any affection for her.

"Kathlyn will do anything," he said. "She's a real sport. The story of *The Leopard Queen* is of a girl who's raised by leopards and only gets found when she's an adult. Returned to civilization, she brings the leopards with her and they're part of her act. But, in the end, she's drawn back to the jungle and has to choose between the animals, that are the only family she has ever known, and the man she loves."

"Mr. Cabot wrote the scenario," the actress said. I had the distinct impression they were both trying to impress Col. Selig, not me. I could see Whitbread from the corner of my eye. He was becoming restless.

Olga spoke in her low-pitched voice. "It *is* dangerous." She gestured to the leopards. "The animals are wild. You must always remember this, but the film *can* be done with real animals. We practice. Now." She motioned to Kathlyn, who hesitated only one moment before stepping into the cage.

"It'll be a great story," Col. Selig said. "But let's leave these ladies to it." He motioned us to follow him back toward the main building.

"Col. Selig, were you aware that Anderson's been trying to lure your cameramen to his studio?" Whitbread asked.

Selig stopped. "Has he?"

"Your men are loyal, though. At least O'Neill is. He turned him down. But Anderson was on the premises the night Hyde was killed. Is there any reason he might want to harm the censor?"

"You mean aside from disrupting our schedules by making it appear someone here might be implicated? Not that I'm aware. He's a competitor, for sure. We're much bigger, though. More of the exhibitors carry our films, Essanay's are taken by a fraction of them. But Edison's studio is bigger than both of us. Unless Mr. Hyde knew of a plan to lock Essanay out of future expansion. Even then, shooting Mr. Hyde would hardly benefit Anderson."

"Could it be that Mr. Hyde was working for Mr. Edison?" Whitbread asked. "Censoring your films or those of Essanay would be another way of attacking you. Did you ever have reason to suspect Mr. Hyde of working for Mr. Edison?"

Col. Selig looked startled. "No, no, I've never thought of that. But Mr. Hyde didn't reject all of our films, only Kathlyn's."

"Perhaps he intended to expand his censorship and someone found out," Whitbread said.

"What do you mean about Essanay being locked out of future expansion?" I asked. "How would that happen?"

"Oh, well, I'm sure it wouldn't," Col. Selig said.

"Do you mean getting sued, like Edison sued you?" I asked.

"Yes, something like that. But, as I said, Mr. Hyde's death hardly seems a way to prevent that."

Unless the censor knew something that would harm Anderson's case, I thought, but didn't say. I was sure Whitbread shared my suspicions. He asked Selig to help him find and interview the other cameramen, to ask about Anderson's visits to the studio. Before I could follow them, Babe Greer came up to me.

"Mrs. Chapman, have you and the detective found out what really happened to the censor?"

I decided to stay behind to see if Babe had any more information. Whitbread might be following the trail back to Broncho Billy Anderson but I didn't really believe the truth lay in that direction. I thought all the threads wound back to my brother and Kathlyn Williams, and I knew that once Whitbread had exhausted all the leads and had answers to all his questions he would be pulled back to the two of them. This time, I had to find the truth *before* Whitbread. Annoying as he might be, Alden was still my brother.

"Miss Greer, do you know of any reason why the film censor, Mr. Hyde, rejected the films of Miss Williams so often?"

She pursed her cupid lips. "Oh, no, I don't. But Kathlyn isn't really a miss, you know. She's married."

"Yes. I understand she's being divorced."

"Divorced. That's not something anyone did where I grew up. It was a small town in the south part of the state. I don't know, but I thought perhaps Kathlyn knew Mr. Hyde in the past. But some time since she's been here in Chicago. She came from New York, you know. I'm sure they do things differently there. Anyhow, I know Mr. Cabot is your brother, but I think, perhaps, Mr. Hyde didn't like that he was…well…working so closely with Kathlyn."

I raised a palm to stop her. I didn't want to hear any more. She was too innocent to say that she thought my brother had an illicit relationship with Kathlyn Williams. But other, older staff had already told Whitbread of the suspicions, and even assumptions, that were generally held about them.

"It's just that it started when Mr. Cabot began working with her. That's when Mr. Hyde started rejecting Kathlyn's films. I couldn't help noticing. I'm sorry."

"Yes. I'm sorry, too."

"All of this can't be good for Kathlyn's suit against her husband…for the money she's trying to get from him. I mean, if he thought she was seeing Mr. Cabot he might use that against her. She told me and Miss Olga that one time. She was begging us to be discreet. It was when there was some gossip."

Perhaps it was Kathlyn Williams who benefited most from the death of the film censor. If Mr. Hyde found out about her relationship with Alden and blackmailed her, by threatening to stop approving her films, that might have been her motive to kill him. Especially if he also threatened to tell her husband about the affair. Could she really be so cold as to kill a man for money? Or perhaps she was the sort of woman who could set men against each other. Had she persuaded, or somehow coerced, Alden to get rid of the threat for her? I was old enough to know some women made the story of Eve tempting Adam to evil believable. Was Kathlyn Williams one of them? Babe reminded me of my own younger self, before I knew how twisted people could become. Babe might believe that Kathlyn had shot the man herself, but I *could* imagine that she might be ultimately responsible, without ever pulling the trigger. Had Alden really gone so far astray?

At that moment, Kathlyn and Olga came out of the leopard cage and headed toward the main building. Kathlyn rushed past, but Olga slowed to look us over with an impudent stare. When she saw Babe watching Kathlyn with concern, she said, "It is nothing. A mere scratch. A love scratch. The cats mark their toys."

Having barely recovered from the lion's attack, I bit my lip at the thought of being marked by a leopard's claws.

Babe looked angry. "Well, that is just too much. Poor Kathlyn. I'll go see if I can help her." She left without a backward glance and I felt a twinge of animosity between her and Olga. I wondered if they had a history.

Olga smiled. "The little one has not the strength of Kathlyn. She has not the *need* of the other. She would not do so well in the cage. She thinks she could do it better than Kathlyn, but she lies to herself."

I wondered if Babe had ever been trained by the mysterious Olga. Perhaps the Leopard Lady made those she trained pass tests, and Babe had failed. That could account for the animosity. I knew I would never want to train with the Leopard Lady. I had quite enough tests being thrown at me by my children.

"Miss Celeste, did you know the film censor who died... Mr. Hyde?" I asked.

She turned her dark eyes on me and seemed amused. She seemed as wild and unpredictable as her leopards. It made me wonder if her life was the basis for the story Kathlyn Williams was filming.

"The man who was shot? No, I did not know him. He had a taste for the heroines in the film stories, I think. I do not appear in the films."

"Why not?" I blurted out the question without thought. My own manners were quickly degrading in the company of these people.

Her eyes lit up a bit as she looked at me. "I cannot pretend," she said. "You will excuse me. The animals, they demand attention."

I watched as she walked away slowly, her head held high and on alert.

Sixteen

Whitbread strode out of the Selig building, followed reluctantly by Fitz. "Come," he said, gesturing to me. "I've been told we should visit a roadhouse to find Mr. Anderson. I want to question him again about his activities. Mr. Fitzgibbons here will provide transport, if he can pull himself away from these film people."

Fitz was flustered. "Oh, now, Whitey, you can't be serious. We can't be taking Mrs. Chapman to a roadhouse. It wouldn't be proper. What would her husband think?"

Whitbread snorted. "Since when does Dr. Chapman have any say in where his wife goes? Mrs. Chapman has accompanied me to less respectable dives than the roadhouse where these film people hang out. It caters to the women as well as the men."

"But they're film people!"

"Oh, really. Some of the inhabitants of your ward offices are far less scrupulous than the owners of this establishment. I'm told it was originally built to cater to mourners from the local cemeteries. In any case, Mrs. Chapman can remain in the motorcar if she fears entry would besmirch her spotless reputation."

"Thank you for your concern for my reputation, Fitz," I added. "But I want to participate...I have to. Alden's far too involved in all of this and I'm worried."

As we continued toward Fitz's motorcar, the chauffeur saw us coming and stamped out his cigarette, preparing to crank the motor. Fitz looked troubled while Whitbread conferred with the driver. Fitz had known us for more than a decade. He could remember when my brother first arrived from Boston, and he knew my sister-in-law Clara, as well. He'd always displayed a certain preference for me, which I found endearing. Clara had remarked on it more than once. But his politics were abhorrent to me. He was a good man, but he was totally lacking in integrity.

"I worry about you, Mrs. Chapman. This world of the film people is not what you're used to, down at the university and all. They have different standards. They'll do things the ladies of Prairie Avenue or the academics in Hyde Park would not approve of. They're somewhat freer in their attitudes, if you know what I mean."

"If you're talking about my brother and Kathlyn Williams, I've already been informed of people's suspicions. He denies it, but I'm not sure I can believe him these days."

Fitz handed me into the enclosed cab of the motorcar and climbed in beside me. "They find it necessary to play a part in public that may not represent their true personalities," he said. "Babe Greer, for example, is the epitome of innocent youth on the screen, yet you'll see her at the roadhouse with her co-workers. So you shouldn't be shocked to see Kathlyn Williams and your brother there. It's where they all go for a bit of leisure. You can see how hard they work all day."

"Work," if you could call it that. I thought of the people who flocked to Hull House for evening classes after long days of manual work or sewing in sweatshops. It was hard for me to sympathize with the so-called work of the film people.

Whitbread joined us and the engine sputtered to life, then the driver hopped into his seat and we were off. We drove until we reached a long, low brick building with a large sign that read "Pop Morse's Roadhouse." I could see a garden on the side with tables and chairs, lit by kerosene lamps. Fitz ushered me through the front door.

Inside, some trouble had been taken to outfit the place with a bit of glory. A long wooden bar with a brass foot rail ran down the left side. Cloth-covered tables were placed around the sizable room and, on the walls, heavy gilt frames encircled painted murals. An upright piano stood on a small stage at the back of the room, beside a sculpture of a woman in an elongated modern style.

Fitz was clearly very uncomfortable as he escorted me to a table then excused himself to get me a lemonade. I could hear Whitbread questioning the bartender about Broncho Billy. The place was sparsely populated at five in the afternoon, but people were beginning to drift in. It seemed to be a cross between a saloon and a restaurant. Two older men in white aprons stood at attention. The waiters, I presumed.

"Ah, Mrs. Chapman. Never expected to see you here." It was Mr. Leeder with a mug of beer in one hand and a cigarette in the other. "You know Babe here, don't you? Mind if we join you?" Not waiting for a reply, he balanced the cigarette while he pulled out a chair for the young actress, then seated himself close beside her. The cigarette-wielding hand rested on the back of her chair as she smiled weakly. She held a wine glass in her delicate fingers.

Fitz soon returned with Alonzo Swift in tow. "Mrs. Chapman, may I present Mr. Alonzo Swift? He's one of the best-known actors of our time." I nodded, thinking that if Delia were here she would swoon.

Swift looked pleased at the introduction, although he murmured something self-deprecating. Fitz knew how to find people's soft spots and then massage them. Such blatant flattery always put me off, but I could see that it worked fine with the handsome actor.

Babe Greer rose from her chair like a moth drawn to a flame, her youthful face turned up toward Swift with pure adoration. I had the impression that Leeder was not pleased with this intrusion, but Swift ignored him, responding to Babe instead. "Darling, it's been a very long day. I definitely feel the need for a pick-me-up."

Leeder grinned at him. "Missing the bars back in Maryland, are you, Alonzo? I heard they'll give you a double or triple there for the same money. Is that true?"

Swift looked at him with distaste. "I don't know what you mean."

"But you were back there last week, weren't you?" Leeder seemed to want to bait the man about something.

Swift turned to Babe and said, "Let's find somewhere more friendly to drink."

She put her arm in his and they made their way to the door. "Ta ta, folks. We'll see you later," she said over her shoulder.

As they walked away, Leeder swigged his beer then rose from his chair to wave. "Over here, come join us," he called to Alden and Kathlyn Williams, who'd just entered the roadhouse. He pointed to his glass. "Another for me, too, thanks."

Fitz was off again, talking to a group of men at another table, and Whitbread was still at the bar. I saw Kathlyn whisper to my brother, but then he handed her a glass and she came to our table. He followed with drinks for himself and Leeder.

It was strange to see Alden in that environment. I still always thought of him as the schoolboy he'd been when we were growing up in Boston. As a child, he dashed around the house as if on fire, with suspenders holding up his short pants. Later, I adjusted my view when he was the young lover of my friend Clara and, in recent years, I'd finally gotten used to him as a rambunctious journalist, liable to turn up at the front of a pack of reporters when anything happened in the city. But now he seemed a different man altogether, with a beautiful film star by his side, at home in this roadhouse with all these other film people around him. It seemed to me, after my experiences at the studios earlier in the day, that these film people lived in an alien world of make-believe that only they appeared to take seriously. When had Alden stepped over into that world and what had he become, to fit in there?

Leeder was teasing Kathlyn about her work with the leopards. "So, how did your training with Olga and the leopards go? I expect in no time she'll have your head in her lap just like she has those cats. She's a weird one, if there ever was one. Selig ought to do Macbeth and have Olga as one of the witches, the weird sisters. Can't you see it? 'Fee-fi-fo-fum, I smell the scent of the evil one.'"

Alden rolled his eyes and Kathlyn looked a bit uncomfortable. I supposed she had to stay on the good side of someone like Leeder, who produced a lot of the films she starred in. "Olga's really good with the animals," she said. "I have every faith in her instruction to keep me safe."

"Of course, if your boyfriend here would stop making up these spectacular thrill rides in his scenarios, we all might live a lot longer, don't you think? Oh, say, Mrs. Chapman, sorry. He's your brother, isn't he?"

Alden frowned.

"He's not my boyfriend," Kathlyn said. She spoke before Alden could get a word in. She seemed determined to jolly Leeder along, not taking him seriously. I could nearly hear Alden grinding his teeth as he sat in enforced silence. Apparently, there was a lot he would do to support his career in films, even kowtowing to the likes of this producer.

Leeder moved his seat closer to Kathlyn and put his cigarette hand on the back of her chair, as he'd done with Babe. The actress sat up taller and pursed her lips. She refused when he offered to get her another drink. Alden bristled across the way, staring into his beer.

Leeder sat back, displeased with the lack of reaction from Kathlyn. "Say, I know what you'd like. Have you seen the copper fixtures in the other room? You'd like that. I know you have a fondness for *copper*." He smiled and put a hand on her arm. "Want to come have a look?"

She pulled away and Alden pushed back his chair to stand. "Enough, Leeder. You know what Mr. Leeder here is called behind his back, Emily? 'Leeder the lecher.' That's right. He's always touching the women, aren't you, Leeder?"

Leeder turned red and pulled his arm away from Kathlyn. "You little simp," he said. "Just because you write little stories you think you're making her career, well I've got news for you, scribbler. The glop you come up with isn't worth the paper it's written on and if it weren't for me, getting the effects, her films would be nothing."

"You slimy bastard," Alden said. "You're only on the payroll because you've got something on the colonel. The slop you turn out is only saved by the likes of Kathlyn and me. You'll see soon enough."

"Oh, you may think so, but you're going to find out different." Leeder rose from his seat, clenching his fists. I looked at Alden with amazement. His fists were also clenched and raised. When did he get to be so pugilistic? Was this the sort of argument he'd gotten into with the dead censor? I saw Whitbread glance over sharply from the bar. He headed toward us.

Kathlyn Williams stood up between the two men. She stared into Leeder's eyes. "Mr. Leeder, that's quite enough. We all have to work together again in the morning. I suggest you go home and sleep it off. We have a big day tomorrow." She turned to look at Alden. "You too, Mr. Cabot. You asked me to give you a ride home. I'd like to find my driver and leave now."

"Is there a problem?" Whitbread asked. He'd reached the table, where he loomed over Mr. Leeder. Alden took Kathlyn's arm and escorted her to the door. Leeder shrugged and moved away to another table. Fitz joined us again.

"What was that all about?" Whitbread asked.

"I have no idea," I said. "For people who work long hours together, they don't seem to like each other very much."

Fitz looked a bit red in the face but he always had a somewhat blowsy complexion. He'd been consuming small glasses of liquor followed by mugs of beer, and I wondered how much he'd imbibed.

"I heard part of it," he said. "It was all that about the copper that caused it."

"Copper?" Whitbread frowned.

"He said he wanted to show her some copper fixtures or something in the other room," I said. I wondered if it was a code or some slang I didn't understand.

Fitz turned even redder. "No, it's the Copper King. That's what he was getting at." He gave Whitbread a pleading look but the detective just frowned so he had to continue. "It's Kathlyn Williams, you see. From early in her career, it's been well known there's an older man from Montana, where she grew up. He was her patron, paid for her acting classes, and things like that. Of course, some say there was something improper about it, but she went on to marry another man and all. It was a while ago. Anyhow, he's known as the Copper King in Montana. Leeder was teasing her about it."

Leeder was trying to embarrass her, and Alden was familiar enough with the story to know what he was doing. Kathlyn Williams did indeed seem to be the type of woman who could easily sow discord among men, and Alden was putty in her hands. I was disgusted with my brother.

Seventeen

Whitbread told us Broncho Billy was such a frequent and distinguished visitor to Pop Morse's Roadhouse that they'd mounted a hitching post outside the door expressly for his use. He often rode over from the Essanay studios and was due to arrive at any moment. I chose to follow Detective Whitbread outdoors to wait for him. I was missing another supper with my family and my thoughts began to stray in their direction. I was getting tired of the flamboyant film people and longed for the quiet of my own home.

It wasn't long before Anderson appeared on a brown mare that walked slowly down the road. He wore a cowboy costume with a tall peaked hat and a red kerchief around his neck. Whitbread called to him and he joined us after tying his horse to the post. By the way he tried to peer into the roadhouse over Whitbread's shoulder, I could tell he was anxious to join the crowd inside.

People passed in and out, but Whitbread blocked his way to the door. "Mr. Anderson, you lied to us," he said. "You claimed that you hadn't been back to the Selig studios, but we have a witness who saw you there this week. In fact, you were there the night Mr. Hyde was shot."

The welcoming smile faded from Anderson's face. He took off his hat and brushed at it with his hand, then slapped it against his thigh.

"Mr. Anderson?" Whitbread's eyes narrowed.

"OK, well, you've got me. I confess...I was there. I didn't think she saw me and I didn't want Selig to know. Might get some of the cameramen in trouble. It's the chance of a lifetime and I just wanted to let a couple of them in on it. But I didn't see the censor when I was there, I'm sure of that. You won't tell Selig, will you? Don't want to get the men in trouble."

"Mr. O'Neill told us he rejected your offer."

"Oh, *he* told you?" Anderson was surprised.

"That's right and Col. Selig is already aware of your efforts. Did Mr. Hyde see you, perhaps? Did you shoot him to keep it a secret?"

"What? No, of course not. You can ask O'Neill. Hyde was shot in the building, right? On one of the sets upstairs, I heard. I met O'Neill *outside*, on the backlot. Ask him. I never went into the building. I don't have a key. And I didn't have any reason to kill the censor. He wasn't censoring *my* films."

"Someone suggested that Mr. Hyde might have been working with Thomas Edison," I said. "You denied it yesterday, but they thought Edison might be preventing Essanay, as well as Selig, from releasing films."

"What? You mean Edison might sue me like he did Selig? Where'd you hear that? Was it Selig who told you that?" He seemed genuinely confused, but he was an actor after all, just like the rest of them.

"Mr. Anderson, lying to the police is a serious offense. I'll let you go now, but I want you at the Harrison Street police station at ten o'clock tomorrow morning, to make a statement about that night and about your relationship to the dead man. Do you understand?"

"But—" Anderson looked at Whitbread's face and thought better of trying to make objections. "All right. I'll be there."

"Did you see anyone else that night besides Mr. O'Neill?" I asked.

"That night, no…only Kathlyn."

"Kathlyn?" Whitbread asked.

"Yes, Kathlyn Williams. I didn't think she saw me. It was just as I was leaving. I saw her at the door of the studios, unlocking it. That's why I thought she was the one who told you I was there…I thought she must have seen me after all."

Eighteen

S o, Kathlyn Williams *was* there that night. Was she the one who killed Hyde? Or had Alden followed her and done the deed himself? Just as I feared, the trail was again leading back to my brother.

After letting Anderson go, and verifying that Kathlyn Williams had already left the roadhouse, Whitbread railed against the perfidy of the film people then went to find Fitz. He said we had another appointment in the city.

It turned out that Whitbread had persuaded Fitz to set up a meeting at the mayor's home just north of the Loop. When we arrived at the three-story row house we were shown into a parlor on the first floor. Soon, Mrs. Busse entered, wearing an evening dress of soft maroon velvet. She was a wispy little woman with light brown hair and a quiet manner. How she'd married one of our flamboyant political figures was a puzzle. I was glad the mayor was absent as I detested his politics.

"Good evening," Mrs. Busse said, after introductions. "Mr. Fitzgibbons asked me to meet with you about the death of my cousin, George Hyde. We're so sad about his passing. I'll return to Hickson, Indiana to arrange the funeral as soon as his body is released."

In answer to Whitbread's questions, she confirmed what we already knew about Hyde. Fitz sat beside her on a silk-covered sofa, holding her hand in sympathy.

"I never met his wife," she told us. "I'd already moved to Chicago when they married. I'm told she was a pretty girl who was very kind and well mannered. It was a terrible shock to everyone when she ran away, and more so when George found her and appealed to her, but she still refused to return with him. Everyone thought it was very generous of him to offer to take her back. They'd been married for three years. But she refused. It was a great scandal, of course, and he could barely hold his head up. That's when his mother...my aunt...wrote to ask if I could help, and Fred was so good about it. He's so generous with that sort of thing. When we heard that George had forsaken everything and spent hours and hours at a nickelodeon, Fred said he'd be perfect for a censor. His relatives in Indiana helped him sell his house and business so he could move here."

Fitz gave me a worried look, but I had no intention of suggesting to a grieving relative that her cousin had paid her husband money for the appointment. I stared at the ceiling and held my peace.

"The truth is, I thought he was feeling better lately," Mrs. Busse continued. "Last month, he came to one of my suppers and he was actually smiling. He was so grim when he first got to the city. He said the job had turned his life around, so he must have liked it."

"Did he say anything else?" Whitbread asked.

"Just that he might look for bigger lodgings. He had a room in a boardinghouse. He asked about real estate and where would be a good place to purchase. I took that for a good sign...that he was recovering from the blow."

"What about money?" I asked. "Had he come into some money by any chance?" I wondered about blackmail. If he were blackmailing someone, that might be a reason to kill him.

She frowned. "Not that I know of. I thought he must have had some money left from his business in Indiana. I assumed that was what he'd use." I wondered how much he would have had left after paying off the administration for the job. Perhaps

Fitz would know. Somehow, I doubted what was left would be sufficient but, then, based on my years of experience, I had a low opinion of the graft that seemed so unavoidable in city government.

"Mrs. Busse, was your cousin acquainted with Mr. Thomas Edison?" Whitbread asked.

"Mr. Edison? The electricity man? Oh, no, I don't think so. I'm sure he would have mentioned it, if he was."

If Hyde *had* been working for the East Coast magnate, there was no particular reason he would have confided in his cousin. But, if he was planning to purchase real estate, perhaps he was being paid clandestinely. It was possible.

We thanked Mrs. Busse for her time and piled back into Fitz's car. He said he would deliver me all the way to Hyde Park, for which I was extremely grateful. It had been a very full, long day, and my head was spinning from all the new information we'd uncovered. On the way, we dropped Whitbread off at the police station, and I arranged to meet him there in the morning to hear Broncho Billy Anderson's statement.

But our plans were disrupted for, in the morning, I received a telegram that read:

LEEDER DEAD IN LEOPARD CAGE AT SELIG
COME SOONEST WHITBREAD

Nineteen

It took me more than an hour via train and streetcar to return to the Selig studios that morning. A black horse-drawn hearse stood just outside the gates. I knew what that meant. It pulled away, bearing the body, as I approached the uniformed officer to let me through. There was a crowd of reporters being held at bay. They shouted questions about whether wild animals were on the rampage inside and whether well-known film stars like Kathlyn Williams or Babe Greer or Alonzo Swift were hurt.

After one look to verify that Alden was not among them, I slipped past the guard. I wondered vaguely whether the story of the crimes at the Selig studios could be used to get my brother back into the newspaper business, given that he'd have the ultimate inside scoop, then was shocked by my own imaginings. A man had died, yet I was already thinking of how that might help Alden get his job back. I was becoming as cynical as the yellow press and the film industry.

Inside, most film people were restricted to the main building and I could see many of them pressed against the glass of the third floor trying to see what was going on in the backlot. In the corner, by the jungle set, were the cages where we'd seen Olga and her leopards the day before. The velvet of the chaise lounge was ripped and the blood had turned rust brown, staining the cloth and the ground. As far as I could see, the leopards were missing. As I approached, I heard Olga and Big Otto arguing with Whitbread that the lives of the big cats should be spared.

"It is not the fault of the leopards," the broad-chested bald man protested, spreading his beefy arms.

"They were locked in," Olga said. "That man had to unlock the cage. It was no affair of the cats. They mind their own business."

"Yes," Big Otto added. "What do you do if someone comes into your home? You defend yourself, no? The cats, they defend themselves, that is all."

Whitbread held up his hands. "It's not for me to decide what happens to the animals. I'm here to find out what happened to the man who was killed. Go talk to Fitzgibbons over there. Maybe he can help you."

Big Otto and Olga took off, following his pointing finger to Fitz, who stood talking to Col. Selig. Whitbread noticed me. "All they're worried about are their confounded leopards. A man is dead, torn apart by those animals, and all they're worried about is saving the creatures."

"What happened?" I asked. The scene of the carnage still smelled of blood and I noticed some tufts of hair on the floor of the cage that made me turn my back on it all and swallow hard. It wouldn't do to start imagining what it had looked like with Leeder still in there.

"Last night—after he left the roadhouse, completely drunk, from what people say—Leeder returned here. Then, for some reason, he went into the leopard cage. Or he was put there. The animals attacked. The results were gruesome. He must have made noise, but no one heard anything, and it was not until Olga and Big Otto arrived this morning that he was found. She went in and got the leopards out and moved them somewhere else before they called us. Leeder was long gone, so they left him there. The coroner just left with his remains."

"I saw the hearse outside."

"Just as well it's gone. There'd be no point in your seeing such a sight."

I clutched one of the black iron bars and looked into the cage. It almost turned my stomach but I squeezed my eyes shut, then opened them again, determined to remain calm. "A second death in the studios. I don't suppose this was a suicide." I couldn't help thinking of the superstition about how things come in threes. It wasn't helpful, but I instinctively wondered who would be next.

"There are many ways to take one's own life. You were talking to Leeder last night. What was his mood?" Whitbread asked.

"I don't know. He was mostly busy irritating people."

"Your brother had words with him?"

"Yes, they insulted each other, but Kathlyn Williams came between them and insisted they stop. Apparently, it was not unusual for them to be at odds. But they regularly worked together despite that," I said.

Whitbread examined the padlock for the cages. "The key was used…to unlock and then relock it. It seems he was most likely lured or forced into the cage, then locked in. According to Miss Celeste and Mr. Breitkreutz, such an intrusion would be seen by the leopards as an attack, so they reacted in self-defense. Those people moved the leopards before we arrived, they're that afraid we might shoot them on sight. It seems anyone who knows Olga would know where the key is kept. There's a shack over there where they hang it. The key's still there."

"Would you have shot them on sight?"

He patted the pistol strapped at his waist. "Of course, if they were loose. If they're caged, then not immediately. As to whether they'll be gotten rid of for their actions, that's not my decision. Not sure if a judge or a bureaucrat will decide, but it won't be me."

"What a horrible thing to do to someone," I said. "Do you really think someone deliberately locked him in with those leopards and left him to die? Wasn't anyone else around?"

"They say not. Emily, this is a *very* peculiar group of people. It is hard to believe anything they say. They seem to be able to believe any nonsense that suits them. Col. Selig has already tried to suggest that Mr. Leeder locked himself in as some kind of joke, or the kind of demonstration that Houdini might do, and that his inability to get out alive was merely the failure of some trick. I find that impossible to believe, but he insists. This place is nothing short of a madhouse."

I turned away from the cage and looked back at the studio building. Col. Selig was standing on the steps listening to Olga and Big Otto. I saw a group including Alden, Kathlyn Williams, Babe Greer, and Alonzo Swift huddled near the door. O'Neill and some other cameramen sat on a low wall with their cameras on the ground in front of them, tripods resting against the wall or a shoulder. Two men with megaphones by their sides stood in front of them. Other film people lined the windows of the building behind. Had one of them really lured Mr. Leeder into that cage and locked him in? If someone *had* done that, would they stand around waiting to be arrested? I wouldn't. I would get as far away as possible.

Whitbread marched over to the bystanders. "We'll want to speak to each of you. We need to know when you last saw Mr. Leeder and an account of where you were last night. Col. Selig, may we use your office?"

I went upstairs with them and found paper and pencil with the help of Col. Selig. There was a uniformed officer taking notes as well, but I wrote faster. Many times in the past, I'd provided Detective Whitbread with legible notes that captured what he wanted. We'd worked together for many years and we thought in a similar manner. Also, he had certain little signs—the lift of a finger, the raising of an eyebrow, even an expressive silence—that I translated into underlines or overstrikes to remind us of the moment. It was one of the reasons I'd long ago persuaded him to allow me to sit in on interviews if he chose to include me in a case. Other reasons included my sex, which often allowed me to go to restricted areas and overhear female gossip for him. And then there was the issue of class. He was well aware that some of the members of society would talk to an educated young woman from a good family when they would spurn a mere policeman. Rather than resent such attitudes, Whitbread would spare no scruple to get around them.

Olga was the first to be interviewed. She repeated that she'd arrived with Big Otto and found the dead man. She refused to divulge the current location of the leopards. I later learned that she had rooms in a neighborhood near the studios and I wondered if Whitbread would raid the place in search of the leopards. I suspected he wouldn't risk his men in such an endeavor, unless he was forced to it. He grunted when she left and commented that the press would undoubtedly report the death in all its gory details, and that the public might demand leopard skins.

From Big Otto, we learned that he came from Munich but had lived in this country for more than twenty years. His original arrangement with Selig had been in the form of a loan but, when he was unable to repay it, Selig took over the circus and allowed Otto to stay on as trainer, with room and board as well as a salary. Otto was looking forward to moving the animals to California. Whitbread frowned at that. He would not allow such a move until the studio deaths had been explained. Big Otto also roomed in the area.

The night before, he brought Olga home from the roadhouse late and then met her for breakfast in the morning. He denied knowledge of the whereabouts of the leopards and had no useful suggestions for how Leeder had come to be in the cage. He didn't recall when Leeder left the roadhouse and he, himself, would never have entered the cage with more than one animal prowling about. He explained that it was possible to lure a single animal to an end of the cage where a panel could be lowered to cut it off from the others before the keeper dealt with the single animal. Not an attractive sounding job, at least to me.

Next, Col. Selig expressed his utter desolation at the loss of Mr. Leeder, especially in such a manner. "I assure you, Detective, we try our utmost to protect all of our staff. Why, this is my family. It hurts me when one of them is hurt. I saw Arnold last night at the roadhouse. He was drinking heavily. You know he was due to film a scene with Kathlyn Williams and the leopards today, don't you? That's why Kathlyn was working with Olga yesterday." He was looking at me when he said that, aware that I'd talked to the women. I thought of the bloody scratch Kathlyn Williams had received, and Olga's comment that leopards liked to "mark their toys."

"Are you trying to suggest that Mr. Leeder was inebriated and let himself into the leopard cage?" Whitbread asked.

"Well, I don't know, but it's possible. He got awfully involved with the scenes he shot. You know, there's some small competition going on for shooting the jungle scenes. You see, our pictures with the *real* animals are becoming quite famous. No one else has anything like it. And I've told my people I'm going to take the animals and a group of them out to Los Angeles to specialize in adventure stories with real animals. So, our *Hunting Big Game in Africa* and *The Leopard Queen* films are just the beginning. I'm a bit concerned that Mr. Leeder might have become overly enthusiastic about that proposal. He wouldn't be my first choice as producer for those films. As a matter of fact, Mr. Boggs, who's already out in Los Angeles, will most likely take charge, but Mr. Leeder wanted to be in the running. That's why he really wanted to direct the two films here, before we move out West. I just hope that didn't lead him to take foolish risks while under the influence of alcohol." Poor Col. Selig looked quite sick at the thought.

"That's a possibility," Whitbread said. "We'll keep it in mind. Thank you for the information. By the way, do you know where the leopards are now?"

"I have no idea. I'd have to ask Miss Celeste."

"Right. We've done that. Thanks. You can go."

"Before I go, Detective, when do you think we can resume shooting?"

Whitbread rolled his eyes. "I don't know. Tomorrow, maybe."

"Oh, thank you." Selig looked relieved. "It's just that we've got to get started on the Oz film and it's slated for tomorrow."

When he was gone, Whitbread grumbled. "Oz. A man is mauled to death on his premises and he's worried about Oz."

Twenty

As Col. Selig left, Fitz appeared in the doorway. They stopped to confer, then Fitz stepped in. Whitbread was not happy to see him.

"It's the mayor, you know. When he heard what happened, he insisted that I come along to find out what's going on and then to report back to him directly." Fitz was dressed in his usual suit plus overcoat, this time accented with a yellow silk tie and pocket handkerchief. He fingered the round bowler hat in his hands but took a stance that indicated he would not be denied access. I shuffled to a new page of the paper I was using to take notes, hoping the ensuing explosion would not be too horrific. My impulse was to brace myself and not look up.

To my surprise, Whitbread raised his hands in surrender and collapsed back into his chair. "The leopards have eaten the producer, Mr. Leeder, and we're attempting to discover who could have locked the man in their cage and left him at their mercy. Perhaps you can assist in our attempts to understand why anyone would do such a thing. It is madness. Simply madness."

Taking advantage of this uncharacteristic plea, Fitz moved into the room and pulled a chair next to mine. A uniformed officer appeared at the door but, before Whitbread could speak, Fitz said, "Could you question Alonzo Swift next?"

Whitbread's jaw dropped open as he turned toward Fitz. I admired the Irishman's temerity and I saw him attempt to smile, but he quickly explained. "He's needed for a scene upstairs. They're all set up for him so they asked if we could take his statement and let him go."

Whitbread rolled his eyes and waved to the officer at the door. "Mr. Alonzo Swift."

When Swift entered, he appeared to be tired, with red eyes and a haggard look. But his hair shone with cream, and his handsome square jaw was neatly shaved. He wore a suit of fine worsted wool that had sharp pleats in the pants and well-padded shoulders. After he sat down, gold cuff links peeked from his sleeves when he clasped his long fingers over one knee.

"Mr. Swift, when did you last see Mr. Leeder?" Whitbread asked.

Swift's Adam's apple bobbed as he swallowed. "At the roadhouse, last night. But we left before he did."

"We? Who were you with?"

"Oh, Miss Greer, of course...Babe Greer."

"You and Miss Greer left together? Where did you go after you left?"

Swift leaned forward. "We had to leave together. It's part of the romance." He released his hands and fingered his collar, as if it were too tight. "You see, we're a couple. Well, not a real couple, but for the press. We're in a lot of romantic comedies together, so Col. Selig and his publicity people like to put it out that we're courting. It makes it exciting for our fans, don't you know. So we'll drive somewhere, or go to a fancy restaurant, or a club or something, and they'll alert the press so they can be there to take pictures. It brings in more people to see the films we're in together.

"Last night we went to a nightclub together after we left the roadhouse and, I confess, I drank a bit more than I should have. It's been a busy week and with that censor dying...and now, I suppose, Leeder...although, of course, we didn't know that last night. Anyhow, I drank a lot. So Babe...Miss Greer...drove my motorcar back to the Bedford. I have a suite there and we went back to my rooms."

I caught my breath. Such an admission was certainly damaging to Babe Greer's reputation but I took it down in my notes without comment. The silence from Whitbread and Fitz was stony.

"What time did you reach the hotel?" Whitbread asked finally.

"Well, that's the thing. You see…I'm afraid I was a little passed out."

"A little?" Whitbread asked.

"I was passed out. So I don't remember. But Babe is a great driver and the bellboy helped her get me upstairs, where I'm afraid I just passed out again on the bed. But Babe, dear girl that she is, camped out on the sofa and ordered coffee in the morning. And she even drove us back to get up here in time for our early calls… but then we heard about poor Leeder. It's pretty awful, don't you think? I told Selig I'm not interested in those animal pictures he's so wild about. Comedy, yes. Drama's my forte. But animals…no, I don't think so."

He was oblivious to the damage he'd almost done to Babe Greer. His ignorance seemed sincere, but then he *was* an actor.

"Is your romance with Miss Greer merely an act then?" I asked. I knew Whitbread would want to know the answer to that question as much as I did.

"Well…not exactly." Swift turned red. "Of course, Miss Greer is a fantastic young lady and we've been discussing our future. So, no, it's not an act…at least not entirely."

"Mr. Swift, last night I heard that Mr. Leeder was sometimes known as 'Leeder the lecher' by the film people. Were you aware of that?" I asked.

Whitbread's wiry eyebrows rose at my question while Fitz cringed in his seat. Alonzo Swift seemed embarrassed.

"I would have to say…I have heard that, yes. Mr. Leeder had a tendency to touch the actresses in a familiar way, presumably to show them how he wanted them to stand. Some of them didn't like it."

"What about Miss Greer? Was she the object of his attentions?"

"You'd have to ask her, but I believe so, yes."

Whitbread jumped in. "Did you resent it that he tried to take advantage of Miss Greer?"

"Of course, but, no…no. Babe's well able to take care of herself. She wouldn't let him take advantage of her."

I thought it was rather ungallant of him to phrase it that way. But perhaps he was more concerned with proving he had nothing against Leeder than with defending the young actress.

"What about Mr. Hyde?" Whitbread asked. "Did you know him? Did he perhaps show too much interest in Miss Greer?"

"The censor who was found shot? Oh, dear me, no. I didn't know him. Babe may have but she never mentioned him."

"Is there anything else you can tell us about the dead men? Or who might have wanted to harm them?"

"No. I heard the censor was giving Kathlyn Williams a hard time but Selig was handling it. Leeder was just one of the producers."

"Very well. We'll ask Miss Greer to come in now. I'm sure she'll tell us the same story about last night."

Swift looked a little doubtful as he rose from the chair. "I'm afraid I really did drink too much last night," he said.

"Poor darling, he was totally knocked out," Babe Greer told us when she was asked about the previous evening. "I had to drive, but that was fine, because I love to drive. Have you seen Alonzo's motor? It's a lilac saloon with the most beautiful mauve leather seats. He was passed out before I finished cranking the engine. I can do that, you know. In fact, I'm a better driver than he is, any day."

When asked about Leeder, she said, "He was still at the roadhouse when Alonzo and I left. I thought he must be meeting someone there…usually he's the life of the party. Poor Arnold. What a horrible way to go. I don't trust that Olga. Did you see how Kathlyn Williams got scratched by those nasty animals yesterday? That's Olga's idea of practice."

She had her own opinions about Leeder's reputation as well. "'Leeder the lecher,' sure, I've heard it. He was like that, always hanging over you or brushing past you. In this business, a girl has to be able to shrug that off, though. He's not the only one, believe me. You have to be careful not to be caught alone in a closet with those types, that's all. He didn't bother me and I certainly didn't complain to Alonzo. If I were going to complain to anyone, it would be to Col. Selig. But you don't want to get a reputation as a complainer. That's not good, either."

"Miss Greer, were you with Mr. Swift all night last night? Can you tell us that he was never out of your sight?" Whitbread asked.

She blushed. "Well, yes. I can. I hope you'll be discreet. Although, really, everyone knows. I expect we'll announce our engagement any day now."

Fitz, who'd been sitting silently, moved in his seat, and shuffled his feet. I looked at him, but he stared at the ceiling as if he saw something there.

Babe continued. "I think Alonzo and Col. Selig are just working with the publicity people to decide when's the best time to make the announcement. For the films, you know."

"Yes, Mr. Swift told us the romance between the two of you had been suggested by the publicity people," I said.

She giggled. "I know. Isn't it divine? Of course, I thought it was wonderful. What woman wouldn't want a romance with Alonzo Swift? He's so handsome."

I thought of Delia and wondered if she'd be disappointed to hear of an engagement. Perhaps other fans would be as well. I wondered whether that kind of reaction would cause Selig and his publicity people to delay the announcement.

Asked if she had anything to add, Babe was quiet for a moment.

She gave me a guilty look, then turned to address Whitbread. "There's one thing. I saw Kathlyn Williams open an envelope while we were still at the roadhouse. She took out a letter and read it, then she turned very pale. I tried to ask her what was wrong but she ignored me. Mr. Cabot was with her, so I thought if anything was really wrong he'd be sure to take care of her. But it was odd."

When she left, Whitbread told the officer we would see Miss Kathlyn Williams next. I hoped she would clear Alden of any involvement with the murder. The night before, many people had heard the argument between Alden and Arnold Leeder at the roadhouse. But I feared that, in order to clear Alden, Kathlyn Williams would be forced to reveal a liaison with him.

Fitz coughed. "Before you go on, there's one thing you might need to know." Whitbread and I both looked at him. "These film people, you see, they live by publicity. This little romance between Alonzo Swift and Babe Greer is just the sort of thing the papers love. The reporters follow the actors around, and they take pictures and write stories that the ladies eat up, about love in bloom and that sort of thing."

"Yes, so, what's your point, man?" Whitbread asked.

Fitz glanced at the door to be sure we weren't disturbed. "Well, Alonzo Swift had a career in the theater back East you know. He was a matinee idol on the stage for years. And, the truth is, he also had...has a family."

"He's already married?" I asked.

"He has a wife and four children in Maryland."

"And no one knows?"

"Col. Selig knows. And his publicity people, they know. They just keep it quiet. It's not really a secret."

"It is to Babe Greer," I pointed out.

Just at that moment, Kathlyn Williams was ushered into the office.

Twenty-One

Kathlyn Williams looked frazzled and worn around the edges, but she had presence, nonetheless. Her blonde hair was curled around her face and pinned up in an attractive French style. She wore a navy walking suit with a white silk blouse trimmed with lace, a little bundle of it fluffed up under her chin. Her hat was wide brimmed and decorated with white silk ribbons. Her eyes looked a deeper blue without the bright lights they used for filming. I thought Clara was every bit as grand looking, but Kathlyn's figure was curved and rounded into a more voluptuous form than any academic woman I had ever met. I was conscious that I myself would appear as barely a penciled figure beside the rich hues of the film star. How could any man not be tempted? And yet, I knew both Whitbread and my husband would be blind to her charms. Why couldn't Alden be as well? But Whitbread and my husband would never be observant enough to be newspaper reporters, either. I suppressed a sigh.

The men had risen at her entrance and Fitz helped her to a chair. Not that she needed it. After all, this was a woman who'd stepped voluntarily into a cage with the very leopards who later tore Arnold Leeder apart.

"Miss Williams, you are aware of the tragic occurrence in the leopard cage. Can you tell us when you last saw Mr. Arnold Leeder and anything that may assist us in understanding how and why he came to be in that cage?" Whitbread asked.

She sat with her gloved hands in her lap, pulling at a lace-edged handkerchief. "I last saw him at the roadhouse. Everyone was there...last night. I had no idea he was coming back to the studio. He'd been drinking...rather a lot."

"Do you know why he might have returned here?"

"No. Not really. He didn't say anything about coming back here. But we were supposed to shoot a scene with the leopards today." She shivered. "It's a film about a girl who grows up with leopards. I play the girl."

"You were rehearsing with the animals yesterday?"

"Yes. Olga was giving me instructions."

"Isn't it dangerous, what they were asking you to do?" Whitbread asked.

I bent over my notes, anxious to hear her answer. How could she agree to enter a cage with wild animals who were capable of tearing a person apart? Didn't the bloody death of Leeder prove that? What would cause her to take such a risk? I couldn't imagine anything that would persuade me to do such a thing. Of course, I had my children waiting for me at home. How could I leave Stephen to explain it to them, if I were mauled to death? And who would raise them? But I supposed an ambitious woman who had no children and was divorcing her husband, in order to pursue film stardom, might be selfish enough to risk it.

Her face stiffened. I was reminded of her reaction when I asked about her divorce. It seemed she brooked no questioning on certain subjects. "That was the point of having Olga instruct me. She spends a lot of time with the leopards, so she's very familiar with them. Of course, she warned me never to let down my guard. They are always wild creatures when it comes down to it. She told me never to forget that is their essential nature. I assume Mr. Leeder must have let down his guard. He should have known better than to go into the cage like that."

"But you're willing to do so for the film?" I asked.

There was a swish of fabric as she turned to look at me. "For the film, yes. It's part of the job. This is a very competitive business. To succeed, you must be willing to take risks. These films are mostly made in a day. There are no months of rehearsals like there are for stage plays. The schedule is such that many feet of film must be turned out every day. And you have to be prepared to take risks, just as Col. Selig has. He bought this whole circus and brought it here to move fast and get these animal pictures out before someone else copies them. Yes, I'm willing to take a chance on it because, if I weren't, somebody else would. I chose to turn my back on other things to do this, and I'll put everything I have into making it a success."

Clearly, she was passionate in her dedication, so committed to her career she'd turned her back on her husband. It seemed mad to me. What was she doing this for? To appear on a flickering screen in some brief scenes that would be forgotten tomorrow? It was the heat of her sentiment that impressed me, however, and I thought that was what had infected my brother. Compared to the chill intelligence of my friend Clara, the scientist, here was the fiery passion of the film star. I resented the woman, both for my friend and for myself.

"I suppose Mr. Leeder was just as enthusiastic?" I said. "I suppose that dedication led to his end. He was torn apart by those leopards because he was devoted to his films?"

She closed her eyes as if the picture was too much. But, more likely, she was viewing the stalking cats as they'd been the previous day. "It must have been awful," she said.

Whitbread coughed. "Yes, well, let me ask you, we've heard that Leeder's actions toward the ladies in the studios were not always as they should be. Did you have any trouble with him?"

She frowned. "It's true. He was very forward and he tried to take advantage of young women. They didn't dare complain since he often had the last word about which actresses would be used in his films. But Col. Selig has promoted my career, so Mr. Leeder was quite anxious to take advantage of my popularity. I had no need to fear him. Some of the other girls were not so lucky."

I was not surprised by her answer, as I was sure she was well able to handle any man who came her way. I pictured her like one of the wild cats, stalking around, quiet and dangerous.

"Can you think of anyone who might have locked him in with the leopards, then?" Whitbread asked.

"Oh, no. I can't imagine who would do such a cruel thing."

Whitbread let that hang in the air long enough that I heard Fitz move restlessly beside me. Finally, the detective said, "I understand you received a note at the roadhouse last night that seemed to upset you. Is that true?"

She lifted her head, startled, then looked down at the handkerchief in her lap. "No, it was nothing. I left because I was tired. We were going to shoot the scene with the leopards today so I wanted to get my sleep. My driver was outside. He took me home, and then he took Mr. Cabot to Hyde Park. We were both quite done in."

I looked up at that. Alden had gone home to Hyde Park. He hadn't stayed with Kathlyn Williams, after all. I felt a catch in my breath. Perhaps I'd been wrong and he wasn't leaving Clara. I was so surprised I left a long line across the paper where I should have been taking notes. I caught Whitbread's eye. He raised his eyebrows but continued with a few more questions before letting Miss Williams leave and asking for Alden to be called in next.

Twenty-Two

Alden frowned when he saw me. Despite the fact that I had felt obliged to come and help him with the police, he seemed to resent my involvement. He entered and sat opposite Detective Whitbread after nodding to Fitz. He and Fitz had always been friendly. I wasn't sure I approved of the connection, but neither man was bothered by my attitude.

Biting my lip, I concentrated on my notes. I was so relieved Alden had gone home to Clara the previous night that I felt I had to hide my glee. At least he hadn't killed anyone. Someone had enticed Leeder into that cage and let the leopards loose on him, but it wasn't Alden, despite the argument everyone had heard at the roadhouse. There was something else going on. There was something behind the deaths of Hyde, the censor, and Leeder, the producer, but it wasn't Alden's fault. It couldn't be.

"Mr. Cabot," Whitbread began formally. "You had an argument with Arnold Leeder last night. What was that about?"

Alden moved as if he were uncomfortable. "I don't want to speak ill of the dead, but Leeder preyed on the ladies. Everyone knew it. He forced them to let him hang all over them or else he'd see to it they didn't get the parts they wanted. It was sickening."

"Was he threatening Miss Williams in that way?"

"Of course not. Kathlyn's a big star. He was lucky to have her in the films he did. Everybody wants her."

"What about you, then? Was he a threat to you?"

"He might have thought he was, but he was wrong. I've got an agreement with Selig and we'll be working on something bigger than anything Leeder would ever do."

At that moment, there was a knock on the door and Whitbread excused himself to go and have a discussion outside the room. Fitz rose to follow him. "It made you mad that Leeder was teasing Miss Williams about copper, didn't it?" I said to Alden.

Out of the corner of my eye, I could see Fitz look up with alarm from the doorway. He didn't expect me to repeat so bluntly what he'd told us about Kathlyn Williams and the Montana Copper King. But I was tired of film people and their secrets. Alden needed to see what Kathlyn Williams really was, and I would not shrink from pointing it out to him. After a momentary hesitation over whether to follow my conversation or Whitbread's, Fitz hustled out the door, closing it behind him.

I took advantage of the privacy to question my brother. "Fitz tells me Kathlyn Williams is associated with a man who's known as the Copper King in Montana, where she came from. She doesn't want that brought up in the divorce proceedings with her husband. Is that what made you pick a fight with Leeder?"

Alden turned in his chair, his face flushed. "Emily, just stop it. You have it in for Kathlyn, I can tell. What makes you think you're so much better than her and the other film people? What makes you think you can look down your nose at them? You don't know anything about these people or this business or how it works. You just think you're so damned smart you know everything but you don't."

"I know that you've become obsessed with these film people. I know you've abandoned your job, your wife, and your children for this madness. But I don't know who you are any more, Alden. I don't recognize you. What's come over you? Have you become mesmerized by all of this? Don't you see how wrong it is? Wake up. Two men have been killed here. This is no wonderland, it's a trap." Knowing that he had an alibi for the previous night made it possible for me to attack him like this. I was relieved he couldn't be guilty, but I was still very angry with him and couldn't stop myself.

"You don't know who I am because you *never* knew me," Alden snapped. "You think you know everything, but you're ignorant. There, I've said it. For all your book learning, you're ignorant of the world in front of your face."

"I'm ignorant? Book learning? It's not book learning I've been doing these past years and you know it. I've been out there on the streets in the *real* world working with *real* people and *real* problems. The work I've done at Hull House, and with Detective Whitbread, and, yes, at the university, has been to help real people. All you want to do is make up stories and run around feeling important with these film stars. That may make you *feel* important, Alden. It may impress the children but, in fact, it's a useless waste of talent. Real people, grown-up people like me and Clara and all the other people you despise at the university, we're at least trying to *do* something, not just sitting around pretending all the time!"

Whitbread and Fitz came back through the door.

"My sister's just accused me of being a useless waste," Alden told them.

"I've done no such thing," I said.

Whitbread put a hand up. "Enough. We need to conclude this interview. Mr. Cabot, we heard from Miss Williams that you accompanied her in her motorcar to her residence and then the same car took you to your home in Hyde Park. Is that correct?"

Alden frowned, restraining himself with difficulty. He wanted to continue his argument with me, but Whitbread had such authority over both of us that he endeavored to swallow his anger and answer. He looked like he was struggling to pull himself back to remember the events of the previous night. "Yes, I was driven home."

"Fine. If you cannot shed any further light on the death of Mr. Leeder, you're dismissed. For now, at least. Oh, one more thing. Were you aware that Mr. Swift has a wife and children in Maryland?"

"Well, yes, but nobody mentions it because he's a romantic lead. It lets down the public if they know he's already married, so it's kept quiet."

"Did you ever hear Mr. Leeder threaten to expose that fact?"

Alden thought for a minute. "No, but that's just the sort of thing Leeder would do. He was unscrupulous." He looked puzzled. "Usually he did that sort of thing with the girls, though. He'd find out something and threaten to let everyone know if they weren't nice to him. That's why they were all afraid of him. He was a slimy snake."

"You wouldn't be surprised if he did it to a man, however?"

"Not hardly. I sometimes wondered if he had something on Selig. He was nowhere near as good as Turner or Boggs or the other producers."

"I see."

"May I go?" Alden asked.

"Yes. For now." Whitbread clasped his hands under his chin as he sat back in the chair.

"Alonzo Swift could have done it," I said, when Alden was gone. "He could have snuck out after Babe fell asleep and come back up here to meet Leeder. He could have given him a sip from his flask. When Leeder passed out, he could have put him in the cage, locked up and left, getting back to the hotel before Babe woke up." Angry as I was with Alden, I wanted to be sure Whitbread was thinking as I did. Alonzo Swift could have killed Leeder to prevent him from publicizing his marriage.

"What about Hyde?" Fitz asked.

"Well, Swift was in the same scenes as Kathlyn Williams. Maybe he was mad his scenes were censored. Maybe he was afraid he'd lose some of his roles if it kept happening. Maybe it wasn't Kathlyn Williams that Hyde had a grudge against. Maybe Alonzo Swift was the man his wife ran away with." I could see

Alonzo Swift seducing a woman and then leaving her behind. I so much wanted it not to be my brother who'd shot the censor that I'd convinced myself that Swift was the one who deserved the blame. It was obvious he'd misled Babe Greer. I doubted she was the only young woman he'd deceived.

"It's possible," Whitbread said. "Miss Greer insists she was with him, although I can see that she could be mistaken. Or she might be excessively loyal. It's necessary to pursue some inquiries at the Bedford. But do not forget that Olga and Big Otto also had opportunities and they're much more familiar with the animals involved. I've just had a report on the search of their residences. The leopards were found at Miss Celeste's apartment. They're being returned to cages at the studios. One of our men was nearly mauled."

Fitz looked downright sorrowful. The film people had disappointed him. Poor Fitz. But at least Alden was cleared. I decided I would go to Clara, as soon as I could get away, to let her know of Alden's close call and to encourage her to keep him away from the film studios. First, I had to accompany Detective Whitbread as he investigated Alonzo Swift's movements the night before at the Bedford Hotel.

Twenty-Three

After some inconclusive interviews at the Bedford, I took a train back to Hyde Park. As the scenery flew by the window in a blur of early green leaves, I tried to think of how we could prove that Alonzo Swift had left the hotel and driven back to the studios. No one there admitted seeing him, or anything else of interest. Our last interview at the hotel had been with a bellboy, who insisted that Swift's lilac saloon had been left in two different places on the street that night. Whitbread doubted the boy's usefulness as a witness, however, after he admitted he wasn't completely sure whether he was remembering the previous night or some evening earlier in the week. But I was sure Whitbread would be able to prove that Swift *had* returned and locked Leeder in the cage. It was horrible to contemplate such an act but, somehow, I could believe Alonzo Swift might have turned the key and walked away, able to sooth what conscience he had with the knowledge that he hadn't been present at the man's actual death.

The shooting of Hyde was, of course, a different matter, but perhaps Whitbread would be able to find something to link Alonzo Swift to that murder as well.

Nonetheless, I was anxious about Alden. He seemed to be sunk in a quagmire. He was so involved with these loathsome film people. It was an addiction, like gambling. He was imagining some sort of glory for himself that was only a fickle shade, always out of reach. He was succumbing to it, and Clara needed to know just how close he'd come to falling. At least he *had* returned home the previous evening. I wanted to insist to Clara that she demand he cut off his connection with the Selig studios and come with us to Woods Hole. Once there, we could make him see how rash it was to think of following Selig to California. He could find another newspaper job or, at worst, remain at home writing fiction. I trusted that Col. Selig would move his operations to California regardless of whether Alden followed him or remained in Chicago. Good riddance to the lot of them. I'd had quite enough of the mad film people.

I tried to compose a logical set of arguments as I walked along to Clara and Alden's town house. The maid led me to the sitting room on the first floor, where Clara knelt on the floor, pulling books from the shelves and setting them in piles to be packed in a trunk by the doorway. She continued to work vigorously while I described all that had happened that day.

"So, you see, Alden is in the clear since he came home last night. Mr. Leeder was locked in that cage sometime after midnight. But you really must insist that Alden break all ties with that studio," I said. I was relieved that I didn't have to tell Clara about my suspicions concerning Kathlyn Williams. I was so happy to be spared that. There was silence. Confused by her reaction, or lack of reaction, I sat down on a little footstool that I pulled up near the pile of books she was examining.

She slapped a volume on the top of the stack and sat back on her heels to look at me. "Emily, Alden came home last night to beg for money. I gave it to him, but I told him to take his things and leave and not come back. He did *not* stay the night."

Waves of anger seemed to emanate from her and I leaned back, away from the fury, looking at her with my mouth open. Alden had *not* stayed at home last night. He'd left again, soon after arriving. Had he gone to the Selig studios, argued with Leeder, and left him in that cage to die? I swallowed. "Clara, what money? What did he need money for?"

She stood up, wiping her hands with a cloth. "I have no idea. I was supposed to trust him. If I couldn't trust him then how could our marriage last? Those were his words. Trust. I wrote him a check to cash. I have no idea what he planned to do with it, but I'm through asking. If he can take my money, but cannot confide in me...even if he says he'll repay it...it's the end. It's done, Emily. I'm done. That's all. We're finished."

"Oh, Clara, don't you see what this means? He could have killed Leeder. And Hyde. Or, at least, it will seem that way."

"What? That he would kill a person for Kathlyn Williams?"

I was shocked when she spoke the name of the actress. I knew then that I'd betrayed Clara by not telling her what I suspected earlier. Feeling a sharp pain in my gut, I realized Kathlyn Williams was a real obstacle that was cracking my brother's marriage apart. I couldn't believe this was really happening. Kathlyn Williams had been a sore point, like a loose tooth, something I'd worried but tried to avoid touching. Now the truth had been ripped out and the pain could not be ignored. Clara seemed strangely calm, but I realized she'd probably spent a sleepless night coming to terms with this—life without my brother. If Alden had been there, I felt I could have clawed his eyes out for inflicting such pain on all of us.

"Clara, I never thought he would do this." I slumped on the footstool while she stood tall above me.

"I know, Emily. None of this is your fault. This falls entirely to Alden...and me." She collapsed into an armchair and put her head in her hands.

"Oh, Clara, I'm so sorry."

She shook her head. "Alden's been distant and irritable. He's so touchy. Why didn't he confide in me when he lost his job? Why couldn't he tell me? I can see, now, that he was working for Selig instead of the *Tribune* this past month, but why wouldn't he tell me? He talked about how Selig's moving to California and how he wants to go...he has some big idea...but I thought he meant he would go for the paper, or for a paper out there. Why wouldn't he tell me it was to work on the films?" She looked bleakly into the space in front of her. "The children told me about Kathlyn Williams, along with the other film stars they met. They said Alden was writing stories for her. Why did he never tell me that, Emily? Unless it was that he felt guilty."

I didn't know what to say. I couldn't tell her that they were the subject of gossip at the studios. It would hurt her too much.

"I accused him of having a liaison with her," Clara said, closing her eyes. "He denied it. He claimed I had no respect for him and no trust. He said I thought he was a failure and that if I couldn't trust him, there was no point in his staying. I told him to go." She took a breath and blinked away some tears. "I haven't told the children." She bit her lip. "I don't plan to until after we've been in Woods Hole for a while."

Woods Hole. Of course, she'd follow through with our plans and leave him behind. It was the only thing to do. It was sad that the children wouldn't even notice when Alden didn't come. He'd been absent so much lately, it would hardly be a surprise. "I won't say a thing," I said. "But Stephen?"

"Yes, you'll have to tell Stephen." She bent to straighten the pile of books, then stood up again. "I don't believe Alden shot that man. He wouldn't do such a thing with forethought. By impulse, perhaps. He could hurt someone by mistake or in self-defense, but not on purpose."

By mistake. No doubt that would be his excuse. It wasn't intentional, as the destruction of his family wasn't intentional. I hated my brother at that moment. What a mess he'd made. And I knew he expected forgiveness and absolution. Well, not from me. Not any time soon.

Twenty-Four

Stephen and I retreated to the study after the children were sent to bed. There was a soft breeze from the windows, and a few moths flew in, to flap madly against the gas lights hanging from brackets on the wall. The building was old and didn't yet have electricity. I removed my boots and curled my feet under me on the lumpy old sofa.

"But won't Whitbread find out soon enough?" Stephen asked.

"I don't know. Alden didn't tell him he came home but then left again. He let him believe he stayed there. Whitbread's known us for so long, he believed him. He would have expected Alden to tell him the truth. I believed him. It was only when I talked to Clara that I discovered what really happened. He didn't lie, he just didn't explain. I don't think Whitbread would question it. Alden is taking advantage of his friendship. How can he do that? What has he become?"

Stephen rubbed his eyes, tired from a long, hot day I supposed. He deserved to get on that train with our children and head for the seashore for the summer. And so did I. Why should we all suffer because Alden was being a fool...or worse? It wasn't fair. I should withdraw from the investigation, complete our packing, and leave on the train with my family. I sincerely wished I could.

"Will you tell him?" Stephen asked. Of course, he knew that would plague me. How could I not tell my good friend and mentor, Henry Whitbread, that my brother had lied by omission? And if

I did, how could I watch as he arrested my brother for murdering two men in order to protect his mistress?

"Now he thinks that perhaps Alonzo Swift did it," I said. And maybe Swift *was* guilty. I could no longer see the threads of what was happening at that film studio. I was blinded by all the illusions they projected. I told Stephen how Swift was hiding his family from the press.

Stephen snorted. "Four children? How does he hope to hide that? Besides, you said Selig and the other film people actually knew about it. Why kill to keep it a secret? It doesn't make sense."

"You don't really think Alden did it, do you?"

He didn't attempt to answer that. The question just hung there like the gas flame attracting the moths. I couldn't shake off the doubts, but I was appalled that I could think such thoughts about my own brother. When had he changed so much that he would do something our father, the judge, would never have understood or forgiven? It would have broken our mother's heart. He knew better. He'd been taught better. How could he go against everything he'd ever learned?

"Can Whitbread really believe that Alden would murder that man Hyde just to prevent him from censoring the films of Kathlyn Williams? Surely that's absurd. Why did Alden need money?" Stephen asked. "It's not like him to ask Clara for money. He's always been so touchy about that."

"Yes, but he lost his job. I don't know, perhaps it's to move to California with Kathlyn Williams. Although, asking Clara to fund their trip would be beyond the pale. Perhaps he has some crazy idea to fund a film himself. He said something about a deal with Col. Selig. He'd do anything to stay in with these film people. I don't know why."

"Perhaps he just wants to make a new start, Emily. It must have been a blow to lose his job. I know he'd feel that deeply. The film industry may give him a way to hide his disgrace. If he clothes the facts in the idea that he'll go to California and be successful, it might make it more bearable for him. And it may be less painful to leave, than to stay and have to face Clara and the children with his failures. It's hard on a man, Emily, to have to admit he can't support his family."

As usual, Stephen was more sympathetic than I could be. I felt too much pain, as if an organ had been ripped from me. Alden was my little brother. At his best, he was witty, charming, and fearless. He teased me and I rose to his bait every time, but I'd been proud of him. I remembered when he'd jumped into a roiling sea to take a lifeline to Clara and three other people. He'd made mistakes in the past, but I always thought he was strong enough to come back from them. This time, he was destroying even the memories of what he'd been for me. I wanted to take my own children and run away to Woods Hole. I wanted to deny all of it. I didn't want to think that, if Alden could change so much that he was capable of such betrayal, perhaps I could change, as well. I looked at Stephen and wondered if I would ever decide to give him up for something I wanted more. Never. But I would have said never about Alden, too...until now.

"Stephen, you need to take Clara and the children to Woods Hole on Monday. I'll come as soon as I can. I don't know what will happen here. Whitbread will probably discover Alden lied and, if he doesn't, I'll try to get Alden to admit it to him. If Alden did kill those men, and if he's charged in the end, I'll make sure he has a lawyer. But we need to get the children away."

The next day was Sunday. It was an unexpected relief to attend church services with my family and then finish the packing for their trip. I had a bit of a tussle with Lizzie about her desire to see the Wizard of Oz filmed and I had to reprimand her sharply. I think some of my anger with Alden was let loose on her. I dreaded the coming days that would take me once more to the

Selig studios, now that I was sure it would end in the arrest and disgrace of my brother, my children's uncle. After Lizzie's bout of tears was over, Stephen took her to visit her cousin Penny, and returned with the news that he'd agreed she could stay the night at Clara and Alden's house and meet us the next morning at the train station. We arranged a cart to pick up their luggage, then ours and our family, so Clara and her children would go by train and meet us at the station.

Stephen was always the peacemaker in our house and I grudgingly agreed to the plan. It was clear that my argument with Lizzie had left my husband and sons tiptoeing around, to avoid my wrath, and I genuinely felt sorry for that.

We sent the boys and Delia to bed early in preparation for the long trip. I felt myself becoming tense with the anticipation of their departure and my unwelcome task. I had to face Whitbread, knowing my brother had lied. Yet, I didn't want to be the one to expose Alden. How could I do that? I wracked my brain for a way to avoid Whitbread until he discovered the truth himself. But would he, if I didn't come forward? Clara would be gone, so he couldn't ask her and, of course, he'd assume I'd tell him if I knew such a pertinent fact. But I couldn't imagine how I *could* tell him. It would be so damaging to Alden.

Stephen and I sat in the study for some time in silence. Darkness was falling, but neither of us lit the gas. Finally, he rose and sat on the sofa beside me, putting his left arm on my shoulders. I was sitting with my arms crossed on my chest thinking furiously. He pulled one hand out with his own. "Emily, you have to leave this. You'll make yourself ill."

I pulled my arm away. "No. I have to stay. I have to see it through, even if Alden *is* arrested. I must. I can't leave him, and I can't leave Whitbread."

"Emily, he's your brother. Whitbread understands that. He wouldn't force you to betray your brother. You know that." Stephen withdrew his arm and sat back, frowning.

"How is it betrayal? Hasn't Alden betrayed all of us? I'm so angry with him for leaving Clara like that. And lying to Whitbread. He's the one who has to own up to it. I won't let him get away with this. I'll get him to tell Whitbread himself, or else I'll have to."

Stephen lowered his head, raised his eyebrows, and looked up at me with a quizzical expression. "Really? You would do that to your own brother?" He reminded me of a schoolmaster who'd caught a child in a lie. He knew me too well.

I threw up my hands. "What else can I do?" I asked. "I can't just leave."

"Why not?"

I rubbed my face with my hands. "It's Alden," I said, trying to stifle a sob. I thought of our parents—our father, who'd been killed in his study back in Boston, and our mother, by whose deathbed I sat, before returning to Chicago to refuse Stephen's first proposal. I'd taken on their cares when they died. And I thought I could shoulder them alone, until Stephen convinced me otherwise. I felt I was failing my mother and father now. I should have curbed Alden. I should have seen this coming. He'd gone so far off course without me noticing and, with a pang, I realized I barely knew my younger sister, Rose, anymore. She had her own family in Boston.

"Emily, Alden's a grown man. You must let him take responsibility for his actions. You cannot and *should not* try to protect him. And what about Clara? Isn't Clara the one who needs your help now? Come to Woods Hole. Leave Alden to take care of himself. Clara's the one we need to help through this. And Clara's the one who *can* be helped by you."

I pressed my face into his shoulder and his arms wrapped around me. He was right. Clara had a steep road ahead of her and she'd be looking to me for support, while Alden only scorned my efforts. I'd already failed with Alden, that was the truth, and it was too late to save him. He'd changed to be something our parents would not have recognized. I knew they would be heartsick, but there was nothing I could do. Now I needed to look after my own little family. Stephen was right. Alden had to be cut loose to make it on his own.

"But Whitbread," I said.

"Emily, don't you think Whitbread will know, when you don't appear? He's well able to conduct the investigation without you. Your absence will allow him to do his job, as he must. You trust him. You need to leave it to him."

"I suppose you're right. I'll do it. I'll leave with you." Still burdened with guilt, I felt relief as we turned out the light and mounted the stairs. In a few days, we would all be at the seashore. It was a sorrow that Alden would not be with us, but Clara and the children would be, and they needed our help.

Twenty-Five

"Where are they? What could be keeping them?" I asked. "Do you think they missed the train from Hyde Park?" Stephen and I were surrounded by crowds of people moving purposefully through the high-ceilinged open spaces of Dearborn Station. Smoke from locomotives and tweets of whistles resounded in the great palace of transportation. With Jack and Tommy, we were able to get all the trunks to porters who were loading them into the baggage car, while we stood beside the door to the first-class carriage Clara had reserved. Toots of a horn warned of departure, while we all stood in a circle trying to catch a glimpse of Clara, her two children, and Lizzie.

Finally, Stephen spotted her and waved his arm impatiently, signaling them to hurry, but when a breathless Clara reached us, with Ollie in tow, she had bad news. "I'm sorry. It's Lizzie and Penny. They're gone. They weren't in Penny's room this morning and I couldn't find them." She stopped to take a breath as she hung onto Ollie's hand.

Lizzie! My anger turned immediately to fear. She was barely thirteen years old, my little girl.

Stephen took Clara's arm. She was not a woman who fainted, ever. But her face was drained of blood and she stumbled her last steps toward us. "Calm down," Stephen said. "What happened?"

She gulped some breath and shook her head, holding Ollie's hand up. "Ollie says they went up to the film studios...by themselves. He said they told him they were going, but he didn't believe them."

The film studios! Lizzie was so stubborn. But, despite the fact that she was younger, Penny was a much more dependable girl. The Selig studios were more than an hour from our home, reached only after traveling on several different trains and streetcars. "But how? They can't know how to get there," I said.

Ollie spoke, looking ashamed of himself. "Penny knows. She paid attention when Father took us. I didn't think they'd really do it."

"I didn't know how to get there or who to tell," Clara said. "I need to go look for them but I need you to tell me how to get there, Emily. I have no idea where it even is. I'm so sorry."

"Oh, Clara, it's not your fault. It's Lizzie, I'm sure of it. It's at least a train, then a walk, then a streetcar after they left Hyde Park." I thought of how many places along the way they could be lost. "We'll find them," I said. Suddenly, a long whistle burst sounded, signaling that our train was about to depart. "All our luggage is on the train," I said. This was Alden's fault. Yet again. "Listen, you all get on the train and go. I'll find them. I'll bring them on a later train."

"We're not leaving with the girls missing," Stephen said.

"But you must. The luggage is already loaded," I told him. He could be so stubborn sometimes. I had to fix this. I'd allowed Lizzie out of my sight when I knew she was intent on returning to the studios. It was Stephen's idea to let her stay at Clara's. He always underestimated Lizzie's strong will but I should have known better. I shouldn't have agreed. No doubt she hounded Penny till the younger girl agreed to go. Once again, we were all held hostage to Alden's ambitions. He was the one who'd taken the children to the Selig studios first. Another long blast of the whistle startled me. "Stephen, listen to me, you have to go. I can find them. I promise we'll be on a train tonight, tomorrow at the latest." Why couldn't he see that they needed to get on that train?

When I moved to urge the boys onto the train, Stephen grabbed my arm. "No, Emily. We're not going. You go find them. The boys and I will get the luggage and go back to Hyde Park. No, we're not leaving. And, Clara, I need you to stay and help me and the boys." Stephen gave me a long look with a sharp nod in Clara's direction. She was on the verge of collapse, so I pushed Ollie over to hold her up. Stephen was right. Alden had ruined it all…again.

"Emily, go!" Stephen said before he turned away, taking Jack and Tommy with him toward the baggage car.

"Clara, he's right. He needs you here. I know how they might have gone. I'll find them and if I don't I'll get the police to help. You need to get back to Hyde Park with Stephen and the boys in case they return there. I promise, I'll find them." Then I turned to fight my way through the station and out to the street. I was so angry with Lizzie, and I was so angry with Alden, that I barely noticed the throngs as I pushed my way through.

After grabbing a seat on a streetcar that was crowded with lunchtime workers, I sat and thought furiously of what might have happened to the girls. No doubt Lizzie had hoarded her pennies to pay the fare. She would have kept them in her small crocheted purse for the trip to Woods Hole. She must have taken that with her when she went to Penny's. I wouldn't be surprised if she'd raided her brothers' savings as well. Lizzie was ruthless when she wanted something, and she must have been planning this all along when she asked to stay at Clara's overnight. I had no idea if Alden could have been involved. I didn't see how but, I was so furious with him, I placed the blame squarely on his shoulders.

I knew both girls were intelligent and could be careful if they chose, especially Penny. She was more than a year younger than Lizzie, but she was a much more thoughtful little girl. She should have known better than to cause her mother such pain by disappearing. I wondered how much the children really knew about Alden's troubles. We'd tried to keep it from them but perhaps we assumed we were successful when we were not. Lizzie was fearless to the point of foolishness. In that she reminded me of my brother. But Penny was not like that at all. She was a kind, levelheaded girl, but she was also extremely devoted to her father. Lizzie might be determined to see the filming of her favorite story, and want to defy me in the process, but perhaps Penny just wanted to see her father before she was pulled away from him forever.

As I attempted to sniff fresh air from the open window at my back, to counteract the smells of garlic and onion from some of the workmen on the streetcar, I stifled a sob. Lizzie was still only a little girl. I should have kept her by my side. She could wear me down with her pestering, and that was what led me to agree to let her stay overnight at Clara's. I felt a horrible hole in my being as I realized I'd just wanted to stop listening to her bickering. How could a mother do that? How could *I* do it? What if they were lost, or hurt, trying to reach the film studios? What would I do if anything happened to Lizzie and Penny? I had an even worse thought when suddenly the picture of Olga's prowling leopards came to my mind, and then the leap of the raging lion. There was a lion in the Oz stories, albeit a cowardly one. What if they were using a real lion? What if the girls had made it to the studios only to fall victim to an accident with those animals? It would be so like Lizzie to want to get too close to them. I felt myself being stifled in the hot streetcar, fighting to catch my breath. If anything happened to Lizzie it would be my fault...not Stephen's, not Alden's, mine.

"Excuse me, excuse me." We reached Western and Irving Park Boulevard, and I had to fight my way to the exit to jump down before the streetcar started up again. I ran across to the doorway with the "S" in stonework above it. A glance at the backlot showed little activity, so I picked up my skirts and climbed the stairs to the third floor, thinking someone up there would be able to tell me where they were shooting Oz.

Rushing into the great open space, I blinked at the bright sunlight and spotted a group of people in front of the barnyard set. My heart fell when I didn't see the girls. I hurried over, as I thought I saw Alden, foolish Alden, between the silhouettes of two men. I was rudely pushing through them to grab his arm when I saw his hand on familiar braids in front of him. *Thank God!* Lizzie and Penny were sitting on a bench with a blonde woman between them. Kathlyn Williams, of course. They were straining to watch the action in front of them and the usual yelling was going on. Looking up, I saw they were filming the scene of the cyclone and, for a minute, I was distracted.

A haystack was moving through a field. Two men in animal suits and the scarecrow were clinging to the sides, while a little girl, who must be Dorothy, clutched her small dog. She was sitting in an indentation in the big haystack that was being rotated by men pulling on ropes outside the set. The haystack traveled between a broken fence and painted scenery of a field that extended a few feet up from the ground. Behind all this hung a painted canvas representing a sky filled with ominous dark clouds, and that backdrop was moving from right to left, then being pulled around the back and through again. It gave movement to the sky while other men tossed pieces of hay from the sidelines and everybody yelled at the top of their lungs. Conditions in the film studio actually seemed to reproduce a cyclone ripping through the place. I was amazed.

I heard my daughter's insistent voice, competing with the rest. "But there was no cow in the book and no donkey. Why are they there? That's wrong. That's not how it was in the book."

I stopped. My joy at finding my daughter turned to a flaming anger. "Elizabeth Chapman, do you have any idea how much trouble you've caused?"

Lizzie turned toward me with her mouth open, and I could see her eyes widen with growing apprehension. She knew she was in deep trouble. I saw Penny reach up to grab her father's arm. Alden turned with a happy look that quickly dissolved into a frown when he saw how angry I was.

I pushed through the crowd of people and took hold of Lizzie's hand, pulling her to her feet. "Come on," I said, nodding to Alden and Penny to follow. It was much too crowded and noisy to properly scold them there. The producer, Mr. Turner, was yelling about how the little dog playing Toto was not performing his part and the dog was alternately squeaking and barking as he was chased around the room. I was glad no one seemed to notice us.

I could only think of one place where I could express myself without an audience, so I headed for Col. Selig's office on the second floor. Pulling Lizzie behind me I burst through the door. Since the frosted glass panel in the wide oak door had hidden the occupants, I was embarrassed to face Col. Selig who sat behind his desk with Broncho Billy opposite him. Both men rose at the intrusion.

"Oh, I'm so sorry. I didn't know you were here," I said. What a blunder. I squeezed Lizzie's hand and she yelped.

"Ah, Mrs. Chapman...and Mr. Cabot. It's all right. We were just finishing our little talk. Mr. Anderson here was just leaving."

Anderson slipped past Alden and out the door before I could comment.

"You were perhaps looking for a little privacy?" Col. Selig said. "No, no, that's quite all right. I need to go up and see how Oz is coming along, come on in."

I attempted to apologize but he'd correctly assessed the situation as a family dispute in which he had no stake, so he took his hat and cane and hurried to the door. "Take your time," he said from the doorway. "Take all the time you wish. No need to hurry." And he disappeared, closing the door firmly behind him.

"Alden, how could you do this? Do you have any idea of the worry you've caused? Not to mention the practical problems. We had all of the bags loaded on the train! We were supposed to leave this morning. All of the arrangements are ruined. Stephen and Clara had to get all the bags unloaded. Do you have any idea what the girls' disappearance has done to Clara? How could you be so cruel?"

Alden opened his mouth at the beginning of my tirade but, as I went on, his mouth hardened into a stubborn expression. When I stopped for breath he finally spoke. "Emily, I did not bring the girls here. They came on their own."

"Don't lie to me!" It was his fault. Even if they *had* come on their own. And he should know that.

"No, please. Aunt Emily, it wasn't Papa. It was me. I did it. Lizzie told me she wanted to go and I did, too. I wanted to see Papa. I didn't want to leave without seeing him." Penny was tall and dark like her mother. She felt the seething anger in the room more sharply than my own daughter, who I could see was gathering her energies to put up a fight. I felt bad for young Penny.

"Penny, don't you know how worried your mother is? Col. Selig has a telephone. I'm sure he won't mind if we use it on this occasion." I pointed to where the instrument sat on the colonel's desk. I suspected Penny would be better able to operate it than I was. "Please call your mother. I think she should be home by now. Although they had to shift all the luggage to take it back again." I glared at Alden.

Penny gulped back some tears and rushed to the desk. She spoke to an operator to get a connection. Lizzie stood with her hands clasped in front of her, wisely keeping her peace. Her eyes wandered around the room and she looked at the ceiling, avoiding my angry glare. Alden thrust his hands into his pants pockets and stood with rounded shoulders.

Penny burst into tears as she spoke to her mother. I knew it was because she realized how much she'd hurt her, rather than Clara's remonstrations, that made her weep. She beckoned to Lizzie and gave her the telephone receiver.

Lizzie held the piece with two hands and listened with wide eyes. It was the first time she'd used a telephone, I was sure. The deep tones indicated she was being talked to by her father. Stephen would not be as hard on her as I would, of that I was sure, but she was more likely to listen to him. I saw her look surprised, then frown, then become a little weepy as she said she was sorry. Then, with a look of contrition and apprehension, she held the receiver out to me.

"You found them," Stephen said, when I held the instrument to my ear. "That's a great relief."

"You got back safely? Did you manage to retrieve all the trunks?"

He sighed. "Mostly. I think one or two may have gone on to Woods Hole. We'll have to make new arrangements for later in the week or early next week, so there's no need for you to hurry back, as long as you've found them." The tone of his voice lowered. "I think Clara may have decided that she wants to stay until the business with Alden is cleared up."

Across the room, my brother was watching me and I saw him flinch. He knew we were talking about him. I was once again in the position of knowing he'd lied to Detective Whitbread. Now, I would have to do something about it. I told Stephen I'd bring the girls back with me and said goodbye.

"I'm sorry," Lizzie said as soon as I lowered the receiver. "I'm sorry I made you worry. It was my fault. I got Penny to take me because she knew the way. I kept asking her to go with me till she had to do it."

Alden had his arm around poor Penny, who was weeping into his shoulder. I was sure Lizzie *had* made a pest of herself until the poor girl agreed. But Clara's resolve to remain in Chicago now probably had to do with Penny's fears for her father.

"You were very bad," I told my daughter. "You caused a lot of people a lot of trouble and don't think you won't be punished for it. But I need to talk to Uncle Alden right now. So, you and Penny can go back up to where they're filming and watch, as long as you stay out of the way."

A look of pure bliss appeared on Lizzie's face. It seemed wrong that her bad behavior should be rewarded, but the film people lived in such a state of constant chaos, I doubted they would even notice the girls. And, if Lizzie should disturb them with her comments on their deviations from the books, I thought it would serve them right. I had no patience for the film people at that moment.

Twenty-Six

As the door closed behind the girls, I stood in a frozen scene with my brother. I was behind the desk and he stood before it with a sour expression on his face.

"Alden, you lied to me. Not just to me, to Whitbread. I saw Clara, and she told me you weren't home when Leeder was killed. You came home, demanded money, and then left. Money, Alden? What did you need money for? Where did you go? And why didn't you tell us that you left? Did you kill Mr. Leeder?"

I shocked myself with that last question. Never had I believed Alden would do such a thing, but I found myself asking anyway.

A look of dismay crossed Alden's features. He was as surprised as I was that I would ask such a thing. "No, of course not. I did *not* kill Arnold Leeder. What are you thinking, Emily? You know I would never do something like that."

"Then where were you? And what was the money for? Alden, surely you didn't ask Clara for money so you could run away to California with Kathlyn Williams? Tell me you'd never do something so crass and vulgar?"

He stared at me, then turned away. He couldn't look me in the eye.

How could he do such a thing to Clara? "Alden, answer me. Is that what the money was for?" I desperately wanted a different explanation. "Or was it to fund some wild film project of yours? Is that it?" A film project no doubt involving Kathlyn Williams.

"Yes," he said softly. "That's it. I have a project with Selig. Only he needed more money. It's a secret, you see, because it means moving the animals out to Los Angeles." He looked up, but stared at the wall in front of him. "It's for Clara in a way. Clara doesn't need me, she needs to be rid of me. She'll be better off. She and the children. You'll see."

I couldn't believe what I was hearing. I don't know what I'd hoped for, some fantastic explanation of all of it, perhaps. But he had none, just the indigestible facts. He was leaving Clara and getting her to pay for it. How our parents would have been saddened by his actions. "Oh, Alden," was all I could say.

There was a brisk knock on the door followed by Detective Whitbread's head. "Have you seen Selig? No one seems to know where he's gone to."

I said nothing. I just stared at Alden, willing him to tell Whitbread the truth of where he was the night of Leeder's death. Instead, he turned restlessly and said to Whitbread, "He was just here. He was going upstairs to see the filming on the Oz set. Penny and Lizzie are up there. They ran away this morning to come up and see the Oz film, and Emily was very upset when she found them." He shot a glance at me but he had no intention of correcting his testimony for Whitbread. I was speechless. "Excuse me, I have another scene to see to." Alden hurried past Whitbread and out the door.

I stood, raging inside, but undecided whether to call him a liar again in front of the detective. The longer I waited, the more difficult it would be to explain my reticence. But I couldn't do it.

"I must have missed the colonel on the third floor," Whitbread said. "Or perhaps our paths crossed while he was in transit. In any case, it appears his office is available. We have new evidence, and we need to interview Alonzo Swift again. Come, let's go find him." He turned to leave but, when he saw me hesitate, he stopped. "Emily, is something wrong?"

I swallowed. "No, it's nothing. I'm ready."

When he began to lope off, I followed him. I needed to ask Col. Selig about this secret project with my brother. I counted on those questions eliciting an alibi for Alden. That way, his absence from Hyde Park would be discovered without me having to call my brother a liar. Clara had enough to worry about. It sounded like Whitbread had evidence against Alonzo Swift and that needed to be dealt with first.

Upstairs, Whitbread once again had to bide his time before he could talk to Swift. The actor wore a thick layer of makeup and extra wiry eyebrows, mustache, and beard. His suit was brightly colored with wide lapels and a top hat, both covered with sparkly gold. He was being attended to by people tweaking his outfit. Meanwhile, Otis Turner was yelling, as the witch and her minions approached Dorothy. I saw they were at the place in the story where she kills the Wicked Witch of the West with water. The girl tossed the bucket and Turner yelled, "Stop!" Everyone froze. Only the witch jumped away, then someone lit a small smoke bomb and Turner yelled, "Ready, set, go!" and everyone moved again, looking astonished that the witch had disappeared. It took me a moment to realize that, on the film, the witch would have been there and gone...like magic. Lizzie stood with her mouth open, and I saw Fitzgibbons watching intently across the way. I suspected he'd be joining us when we questioned Alonzo Swift.

They quickly moved to the next set where the handsome actor, as the wizard, sat on a throne while young women in short dresses that were a sort of uniform, with tall hats to match, did a dance. Then someone made a proclamation and the wizard jumped down and put the scarecrow on the throne, relinquishing his crown. Another move took them to a box that was meant to be hanging from a balloon, although there were only ropes, and bags of sand, and men above in the rafters to haul the contraption up as Oz floated away, minus Dorothy, who left to chase after Toto once again.

As soon as the production had moved on to Dorothy's finish, and Alonzo Swift had descended, Whitbread took the man by the arm and beckoned to me to follow them back down to Selig's office. Fitz headed towards us, as I'd anticipated. I looked around and saw neither Alden nor Kathlyn Williams. The girls were following the little actress who played Dorothy, and I saw a happy-looking Babe Greer with a hand on each of their shoulders. They would be all right for the duration, so I scampered after Whitbread.

Inside Col. Selig's office, Whitbread stood behind the desk, clearing the space in the middle, then he opened a large paper bag and carefully placed some shredded items on the blotter. Alonzo Swift, Fitz, and I gathered round to view the pieces.

"These were found on Mr. Leeder's body," Whitbread said. "They are naturally much damaged by the attack." He pointed a long bony finger. "This is material from Mr. Leeder's linen shirt." It was a mangled piece marred by dark bloodstains. "These are pieces of a white silk scarf or muffler." In the second mound, the scraps were mostly torn to threads, but a few squares of bright white stood out. Alonzo Swift, who was still wearing his Oz costume, moved restlessly in his chair. I remembered seeing him with a white silk muffler around his neck. "And this is the most interesting of all." Whitbread pointed to a smaller pile of faint blue tatters. "You see, here? This is a bit of paper that indicates 'First Bank.' The rest is torn off, but you can see these are pieces of a check. You see that?" He looked across at Alonzo. "Mr. Swift, do you recognize any of this?"

"No, certainly not," Swift said. "What do you mean?"

Fitz bent forward to try to make out more of the scraps of the paper check. "Yes, Detective Whitbread, what are you getting at?"

"I believe these remnants may help us identify Mr. Leeder's killer. I believe he was attempting to blackmail someone and that he met them that night in order to extort money. I believe the person enticed him into the cage by offering the check but then locked him in and left the animals to do his dirty work."

"You don't mean you think I did that?" Alonzo Swift stared at him, open mouthed. "Why ever would I do such a terrible thing? I'm afraid of those beasts, you won't find me near them, and Leeder was…well, not a friend exactly…but a colleague. Are you trying to say he was blackmailing me? For what? I assure you, he was doing no such thing."

"I'm suggesting that Mr. Leeder knew of your desire to keep information about your wife and children back in Maryland out of the newspapers. He found out about their existence and threatened to alert the press unless you met his demands. I'm suggesting you had to give in to his threats, so you pretended to go home drunk, then returned with a check, which you gave him. But then you locked him in with the leopards and, in a struggle or by accident, you left behind the scarf. Perhaps Leeder grabbed it from you, in an attempt to get you to release him, and he was mauled to death, while you returned to your hotel and claimed to have been there all night. Miss Greer herself either slept through it all or unwisely supported your story, due to her affection for you."

Alonzo Swift stood up straight and shot a glance at Fitz across the desk, then protested to Whitbread. "You're mad. And what's more, you're completely wrong. I never left my hotel room…I was passed out. I dare you to prove otherwise. Mr. Fitzgibbons, help me out here. This is insane. That is not my scarf, I assure you. Every scarf I own can be accounted for by my valet. And, as for the bank check, my bank is Wells Fargo, a fact that may also be easily ascertained. I was not being blackmailed by Arnold Leeder, I promise you."

"And yet Miss Greer appeared to be under the impression that you would soon be proposing to her, despite the fact that others at the studio are aware of your wife and children."

"Detective, we explained that is a publicity matter," Fitz said.

Swift held up a hand. Despite the rather ridiculous outfit he was wearing, he projected a certain amount of dignity.

I remembered then that he'd been a Shakespearean actor before moving to the films. "Please, my marital circumstances are indeed private. However, I can assure you that I have not been misleading Miss Greer. On the contrary, you can ask Col. Selig. For some time, there have been private negotiations under way to obtain a divorce settlement from my wife. In fact, we recently reached consensus and the agreement was signed, as a result of which Miss Greer and I will be announcing our engagement at the release of our next film. Get Selig in here, he'll tell you. Even if Leeder was aware of my family in Maryland, there would be no reason for me to kill him to prevent discovery of so public a situation. Our private agreement will result in a quiet divorce and a generous settlement for my wife and children. The fans will quickly be distracted from those details by the news of my engagement to Miss Greer. These plans have been in the making for quite some time."

"You see, there was no reason for Mr. Swift to wish Mr. Leeder harm," Fitz said. "None at all."

"Excuse me." Babe Greer had been knocking softly on the door and, when there was no response, she finally opened it and stepped inside. "I'm sorry to intrude, but I wanted to be sure Alonzo was all right. Is there something the matter?" She looked quite happy despite her concern for her beau.

"This is a police interview, Miss Greer, and I'll thank you to not interfere. As long as you're here, please enter. Close the door, if you would," Whitbread said. "Mr. Swift has been informing us of his upcoming divorce from the wife who has borne him four children. You were aware of this?"

It was bluntly said, on purpose I knew, but Babe Greer merely blushed and ducked her head. Then she moved to Swift's side and took his hand. "Yes, of course. That's all being worked out, and only yesterday we were discussing the announcement of our engagement. Col. Selig wants us to time it for the release of our next picture."

Fitz relaxed but Whitbread was angry. "I see. Tell me, Miss Greer, do you recognize these scraps of white silk, by any chance? Could they be from a scarf or muffler belonging to Mr. Swift?"

She looked toward the pile of brilliant white scraps spoiled by horrid stains of blood. I thought he was trying to shock her into an admission and frighten her with the thought that the man she so admired might have committed the awful deed of locking Leeder in with the leopards.

"No, I don't think so. They're only scraps, aren't they? But Alonzo isn't the only person with an expensive white silk scarf like that. Why I saw one on Kathlyn Williams only the other day." She clasped Alonzo Swift's hand and looked up into his eyes.

Whitbread was fuming but I was merely shocked. If Alonzo Swift really had no reason to fear exposure, it was difficult to believe Leeder might have blackmailed him. And that meant there was no reason for him to kill the man. The shreds of paper from the check did seem to indicate Leeder might have been blackmailing someone, or that he'd done some business that night. I ground my teeth as I stared at the pieces of paper. Alonzo Swift might use Wells Fargo for his banking but I knew Clara used the First Bank of Illinois for hers, as did I. And I knew their checks were of the same pale blue as the bits of paper before me. That made me afraid.

Twenty-Seven

Where's Col. Selig?" Whitbread asked after Alonzo Swift and Babe Greer left us.

"I don't know, he was here earlier," I said. "He was with Broncho Billy, which seemed surprising." I tried to hide the fact that I was reeling from the news that Alonzo Swift apparently had not killed Hyde and Leeder. Just as I feared, the trail seemed to be returning to Alden, and I still had not told Whitbread about his lie. I couldn't bring myself to do it now. It was too late. I found reprieve when Whitbread decided that I should take the children and leave.

"Mr. Fitzgibbons, you'll be so good as to transport Mrs. Chapman and the girls back to Hyde Park." It wasn't a question, it was an order. Fitz knew it and he frowned, but he graciously agreed, nonetheless. "I'll follow up here with Selig and the others," Whitbread said. "And I must speak to Broncho Billy…Gil Anderson."

Lizzie and Penny were sufficiently repentant and grateful for the time they'd spent at the studios to not make a fuss when I found them. I shepherded them down to Fitz's automobile where they fell into a funk, no doubt anticipating the trouble they would be in when we reached home. I sat with Fitz in the back seat. The girls faced us on little stools that folded down. As we began to pull out of the drive I saw a very long white saloon car parked off to the side. Fitz noticed it as well.

"That'll be Senator Clark," Fitz said. He kept an eye on the girls as he whispered in my ear. "The famous 'Copper King' of Montana I was telling you about."

I twisted around to try to get a look but there was nothing to see. It seemed Kathlyn Williams was still seeing her wealthy patron...in secret. This was the woman Alden was leaving Clara for? I was already very worried about him. What had he done with Clara's check that night? Why would he give it to Mr. Leeder? Was Leeder really a blackmailer? Had he been blackmailing Alden about his liaison with Kathlyn Williams? Or something else? Perhaps it wasn't Clara's check at all. Or perhaps Alden had given it to Col. Selig and he, in turn, had given it to Leeder. Was the colonel the one Leeder had been blackmailing? My head spun with the possibilities.

Fitz gazed at Lizzie and Penny with quiet admiration. "Your children have grown up," he said.

To me, they represented yet another problem. What to do about them when we got home? I was unsure, but I trusted that Stephen and I, between us, could come up with a suitable punishment that would teach Lizzie a lesson. As for Penny, I knew she was a warmhearted girl who was already repentant and that she felt the hurt she'd caused her mother deeply. I only wished some of her sensibility would wear off on my daughter. But I knew Lizzie sat there fearing for herself rather than thinking of how she'd injured others. I shook my head. "Mr. Fitzgibbons, is it true what Alonzo Swift said? Is there really a settlement with his wife?"

"Yes, there is. Selig told me about it yesterday. Of course, some people will still object."

"I should think so. He has four children!" I was outraged even if no one else was.

"Yes, but most people aren't aware of that. Most people only know him from the films and they think of him as Babe Greer's lover. They won't be surprised by the engagement. Most of his fans have been waiting for it anxiously."

How unfair it seemed that people like Alonzo Swift could discard a family at will and suffer no consequences, while Alden and Clara were facing disgrace among their friends, family, and colleagues. Unlike the film star, even their professions would be damaged, as such actions were just not deemed acceptable. I supposed it might be different for Alden if he really planned to leave the newspapers behind. Perhaps in the film world he, too, could escape condemnation.

But he would face far worse if he was charged with two murders.

"You're very fortunate," Fitz said.

His comment shook me from my reverie. I wasn't feeling fortunate, but I supposed he meant my family as he observed the girls. Poor Penny. There was a rough road ahead for her but I didn't dare to say so. "Family is both a blessing and a burden," I said. "Do you regret never marrying? Perhaps it's not too late for you. At least, unlike Alonzo Swift, you don't need to rid yourself of an unwanted wife and children if you find your true love."

"No. But I've always feared my fate, if I tried my luck, would be more like poor Mr. Hyde's than your Dr. Chapman's," he said.

Hyde, whose wife had run away. I wondered what Fitz would think of the fate of Alden and Clara. I knew he suspected. "Kathlyn Williams seems also to suffer the consequences of an ill-fated match," I said. "I only wish she'd had a happier conclusion to her marriage, so as not to endanger anyone else's." I was looking at Penny, who stared out the window with a sad face.

Fitz sighed. "We cannot always be blamed for our feelings. We cannot always have control of them. Things happen that must be lived through and accepted."

I remembered years before, when Fitz confided in me that the wedding picture in his office was of his brother's wedding... to a young woman Fitz himself had loved first. He felt that pain he spoke of, but I was unwilling to concede the point. I was thinking of Clara, not Fitz. "I don't believe it's right to condone a breach with the excuse of strong feelings. To see a family torn apart, to allow a past life together to be ripped to shreds merely to satisfy a new flame of emotion is wrong, Mr. Fitzgibbons, and it is something I would never forgive."

At that moment, we reached Clara's house, where Penny was greeted with tears. Clara looked so pale I insisted we leave all explanations and planning to the next day, and Fitz delivered Lizzie and me safely to our own door. I had lost heart for punishing my daughter by the time we sat down to a makeshift supper. Stephen was exhausted, so we all went to bed early, putting off decisions about the future—when we would leave for Woods Hole and other matters—to the next day.

In the morning, we were still at breakfast when a policeman came to the door. He informed me that Detective Whitbread demanded my presence downtown immediately. The tone of the request was so different from what I was used to from my friend and mentor that I was surprised. I was even more taken aback when I hurried out to the official motorcar and found Clara already seated inside. I knew something was seriously amiss.

Twenty-Eight

Neither Clara nor I knew why Whitbread had sent for us. Uneasy myself, I nonetheless tried to reassure Clara. The Harrison Street police station was cold in the early morning. It had rained overnight, and the day was unusually brisk and windy. Clara and I were led, not to the familiar office on the second floor, but to a larger one on the fourth floor instead. We took the elevator with the desk sergeant, whom I knew quite well, and another officer, but they failed to reply to my greetings and seemed uncomfortable. They deposited us in a carpeted room with a long table and several padded wooden armchairs. It was a room I knew was used to question influential people, and the sergeant left the younger officer guarding the door.

Detective Whitbread entered, followed by a stenographer. They took seats across the table from us. Whitbread had a dull look in his eyes and, rather than angry or wrathful, he seemed as cold as a solid block of ice in winter.

I was about to offer to take notes when he motioned me to stop and formally requested our names and addresses. I let Clara speak, then gave my information, feeling ridiculous, as I was so well known there. What did he mean by this? Nothing good, I feared. "What is this about?" I asked.

Whitbread looked at me. The transcribing officer kept his eyes on his paper, pencil poised. "We will get to that in time, Mrs. Chapman. First, I would like to ask Mrs. Cabot several questions and I would appreciate it if you would remain silent during that discussion. If you speak, I will have you removed from the room."

I felt my heart pump and my pulse beat in my ears. Never, in all the years I'd known him, had Whitbread spoken so to me. When I heard his next question, I knew that he'd discovered my lie.

"Mrs. Cabot, will you describe what happened on the evening of June fourth? When did your husband return home?"

Clara felt the atmosphere and looked toward me. I avoided her eyes. She'd never lied to Whitbread and, as he obviously already knew that Alden had returned to the city that night, there was no point in her lying now. Dear Clara had no intention of lying in any case.

"Alden was quite late. As it happens, I was waiting for him. We were due to leave on a trip to the East Coast this week and I was concerned that he might have changed his mind about coming with us." She looked down at the table, where her hands were clasped together. "He has had many work assignments that take him away from home and which cause conflicts with travel arrangements." She hesitated before she continued. "I was correct in my assumptions. He did have an obligation that would prevent him from coming with us."

"I see. And did he remain at your house all night?"

A faint tint of pink rose from her neck to her cheeks and she fixed her gaze on her hands. "No. He left again."

"So, he was not at your home that entire night?" Whitbread stared at me as he asked this.

"No."

"And did you let Mrs. Chapman know that? Did she ask you?"

Clara looked up and quickly glanced between me and Whitbread. "Mrs. Cabot?"

"Well, yes. Emily asked me about it the next day...in the afternoon. I told her that Alden had come home but then left again. Why are you asking this, Detective? Has something happened?"

Whitbread was glaring hard in my direction. I didn't dare try to explain my actions. I'd known Alden was not home all night and yet hadn't told him.

"Mrs. Cabot, do you have accounts in the First Bank of Illinois?"

"Why, yes. But what does that have to do with anything?" she asked. Then she drew a breath. I knew she remembered the check she'd given to Alden that night.

"Tell him, Clara," I said.

"Tell me what, Mrs. Cabot?" Whitbread asked.

"All right. I told Emily that I wrote a check for Alden that night. He asked for money and I wrote a check, and, yes, it was on the First Bank of Illinois. Is that what this about?"

"What was the check for, Mrs. Cabot?"

"I don't know. He didn't tell me. He just asked for it."

"And the amount?"

"Is this necessary? All right, it was for $10,000. I'm a wealthy woman, Detective Whitbread, and I can well afford it."

I was shocked at the amount. I had no idea it had been so large. What could Alden want it for? What could he have been thinking?

"Your husband asked you for $10,000, without saying why, and you just wrote him a check?" Whitbread was also astonished.

Clara looked like she was going to break down.

"Detective Whitbread, please," I said, hoping he wouldn't have me ejected. "Mrs. Cabot is under a lot of strain. I know you must be angry at me for not disclosing what I knew, but Clara knows nothing of the case. Please, tell us what's happened."

He stared at me for a moment before addressing Clara. "Mrs. Cabot, we have arrested your husband, Alden Cabot, for the murder of Arnold Leeder."

"Oh, no, he would never do such a thing," Clara said.

I closed my eyes. I'd suspected this was the case. But I never anticipated what he said next.

"I'm afraid it *is* true, Mrs. Cabot, and your husband has confessed."

Twenty-Nine

C onfessed?" I said. "Alden confessed?" I pictured the bloody floor of the leopards' cage. I could imagine Alden shooting someone while in a rage, but to lock a man in a cage and then either leave or, worse, remain to hear his victim's screams as he was torn apart by animals, was something I could not fathom.

"No," Clara said. "It's a mistake. He would never kill someone. He wouldn't do it, Detective. You must believe me."

"I'm most sorry, Mrs. Cabot, but I'm afraid it's true. You must steel yourself for some very unpleasant news. I believe it will be better if you hear this directly from me, rather than having it come out in dribs and drabs in the papers. Mrs. Chapman, despite our many years of association, did *not* tell me that your husband left your house that night. Your husband told me only that he had arrived there. I made the mistake of believing Mrs. Chapman would have felt obliged to tell me if she knew something so pertinent as that he'd left again, so I assumed he was with you all that night and could not have been physically present to do the deed.

"It was only when I learned that another suspect was cleared that I returned to the original investigation and spoke to Miss Williams's driver. He freely admitted that he waited for Mr. Cabot at your door and then returned him to Miss Williams's lodgings later that night. The driver left the motorcar there, before returning to his own home on the streetcar."

I suppressed a groan. Alden *had* returned to Kathlyn Williams that night, just as I'd always feared.

Whitbread continued. "Last night I interviewed Miss Williams at her home, where we found her in the presence of your husband. Several people told us she was wearing a white silk scarf on the evening of Mr. Leeder's death. She claimed the scarf was lost earlier in the day but, when presented with the testimony of her driver, she admitted Mr. Cabot had returned that night. I'm sorry to have to tell you, Mrs. Cabot, that they then attempted to swear that they both remained at her home together the whole night. I regret being the one to have to repeat such assertions to you, but I must tell you I believe they lied. Mr. Cabot took a room at a nearby boardinghouse and, in any case, they did not remain at Miss Williams's house that night.

"We executed a search warrant and found these two notes." He placed the two scraps of paper in front of us. Each had been printed in block letters in black ink and then folded many times.

"Blackmail," I said, reaching out to read them. "And the nights of both Hyde's and Leeder's deaths are mentioned?" Each note demanded money be delivered to the Selig studios. The first was for a smaller amount, $300, but the second demanded an envelope with $10,000 be placed in the leopards' cage by eleven o'clock that night and threatened harm to Miss Williams, as well as exposure, if the demands were not met. "Was Leeder the blackmailer, then?" I asked.

"Miss Williams believed so."

"But why was Hyde killed?"

"It's possible he was a victim and refused to pay, or perhaps he was an accomplice to the blackmail. Or he may have been killed by someone who mistook him for the blackmailer. As you can see, the first note gives instructions to leave the money in the bedroom scene at the studio, on the very night Mr. Hyde was killed. Miss Williams claims she never paid that first amount because the man was already dead when she arrived at the designated spot."

Whitbread crossed his arms on his chest. "Faced with the evidence of the letters, Miss Williams broke down and admitted she was being blackmailed. She was confused when she received the second letter because she assumed that Mr. Hyde had been her blackmailer. But she delivered the money for the second demand as instructed. She claimed she saw no one, not even Leeder, at the leopards' cage, so she left. When I pronounced her arrest, Mr. Cabot jumped up, insisting that *he* was the one who locked Leeder in the cage. He said he was the one who brought the check, then he fought with the man, and left him to the leopards. He was arrested and he continues to insist Miss Williams knew nothing of his act."

"I see," Clara said.

I slumped in my chair. I no longer felt the strain of keeping something from Whitbread but that was no kind of relief. I pictured Olga's leopards as they had stalked around their cage. How terrifying to be attacked by them. What kind of person could hear the screams and walk away? Alden? How had he come to be that kind of person?

"Detective Whitbread, I'd like to speak to my husband," Clara said.

"Yes, we should hear it directly from him," I said and began to think of a list of recriminations to read off to him.

But Clara put up a slender hand. "No, Emily, please. I must speak to Alden. You can be present, but *I* need to speak to him, not you."

I looked at her, realizing then that Clara had trusted me to see Alden through this crisis but I'd failed. I felt her spirit withdraw from me.

"Please, Detective Whitbread," she said.

It was as if she were lowering a metal door between us and it took my breath away. I felt empty. Would Clara ever speak to me again with the sincerity and honesty we'd known as friends? It was quite sudden, the realization that she might not. Our mutual confidence had died before my eyes.

I gulped at a lump in my throat while Whitbread instructed a uniformed officer to bring Alden up to speak to his wife. While we waited, Whitbread began to gather the evidence from the table and return it to a paper bag. I bit my lip to force myself to feel something in this frozen silence. "I'm sorry," I said, after I regained some composure.

He continued his actions until he could neatly fold the top of the bag. I thought then that Stephen was wrong when he told me Whitbread would understand my need to protect, or at least not to betray, my brother. It wasn't something the detective would do, himself. His own commitment to the truth was absolute.

"I'm sorry," I said again, panic rising in my chest.

He raised his head to give me a good long look. "Mrs. Chapman," he finally said, "in the fifteen years since we met have you ever known me to willfully persecute any man?"

"No, certainly not," I said.

"Have you ever known me to strain a point to obtain a conviction?"

"No, never."

"Have you ever known me to suffer such actions by any man, if I could prevent it?"

"No...no."

"And yet, rather than relaying the full truth of your conversation with Mrs. Cabot, you lied by omission in order to protect your brother, didn't you?"

I couldn't avoid his eyes. "Yes," I admitted shamefacedly. Clara watched silently.

"Because, despite your knowledge of my character and my actions over all of these years, you feared what? That I would make a mistake? That I would bring an innocent man to justice? Or was it that you believe your brother to be guilty and you sought to hide his guilt? Liars always come to a wrong end, Mrs. Chapman. You should know that. What did you hope to achieve by this misrepresentation? It all comes out in the end. There must be equal justice for all, Mrs. Chapman, and that includes your brother."

"I know. But I still can't believe it and I just couldn't betray my own brother. I'm so sorry. I know it was wrong of me."

"You did *not* betray your brother, Mrs. Chapman, but you *did* betray me. I'm sorry to say that trust which was between us has been broken."

"Oh, no, please don't say that. I'm very sorry. I'm sure I've learned my lesson." Whitbread was such a staple in my life. His tall frame, balding brow, and large brush-like mustache had become such a constant for me. Suddenly, I realized that I'd crossed some bridge and, as I looked back at him, the very structure crumbled, dividing us forever. The light of amusement I'd seen so often in his eyes was gone, snuffed out. He would never open his heart to me again, as he had in the past.

He excused himself and left us. I sat there, regretting the inevitable slide that had taken me away from him. In trying to protect Alden, I was forced to give up that part of myself that had been linked to Detective Henry Whitbread. I knew he would be too professional to let it affect the police work I did with my students, but never again would I feel the warmth of his loyal friendship as I had in the past. I'd made a choice…and a mistake… that were unforgivable to him.

Thirty

I tried to ask Clara what she planned to say to Alden, but she cut me off with an impatient wave of her hand and I realized she didn't want me to speak. Ordinarily, I would have jumped in and questioned Alden as soon as he entered, but Clara raised her hand in a warning gesture to me as Whitbread led him in. She wanted to be the one to talk to him.

Whitbread got Alden seated opposite us, then left again, saying, "I'll be outside the door. You have twenty minutes, no more. After that, Mr. Cabot will need to be returned to his cell."

Alden looked surprised to see us but, after a glance at Clara's face, he moved uncomfortably and stared down at the table in front of him, as if he were afraid to meet her gaze. The air seemed tense, as if it was crackling with potential lightning. I realized Clara was very angry. I could almost feel the strength of that anger flowing from her, so I knew I would be wise to stay silent.

We sat like that for a moment before Clara spoke. "Alden, did Kathlyn Williams lock that man in the leopards' cage? Is that why you claimed that you did it?"

I suppressed a gasp, holding my breath.

Alden folded his arms and sat back in his chair, frowning. He still wasn't looking directly at Clara. He was staring at some point over her head.

Clara looked very pale. "Is that why you said you did it? To save Kathlyn Williams?" she asked.

Alden's gaze dropped to Clara's face and I saw a spasm of pain in his expression. "Not Kathlyn Williams herself, *The Adventures of Kathlyn.* It's all gone now, anyhow. I lost it all."

Clara stared at him. "What are you talking about?"

He blew air through his lips. "*The Adventures of Kathlyn.* My ticket out of all this to California. It was my idea. It's what I was working on so much that it got me fired from the *Trib*. Not that there was anything left for me there, anyhow. They were paying me by the piece, you know...at the paper. They wanted to get rid of me."

"You never told me," Clara said.

"How could I? How could I admit to you that I was that big a failure? But *The Adventures* was going to make it right. I knew Selig wanted to move the animals to California and everybody was vying to go with him. He's made a name for the studio, doing animal films. I told him my idea of doing a series of related films. The story would be a rescue from wild animals every week and then end with the star in another predicament that would make the audience have to come back again the next week to see how she got out of it. He liked it, but he told me I'd have to get Kathlyn Williams to agree to do it. She's the only one of these actresses who'd work with the animals like that, doing stunts."

He looked at both of us. "You think it's just a stupid idea, don't you? You're wrong. But I knew you'd look down your noses at it." He sneered. "Just another failure for Alden, that's what you'd think."

"Alden, stop it," Clara said. "I don't care about your film idea. Why did you say you killed that man?"

"Leeder was a real lowlife. But it started with the censor, Hyde. Everything was lined up. Selig and Kathlyn Williams were both enthusiastic about the scenarios I was turning out. Then Hyde started censoring Kathlyn's scenes. He'd never done that before. Selig got worried about using her because of that. But *The Adventures of Kathlyn* wouldn't work without Kathlyn. And then she got the first blackmail letter, threatening to tell the newspapers about her relationship to that old Copper King from Montana. If that got out, it would ruin her, and ruin *The Adventures,* and ruin my chance to do something with my life. Something the kids could be proud of. We were so close, and then it all started coming apart."

"Alden, how can you think the children could be proud of you, if you confess to a murdering a man?" Clara asked.

He hung his head. "It's all over, anyhow. Everything's ruined."

"It will be if you're convicted of murder," I said. "Did you lock Leeder in with those leopards? Or, if you didn't, why did you say you did?"

"Whitbread was hammering Kathlyn Williams. He wouldn't believe her when she said Leeder wasn't there when she left the payment as per the instructions. He was going to arrest her."

"So, you claimed *you* did it?" I asked.

Alden was looking at Clara, whose eyes were closed. She was shaking her head slowly back and forth. "If he arrested her, the publicity would destroy her," Alden said to Clara. "She has a little boy, you know. She's afraid of losing him to her ex-husband if the business with the Montana Copper King gets out. That's why she was being blackmailed. That would ruin her and it would ruin *The Adventures of Kathlyn,* too. Don't you see, it was already over for me then? If I stepped in, at least she could keep the child and her career. I'd already lost everything—my job, my family. I had nothing to lose."

What a stupid thing to say, I was tempted to tell him, but Clara took a big breath and spoke. "Alden, if you insist on jumping off a ledge, you must see that you're taking the children and me with you."

"No, Clara."

"Yes, Alden. Why can't you spare your own children? How can you do this to them? You must retract your confession."

"No. What's the point? Kathlyn Williams didn't kill Leeder,

but the police won't believe her. She'll lose her son for sure and it'll destroy her career. If I can't make *The Adventures of Kathlyn* I'm ruined, anyhow. Penny and Ollie will be better off without me. What good is a father who can't take care of them?"

"Stop it, Alden," Clara said.

"No, Clara. I won't retract my confession unless I know Kathlyn Williams won't be arrested. What's the point?"

"Alden, you must tell the truth. You can't continue to lie like this," I said.

He turned toward me. "Emily, if you tell Whitbread, I'll deny it. He's already furious with you. What will he think if you tell him a different version and I deny it?"

"You're a fool, Alden. Look what you're doing to Clara and your children."

Clara put a hand up to stop us. "Alden, you're wrong to think the children and I wouldn't respect you because you lost your job. It's just not true. You're wrong to think we're better off without you. Our children need their father and I need my husband. You're fearless, Alden. You've always been that way. You'll risk your life without a thought in the blink of an eye. It takes my breath away."

That made me remember, again, the time he'd jumped into the sea to save her.

"But you can't do that anymore," she continued. "You're a father now. You don't just risk your own life, don't you see? You risk Penny and Ollie, too. And I won't let you do that."

The door opened and Whitbread brought in a uniformed officer to take Alden away. "The time is up. Mr. Cabot must be returned to his cell."

Alden stared at Clara, then allowed himself to be led away. Clara put a hand on my arm. "Thank you, Detective Whitbread. We'll hire a lawyer for my husband. Also, I must speak to Miss Williams. Could you give me her address?"

She squeezed my arm, a signal that she wanted me to remain silent. But I couldn't. "You can't really believe Alden would kill a man just to save the career of a film actress," I said. "It's absurd." I wanted to tell Whitbread what Alden had said, but I knew my brother would deny it. I owed it to Clara to follow her wishes in this. In any case, Whitbread ignored me. Nothing I could say would penetrate his disdain. He opened the door and beckoned a uniformed officer to take us away.

Thirty-One

Clara bit her lip, declining to respond to my comments, as we trotted up State Street and then a few blocks west in the carriage Detective Whitbread had arranged for us. We found ourselves in a perfectly respectable neighborhood and stopped in front of a small bungalow. Clara paid the driver, asking him to wait. When a maid answered the door, Clara asked to be announced as Mrs. Alden Cabot. The girl ushered us into a crowded living room with chintz furniture and drapes. A large braided rug covered the floor. On the whole, it was a homier and less stylish place than I would have imagined for a film star.

Kathlyn Williams entered slowly, wearing a loose tea gown of ivory lace. "Mrs. Cabot? And Mrs. Chapman, please sit down. I'm so very sorry your husband's been arrested. How can I help you?"

She looked strained to me. Her face was very white but, even under strain, she looked every bit the ten years younger than Clara that she was. Her hair was a golden color, with curls that were pulled to the side, where they trailed over her shoulder. She looked sincerely sorrowful, her big eyes alertly following Clara's moves as she settled herself on the sofa. I reminded myself that she was an actress, after all.

"Miss Williams, I'm aware of why my husband has confessed to the murder of Arnold Leeder. He was afraid the police were about to arrest you and he wanted to spare you that. I will not go against his wishes at the moment, but I need you to tell me, and

Mrs. Chapman here, everything you know about what happened to both Mr. Hyde and Mr. Leeder."

Kathlyn Williams frowned and her eyes slid back and forth between Clara and me as we sat on opposite ends of the sofa. "I don't know if I can," she said.

"I understand you're afraid to discuss certain things that led to your being blackmailed, for fear of public exposure, but I assure you that is not my intention," Clara said, then turned to me. "Emily, I must ask you to swear to keep in confidence anything you hear from Miss Williams today. Please, for me. Promise complete secrecy."

"I promise," I said.

Kathlyn still seemed reluctant. Clara shook her head as if she were barely restraining some great energy. "Miss Williams, I have two children of my own. Their father is currently in a jail cell. It would seem these things have come to pass because he's determined to aid your cause. I ask you, as a mother, to help Emily...Mrs. Chapman find the truth. Alden is determined to stay on his current course until he's sure you won't be arrested. Emily may be able to help us discover the truth. She has some experience and she's worked with the police for a long time. You must tell us everything."

Kathlyn Williams took a deep breath, but I thought she set her features in a way to suggest she would stubbornly dig in her heels, when suddenly a door swung open and a child of three or four years of age ran to her.

"Mama," he said, grabbing her knees, and attempting to climb into her lap.

A young woman in an apron followed close behind. "I'm so sorry, ma'am, he got away from me." The boy laughed at her in triumph as he extended his arms to his mother.

"It's all right, Mary," Kathlyn Williams said. She lifted the boy onto her lap, turning him to face us, and straightening his little jacket. He reached up to grab an earring and she gently pulled his hand away. "Mrs. Cabot, Mrs. Chapman, this is my son, Victor, who should be helping Mary in the kitchen. Be good, Vic. Say good day to the ladies."

He did so and we replied in kind. Clara asked him how old he was and he told her he was four. She complimented him and told him she had a son at home who was ten. After a few moments, Kathlyn Williams put the boy down again and sent him off to follow the nursemaid back to the kitchen where he could have a treat. He bowed politely to us before leaving.

Even though Alden had told us she had a child, I was deeply surprised. I'd been shocked to hear that Alonzo Swift had a wife and four children, but I'd never suspected that Kathlyn Williams, who was in the midst of divorcing her husband, could also have a hidden life.

"So, that is your son," Clara said.

"Yes. Alden told you?" Kathlyn asked.

"Alden told us, and we know you were being blackmailed. Since Emily and I know that much, surely you can tell us the rest, so we can try to find out what happened."

Kathlyn twisted a lace-edged handkerchief in her hands. "I must keep him. I can't let his father take him away…he wants to. It's not that Harry cares so much for the boy, but he wants to hurt me. He wants to make me pay. But you can see why I needed to sue him for money in the divorce proceedings. It's not just myself I have to support. My husband, Harry Kainer, is in New York. He has other women. That was true even when I was living with him. He kept me penniless while he went out on the town. He expected me to be the nice little wife, sitting by the fire, while he was out gallivanting. Finally, after Victor was born, I decided that I was through with Harry and his ways." She looked away from the door her little son had left through to face us. "I don't know what I expected, but being a mother at home wasn't enough for me. I wanted to go back to the stage but Harry wouldn't allow me to. I was stuck until Bill Clark—you've probably heard him

DEATH AT THE SELIG STUDIOS

referred to as the Copper King—saw how unhappy I was and helped me."

She grimaced. "I know what it looks like, but it's not like that. Mr. Clark's a big shot...he was a senator not long ago...back in Montana where I grew up. He had no children of his own and he has lots of money. He saw my talent. He got me into the New York Academy of the Arts and he followed my career after that. When I got married to Harry, he was disappointed. I know he was. But he didn't say anything. It was only after Victor was born and he came to see me that he noticed how unhappy I was. He was the only person who saw how very miserable I was. He told me then that he'd help me and Victor...if I wanted to leave. He made it possible."

"But then that became a reason for blackmail," I said.

She looked down. "Yes. At first, I couldn't believe it would mean anything to anyone...until I saw what was going on with Babe and Alonzo. Of course I knew Alonzo had a family back East. I tried to warn Babe, but she told Col. Selig and he called me in and told me I was never to mention it again or Alonzo would be ruined. Well, if they thought that about Alonzo's situation, what would they think about mine? A divorced woman with a child? So I knew, then, that I had to keep my situation quiet. Even Col. Selig didn't know. Only Babe did...because she told me about her own problem...I confided in her."

"Alden knew," Clara said.

Kathlyn put a hand to her hair, patting the curls in place on her shoulder. "He found out by mistake. But I knew I could trust him. He wouldn't tell anyone. He wants Col. Selig to film *The Adventures of Kathlyn* and he needs me to do that." In pausing, Kathlyn seemed to deduce our assumptions about how Alden had gotten close enough to learn her secret. Clara closed her eyes gently as if she felt pain.

"It wasn't like that," Kathlyn said. "We were working together on *The Adventures*. That was a secret, too. You see, Col. Selig wants to move some of us out to California to do animal pictures, and Alden and I had a great idea. Well, really it was Alden's idea. He wrote a set of stories about a princess who gets lost in the jungle and has all kinds of adventures before she finally gets her crown. It's set in India, so there are tigers and elephants and all. He was going to call it *The Adventures of Kathlyn*. But he had the stupendous thought to make it a serial, with a new episode every week. It would be an ongoing story that would bring people back to the theater every week. It was a radical idea, so we didn't want anyone else to get hold of it and present it to Col. Selig before us."

"Did Mr. Hyde know about this?" I asked. I was still trying to put it together, how these secrets could lead to murder.

"About the serial? I don't see how. I don't know what he knew, though. Suddenly, he just took a dislike to my scenes and kept rejecting them. It was a big problem because Alden had written the scenarios all for me, in particular. I mean, I suppose he might have found someone else to star, but I helped with the stories. I suggested predicaments she could get into, based on what I knew would work. Besides, Alden knew I needed the money to support myself and Victor."

"Then you received blackmail notes," I said.

"Yes, and I told Alden. The first one was for $300. I scraped that together and I put it in an envelope that I took to the studios…like the note said to do that night. But the censor was already dead when I got there. He was shot and left lying on the bed. It was awful. I should have called someone, but how would I explain why I was there?

"So I ran home. I ran the whole way, it must be two miles, but I was too frightened to find a cab and I hadn't dared to use my driver. When I got here, Alden was waiting. I'd forgotten we were going to have a session on *The Adventures of Kathlyn* that night. He made me tell him what happened. I didn't know what that censor had against me. We thought it was because he knew about Bill Clark. Mr. Hyde's wife left him for another man, so maybe he thought I left my husband for Bill. It's not true. I knew Bill Clark before I ever met Harry. But maybe the censor heard that Bill came to see me, just to check on me here in Chicago, and he thought I left my husband for him.

"Anyhow, Alden went to the studios early the next morning and found the dead man."

"So he was putting the gun in the dead man's hand when Leeder saw him," I said.

"He was just trying to help me," she said. "He knew about Victor. He knew that, if my husband thought I was seeing Bill Clark, he'd try to take Vic away. Alden knew that was what I was scared of and that was why I tried to pay off the blackmailer." She turned toward Clara. "He just wanted to stop the censor from rejecting my films. He was afraid Col. Selig wouldn't do *The Adventures of Kathlyn* if they'd be rejected by the censor."

"He told us," Clara said.

"But the blackmail didn't stop," I said.

Kathlyn looked at me. "No, I thought it had. I was relieved. So I was shocked...at the roadhouse...when I got another note. It was slipped into my purse. I don't know who did it."

"You told Alden?" I asked.

"I was hysterical. This time they wanted $10,000. I don't have that kind of money. And they knew about Victor, I know they did. It said my husband would find out about Bill and I would lose everything, not just money. I panicked. If they'd given me more time, I could have asked Bill for the money, but the note demanded the money be placed inside the leopards' cage that very night...by me."

"So Alden came to me for the money, and he couldn't tell me why because it wasn't his secret to share," Clara said.

"I'm so sorry. I made him promise he wouldn't tell anyone. But I promised him I'd go to Bill for the money and pay it back. I would...I will. I'll pay back that money."

Clara looked up. She'd been contemplating her hands as she listened to Kathlyn's version of the story. According to her, it was more the need to protect her son, than her career, that forced her to pay the blackmailer. But, if it had been that important to her, would she have killed to protect the boy? Wouldn't a mother do that to protect her child?

"What happened after Alden returned with the check from Clara?" I asked.

Kathlyn wrapped her arms around her waist, hugging herself as if she were cold. "I had to take it just like the note said. Alden offered to deliver it, but I thought that wouldn't be enough. I was sure *I* had to be the one to bring it right into the leopards' cage."

"Alden drove the motorcar. The driver always leaves it out on the street. Alden had driven it before." She looked up guiltily. "We'd go out and drive around and talk about the serial," she said, looking at us for a reaction. "We were just planning for how we'd propose it to Col. Selig. It would mean so much to both of us. We wanted to be the ones who were sent out to California to do the animal pictures." She shook her head as if she were seeing herself and Alden driving around all night and was now regretting it. "It seemed so important then."

"Well, Mr. Leeder wanted to go to California too, didn't he?" I asked.

"Oh, everyone did…everyone does. It's going to be the future."

For a moment, I wondered whether that could have been a motive to get rid of Arnold Leeder. I looked at Kathlyn Williams. Could she have lured the man into the cage and locked him in, then walked away into the night to where Alden was waiting in the car? Could she do that? But then I shook my head. No, Leeder played a different role in the film company. A producer wouldn't be competition for an actress and a writer of scenarios. Still, someone *had* apparently wanted him dead.

"You're sure you didn't see Leeder?" I asked.

She frowned. "Yes, I'm sure. I saw no one. I slipped the envelope between the bars and said a prayer. Then I left. I saw no one."

"But Alden's claiming he's the one who put the money in the cage," I said.

"He knew that, if they arrested me, Victor would be taken away from me for good. That's why he confessed. Please, believe me. I didn't kill Arnold Leeder and neither did Alden. I'll do anything to help you clear him."

"But I've promised Alden we'll do that without your being arrested," Clara said. "He's concerned about your son."

"I can't abandon him to Harry," Kathlyn Williams said. "But I can't let your husband take the blame for something he didn't do."

Didn't he? I wondered. "What happened that night...after you left the envelope?"

"Alden waited for me, then drove me back home. He left me and returned to the boardinghouse where he'd taken a room. We thought the blackmail was paid. I swear to you, Mrs. Cabot."

I wondered. It seemed to me that, even if Kathlyn Williams testified to Alden's innocence, she might not be believed. They could be seen as conspirators and, even if they weren't, who could say that Alden hadn't used her motorcar to return and lock Leeder, the blackmailing rascal, in with the leopards, as he no doubt deserved? Even if Kathlyn Williams told the truth, Alden would not be saved.

Thirty-Two

The cab was waiting at the door. We were silent for the first part of the drive. Once we left the noise of the Loop behind, and were traveling the quieter streets of Hyde Park, Clara told me she'd wire one of her brothers, who was a lawyer. He'd help her find someone to represent Alden. She waited expectantly for me to say what I planned to do.

I hardly knew what to say. My break with Whitbread made me useless. He'd be willing to continue our academic projects, but I knew he'd never include me in this investigation, after what I'd done. Perhaps he'd never include me in any investigation again. Whitbread's integrity was unblemished and he couldn't comprehend anything less from his confidants.

"Clara, what if the lawyer can't disprove the allegations against Alden? In that case, won't you have to ask Kathlyn Williams to testify on his behalf?"

"No, Emily. We won't do that. I promised Alden we wouldn't allow her to be arrested. She told us her story under the promise of secrecy. You cannot tell anyone, not even Stephen. I certainly won't reveal Kathlyn Williams's secret to either my brother or the lawyer. That's how it must be. I only persuaded Alden to tell me the truth by agreeing to this. He believes she didn't do it, so what would be the point of putting her through an arrest, which would surely lead to her losing custody of her son? We must find another way."

If Alden hadn't committed the murders, we needed to find the real killer. I knew that was what she hoped to hear me say. But what if there was no one else? What if Alden *was* guilty? Or Kathlyn Williams, for that matter.

"Emily, I'm counting on you," she said.

I stirred, moving to lower the window, hoping to catch the scent of a spring breeze. Based on the past, she thought I could uncover the truth here, but I had no such confidence. "I'll do whatever I can," I said, hoping it would be enough.

At home, I told Stephen of Alden's arrest but I didn't tell him about our visit to Kathlyn Williams. Neither one of us wanted to discuss travel arrangements, and I found myself curled in a corner of the sofa in his study that night, thinking hard about the deaths. I knew Stephen, like Clara, took it for granted that I would go out and find the real culprit, but I had no such expectation. Even when I told him how angry Whitbread had been, Stephen disregarded that and assumed I would return to the Selig studios to investigate.

But what would I find there? I couldn't see a resolution to the conundrum. Alden had confessed to killing Leeder because he was blackmailing Kathlyn Williams. If he hadn't done it, and if Kathlyn hadn't done it, as Alden insisted, then who was left? And who had killed the censor, Hyde? And why? After the first death, we assumed Hyde was the blackmailer but, if it was actually Leeder who was the blackmailer, why was Hyde killed, and by whom? Did Leeder kill him? Was Hyde himself being blackmailed? If so, I wondered what he'd done to be blackmailed. He sounded like such a pathetic figure. Could it be that he'd been working for Edison somehow, conspiring against Selig, and Leeder found out? Or had Hyde threatened to expose the blackmailer? Were there others being blackmailed, besides Kathlyn Williams and George Hyde? Col. Selig? Olga or Big Otto? Apparently not Alonzo Swift, as he'd come to a settlement with his wife. How would I ever be able to find out? My head spun with all the possibilities.

I knew I'd have to make another trip to the studios, even though I despaired of achieving any useful result. I felt empty, like a hollow shell. My family might think I was solid but it was an illusion. In point of fact, I could make as much impact as a wisp of smoke on the events that were barreling toward a bad end for Alden. I could do nothing to stop what was unfolding.

Thirty-Three

A re you well, Mrs. Chapman?" Babe Greer asked me when I walked onto the backlot of the Selig studios the next morning. "I was so sorry to hear about your brother. Did you know Col. Selig's missing? No one's seen him since the day before yesterday. Detective Whitbread has come by several times—yesterday and first thing this morning. He seems quite short tempered about it."

"Is Detective Whitbread here now?" I asked. I feared he'd warn me off if he saw me.

"No, he's been and gone. I think he was going to the Selig offices downtown on Randolph Street. Of course, it may be that Col. Selig is there but, in the meantime, did you know they're filming the *Leopard Queen* scenes with the very leopards who attacked Mr. Leeder? Isn't that a scandal? I said so to Alonzo, and he agreed with me. I wouldn't go anywhere near those cats. What if they attack again? Really!"

I felt repulsion at the thought, myself. The animals that had ripped the producer apart were back and working, as was Kathlyn Williams. "What about the *Wizard of Oz*?" I asked.

"Oh, they finished all that yesterday. They've torn it down already, it's gone." Babe sounded satisfied as if she, too, lived for the constant change of scenery and props that was the film business. I was glad the excuse for the children to sneak up to the studios was gone and I resolved to be sure to mention the obliteration of Oz when I returned home.

A group of people were milling about the jungle set. As I walked in that direction, I passed the long, low cages for the leopards. They were empty. Big Otto stood in a spot beyond the cages hosing down a small elephant that slowly swayed its head from side to side, relishing the spray. The fetid smell of animals hung over the area.

Beyond the crowd of people, Otis Turner stood waving his arms and talking through his megaphone, while Kathlyn Williams lay on a rock as if asleep. The leopards paced around superciliously, stopping to rub against Kathlyn's body now and then. Olga stood beyond the sidelines, occasionally whistling, or motioning with her hands to communicate with the cats.

I wondered at Kathlyn's composure. A man had been killed by those leopards just a few days before, yet there she was, lying still in the midst of them.

"They gave her a sedative," Babe Greer whispered in my ear. "The cats, too. Seems like they've got some tabby naptime medicine. Olga fed it to them. They'll do anything for her." Two of the cats continued to stroll, marching back and forth as regular as a clock pendulum, while the third one slept at Kathlyn's feet. In response to prompts from Turner, the actress raised herself up and began to stretch, showing a strong resemblance to the cats.

"She's either very brave or very foolish," Babe Greer whispered. "Alonzo says they're man-eaters now that they attacked Mr. Leeder. They get a taste for human flesh, he says." She shivered. "Do you think Kathlyn will be implicated in the murders? Maybe that's how she can do it. Maybe she doesn't care anymore, knowing she'll have to stand trial, too."

I looked at her eager face. "I think Alden has saved her from that," I said. "He confessed and he insists she knew nothing of his acts." I'd promised Clara I would respect her agreement with Alden. If he had to make such a mess, at the very least Kathlyn's child ought to make it through unharmed. Something good had to come from all of this. Babe Greer's interest had all the marks of common human curiosity and gossip. I didn't want to feed it, so I turned away and headed back toward the leopard cages. There must be something I could do to discover who the real culprit was.

Babe Greer stared at me as I walked away, but she remained with the others, all of them waiting breathlessly for Kathlyn Williams to be attacked. I would hear about it if that happened, I didn't need to see it.

By the time I reached the cages, Big Otto was cleaning them out. An old blanket had been placed over the chaise lounge to cover the blood stains. He had a pail and shovel to remove the leopard droppings, and a pitchfork to bring in more hay from a small wheelbarrow by the door. I felt the cool iron of the black bars of the cage. Big Otto eyed me suspiciously.

"Is it true that the leopards develop a taste for human flesh, once they've killed a man?" I asked.

He rolled his eyes in his bald head. "Only if they eat the body," he said and I shivered at the thought. "We found them before they could do that. They go for the jugular, the big vein in the neck." He pointed to his own neck, rocking his head to the side. "One of them got him there, and bit his head too. But they'd already been fed, you know. They weren't hungry, we feed them well. Someone must have prodded them to make them angry."

I stared at him. Someone had prodded them? Someone had left Leeder in the cage, then gone outside and used a stick to disturb the beasts? How horrible.

"What would you do if you were sleeping in your bed and somebody broke in and started poking at you? When you saw a stranger, wouldn't you attack him to defend yourself? It is what they did. They were prowling around all upset when we got here. They didn't attack to eat him, it was provoked. That's why we moved them. Olga could tell. It was not the fault of the cats."

I watched in silence as he finished his work, then he turned to a rope and pulley at the side of the cage. "You see this? This is how you get them out one at a time. That's the way to do it. You put meat there, at the end. You hoist this." He pulled on the rope and a metal sheet that formed a gate inside the long cage was lifted. "As soon as one is through, you drop it." He let go of the rope and the metal hit the ground with a clang, forming a barrier between the main cage and the smaller, lower part at the end. "It's all safe, unless you want to do harm." He grunted. He was offended that Leeder's death might have been blamed on the cage itself.

"My brother has confessed to luring Mr. Leeder into the cage and locking him in," I said. Alden had said nothing about poking the animals to make them attack, though. He'd told Whitbread he just left the man there, expecting nature to take its course. From what Big Otto said, perhaps that was not enough. If he *had* locked Leeder in the cage, could someone else have come and provoked the animals?

Big Otto straightened up and looked at me. "I'm surprised. I think Leeder was a big showoff. I thought he might have come in with a lady…to show her how he's a big strong guy, he can play with leopards. I've seen him do this before with other ladies. Olga and me, we told him not to do that. But he's a big ladies' man, big showoff."

"You'd seen him in the leopards' cage before?" I asked. I knew Leeder had pursued women, but *in* the cage? We thought he'd been there to blackmail someone, not to romance a woman. "Did anyone besides you and Olga know he did that?" I asked the big man.

"The girls he took there, for sure." Big Otto shrugged. "You want to know, ask Olga." He picked up his pail and shovel and walked away toward the shed where the key to the cage was kept.

I stood deep in thought for some minutes, then I heard a swish behind me. I turned and jumped away, as Olga sauntered along with the three leopards on leads. She took them to the shack where she retrieved the key, then led them back to the cage, detaching their leashes from their collars as she released each one into the cage. They appeared to suffer her touch haughtily before loping off into their home.

"Good girls," she said in her throaty voice as she locked the door. "You will be beautiful on the film, beautiful." Draping the leashes over her arm, she turned toward me.

"Miss Olga," I said, "Big Otto told me that Arnold Leeder had entered the cage in the past, to impress young women. Is that true?"

She spat on the ground. "He was a pig. He tries to scare the girls to seduce them. He threatens to put them with the cats."

"My! Did he threaten Kathlyn Williams that way?"

"Kathlyn? No. She goes of her own accord. She can walk with the cats. They have an understanding. Leeder was just a pig. He understood nothing."

She certainly seemed to have disliked Leeder. I wondered how deep that dislike ran. Had Leeder propositioned her? Or perhaps he'd blackmailed her for something. "Have these leopards ever harmed anyone besides Mr. Leeder?" I asked.

She frowned at me and her whole tall figure tightened up with anger. "What do you accuse us of? You leave the cats alone, they leave you alone, it's simple."

She seemed very defensive, which made me wonder if there *had* been other incidents. Could she have been blackmailed to hide them? It frustrated me to know Detective Whitbread would be able to demand the woman's cooperation in a way I couldn't. Before I could challenge her, Babe Greer came running up and took my hand in hers.

"Mrs. Chapman, I'm so glad you're still here. I'm so excited. Col. Selig's decided that now's the time. He left instructions that Alonzo and I should announce our engagement on film and that we should do it now. Isn't it wonderful? There's to be champagne and flowers and Alonzo will get down on one knee and give me the ring. It's all being set up in the drawing room where they film the melodramas. You must come and be an extra. We'll all be in evening gowns with diamonds—of course they're paste—but the ring is real. They'll look just wonderful. Olga, you must come, too. It's to be a big scene with everybody in it and they need people to fill in the crowd. They'll film it and release it next week, along with our latest comedy. Come on. Costuming is waiting."

I hesitated, unwilling to be filmed. I was not an actress, and the idea appalled me, but she insisted. "Really, you must come. Olga, you'll come, too?"

The Leopard Lady nodded. "I will change to the evening gown," she said.

Babe turned back to me, seizing my right hand in both of hers and pulling. "Mrs. Chapman, you must come. The colonel's arranged everything."

"He's back, then?" The prospect of interviewing the head of the film studios made me follow her.

"Not yet. He's not back yet, but he'll be back soon and he left all the directions."

I allowed myself to be pulled across to the main building. We mounted the stairs to the second floor where the wardrobe mistress was in charge. She directed us to a large room full of gowns. I tried to protest that I wasn't part of the studio, but Babe insisted that they needed more people in the background. In the end, I decided it would be fun...a little adventure.

We were plucked and prodded, then buttoned into splendid dresses with low-cut bodices. Corsages of carnations and white roses were even provided for each of us. The gown they put me into was of a heavy ivory damask with long strings of pearls running from my neck to my knees. They produced a huge wide-brimmed hat of shiny black straw with creamy silk and gauze around the brim. Dangling fake diamond earrings and long kid gloves, with shiny bracelets clasped around my wrists, finished my costume. Then I was pushed out the door, to allow them to work with the other people being gussied up—more women in gowns; and men in morning suits with striped pants, waistcoats, and cutaway jackets. Large boxes at the door held carnation boutonnieres for the men.

We waited in the hallway until we were all led up to the third floor. In the bright open spaces, women in gowns and magnificent hats were paired with men in top hats and herded toward the drawing room set, which was arranged with gilt furniture with embroidered seats. People began to be placed around the set, just as if they, too, were pieces of furniture.

Babe waved to me from across the room. She was being posed beside Alonzo in front of a mantelpiece. There was a six-piece orchestra in one corner, and waiters, balancing trays filled with flutes of champagne, brushed against me as I made my way to her. Otis Turner was giving orders, setting everyone up. He and his cameramen were the only ones in ordinary dress. I saw Kathlyn Williams in a stunning low-cut gown beside Olga and Big Otto on the other side of Alonzo.

Yelling at the cameramen, Turner was warning people not to drink the champagne until the toast, which would be given by Charles Clooney, who usually played the villain. Turner grabbed Babe and Alonzo and placed them before the camera to rehearse. I stopped to watch Alonzo go down on his knee while Babe looked away shyly as he mimed slipping a ring on her finger. I thought of the day when Stephen had proposed to me and how embarrassed we would have been for such an audience. Especially since I'd refused his first proposal.

"Mrs. Chapman, have you seen Col. Selig?" There was a light touch on my shoulder to get my attention and I turned, at first not recognizing the young man. It was Tom Mix, dressed in a light gray morning suit, and holding a shiny top hat in his gloved hand. He looked so different, not being in his usual cowboy attire, that I barely recognized him. I wondered what my son Jack would have thought of his cowboy hero dressed in such an outfit.

Another vaguely familiar face pushed through after him. "I've got to see him. You're with the police, aren't you? Do they have him? Where is he?"

At the sound of his voice, I recognized Broncho Billy. "No, I'm sorry. I have no idea where Col. Selig is."

"Is that policeman here?" Broncho Billy asked.

"I don't believe so. I heard he was down at the Randolph Street offices."

"Selig's not there. We've already tried." Broncho Billy pulled a slip of paper from his pocket. "I can't be too late. I must reach him. Look here, Mix, is there somewhere I can go to send a wire? I've got an address. I think I can get to him in time."

Mix excused himself and his companion, then elbowed through the crowd, presumably to lead Broncho Billy to Col. Selig's office so he could send his wire. I wondered what it was all about. Suddenly, I was aware of young boys handing out little pouches of confetti, warning as they did, "Not till the toast," and, "Wait till Mr. Turner says," and "Wait for Mr. Turner to say it's time."

"Attention. Attention," Turner projected through his megaphone. I cringed at the noise, balancing a glass of champagne and the packet of confetti. Babe Greer slid up next to me. "Isn't it exciting, Mrs. Chapman? I'm so glad you're here. Just think, you're going to be in a moving picture. Won't your children love to see it!"

I gasped at the thought. I could just hear my children insisting we go to a nickelodeon to see me. That was not what I'd hoped for, and it certainly wasn't what I'd worked for, all those years at the university and the settlement house. It was too ridiculous.

I gritted my teeth with dismay, then forced myself to nod and smile at Babe. She looked glorious in a gown of ivory satin and wore a sparkling net in her hair, as well as a coronet of white roses. Swirling filigrees of some silvery substance decorated the bodice and hem of her gown. Her arms were bare of gloves, so that the ring could be slipped on her nervous finger. She squeezed my arm before hurrying back to her place by the mantel.

Meanwhile, Otis Turner was apologizing for Col. Selig. He said the filmmaker had intended to be present for the occasion but was called away. Then Turner explained how the scene would be filmed, admonishing us *not* to release the confetti until they were done with the proposal and toast. As the crowd parted for the camera, I looked around. There must have been two hundred people, two dozen waiters, and three cameramen all packed into a lavishly decorated set. Yet, it had all been conjured up in only an hour. And all by the hidden hand of Col. Selig. It bore the marks of his design, even if he was mysteriously missing. It reminded me of the scene in the *Wizard of Oz* where all the townspeople were gathered to watch the wizard sail away on his balloon, without Dorothy. I began to wonder about Col. Selig. Who else could manipulate so many people without seeming to do so? Could *he* have caused the murders without being present, just as he'd arranged for this huge scene to unfold in his absence? Could he have had Hyde killed, without pulling the trigger himself? And Leeder? Col. Selig was like a puppet master who controlled the puppets without strings. Was he the man behind the curtain of the murders? But what would have been his motive?

I turned my attention back to the scene being filmed and saw Alonzo Swift get down on one knee and offer the ring to Babe Greer, just as he had in the rehearsal. She looked meekly away but stuck out her hand, fingers splayed to receive it. They did this while Turner yelled at them and other people milled around till the camera stopped. Then the scene was repeated twice more, before Charles Clooney raised a glass for a silent toast, moving his mouth, and looking around as we all raised our glasses and the camera turned on us. Then we were told to drink up. That, too, was repeated twice more with waiters racing to refill the glasses between times. It was a strange mixture of real and unreal, as we celebrated a real engagement multiple times. I could see, by her joyous expression, that Babe was pleased about it, although I was only confused. Perhaps it was the champagne. I began to feel it running through my veins and rising to my head. With a false toast, paste jewelry, and costumes in a pretend drawing room we wished them well.

After the toast, we waited again while waiters circulated to refill glasses before the throwing of the confetti. We were warned this would only happen once and the scene was rehearsed twice up to the point of releasing the confetti. By the time they were ready for the real thing, I was feeling ridiculously unsteady on my feet. I clutched at a nearby chair and found it less than stable. Juggling my glass and my pouch of confetti, and feeling the room begin to spin, I moved to sit down. When the final yell to throw came, I managed to toss my bits of paper into the maelstrom that descended on the couple, but then felt the room swirl away from me, as darkness moved in swiftly from all sides.

Thirty-Four

My head felt top-heavy, too thick for it to be worthwhile to open my eyes. I made a slight attempt but gave it up as too strenuous. Much better to leave the light out of my little black world. I knew instinctively that movement would bring pain and I didn't want to chance it.

I couldn't escape the smell, though. It was a barnyard smell, sharply repugnant. But I had to breathe. I was lying on my right side. I tried holding my breath but, when I let it out and took it back in, my nose was tickled. There was hair tickling my nostrils. My poor suffering nose—twitching hairs and an unpleasant smell. I slid my face against a scratchy blanket and half opened my eyes, looking through my lashes. There wasn't much light, but a lamp must have hung somewhere behind me. The darkness was my friend, full daylight would have been painful.

I wasn't in my own soft bed, though, and where was Stephen? I let my eyes close again as I began to realize I didn't know where I was. Better to sink back into darkness. Some fidgety little spot of attention and worry had been awakened, though, and it would not sink back down. Where was I? In the deep darkness, I could hear a swishing noise, more than once. A swish, tap, tap, swish, then a swish tap, swish, tap, swish, tap, tap, swish. Soft sounds from different directions, above my head, down at my knees, behind me now. At least it wasn't the children. They were never that quiet, especially Tommy. Delia, maybe?

The idea of the children prevented me from giving way and losing myself in the velvet darkness again. They were fine, I was sure. Still, I ought to be aware. Shouldn't I check on them? The air by my nose got hot and moist. With an effort, I opened my eyes to a slit. I immediately closed them again. I'd seen a black wet snout and amber eyes with black pupils, then white and brown fur with deep black spots. A black-rimmed mouth was slightly open, panting. There'd been just the gleam of yellow teeth.

I felt a thrill at the base of my neck that extended up to the roots of my hair and down to the toes that curled inside my shoes. It was a leopard. I was with the leopards. I vaguely recalled the filming of Alonzo and Babe's engagement, the toast, then falling, falling. Someone carrying me, then later supporting me along. Falling. But how had I gotten into the leopard cage? With great effort, I smothered my desire to jump away. Still...I had to be very still.

My heart raced suddenly, but I kept my eyes closed, quietly clenching my toes and fists. I felt dizzy. I tried to picture the leopards' cage. It was the big square cage where I'd seen Kathlyn Williams, and I remembered it connected to the smaller, shorter cage that Big Otto had shown me. There was a gate that could be lowered between them to get a single leopard out at a time. I must be on the chaise lounge in the big cage. I tried not to imagine the blood stains under the blanket I was lying on. This was where Leeder had been attacked. I could hear everything now. Two of the cats were moving back and forth, while one lay heavy on my feet, just as I'd seen them do with Kathlyn Williams.

My head was still foggy. I must have had too much champagne. I was afraid to raise my head, afraid to move, because I had no idea what the leopards might do. Otto said they would attack the jugular vein. My neck lay exposed on the lounge. I had to keep myself from moving to protect it. I prayed someone would come before the cats decided to react to me. I tried to become part of the sofa, tried to relax. I could feel my calves begin to cramp from my anxiety.

Suddenly, I heard a voice. "Mrs. Chapman, are you here? Olga, what have you done? Did you—" Kathlyn Williams's voice stopped and I heard the sound of a struggle and then a scraping noise. I wanted to call out. I peered through half-closed eyes and nearly jumped when a tail waved an inch from my nose. The leopards. If I startled them they would be on me before anyone could react. I froze.

Through my blurred vision, I noticed a leopard's head move toward my feet. The bars of the cage rang unpleasantly. No! Someone was purposely riling the leopards, hitting the cage with a stick. I heard a snarl...it was deep throated...then one of them jumped, and another growled. I didn't dare change my position to see, but I was sure whoever it was must be prodding the cats with a stick through the bars of the cage. I heard repeated sounds of growls and jumps. They were so agitated it felt like there were sparks in the air...like when you hit a burning log. The animals threw themselves at the end of the cage near my feet.

They continued to prowl in an excited fashion, but now the knocking of the sticks came only after the cats jumped. Perhaps the person had left. I opened my eyes a bit, convinced that if I didn't do something, the leopards would attack. They seemed to be building up to it.

On the ground, in a pool of light just in front of the cage, I saw Kathlyn Williams in her silk dress, face down. Was she friend or foe? I had no choice but to try to enlist her help. I hissed at her a couple of times. One of the leopards stopped pacing, and I shut my eyes when it came and thrust its nose at me, but it went away again and I risked it. "Kathlyn...help...Kathlyn."

She moved a bit, then pushed herself up into a sitting position, her head hanging heavy. My instinct told me that the cats were building up to something. One of them sprang toward the end of the cage. I risked a move to look. There were sticks thrust through the bars of the cage down there. They must have been used to knock against the bars, and then to hit the animals. It seemed they'd been left there as obstacles to annoy the cats.

Kathlyn looked at me with horror and stumbled to her feet. "Keep still," she whispered. "Slow and still. That's what Olga says, slow and still." She looked around helplessly. "I'll get the key." She stumbled into the darkness and the leopards jumped at the bars of the cage near my feet as if trying to get to her. She was back quickly. "It's not there. Whoever put you in there took it." She clutched her head and looked anxiously around.

"The gate," I whispered. I was remembering what Otto had showed me. The smaller cage that could be separated by the gate was beyond my head. If I could get in there, I could drop the gate and get away from the cats.

"Yes." She stepped closer to the cage at the end near my head. The leopards rushed to see what she was doing and scratched at the bars, leaping up now and then. "Here's the rope, I'll open it." She knew what I wanted to do—to get into that smaller cage and shut the connecting gate. There was the sound of a slide as she opened it. "They can get in, too," she said, sounding frightened. "Maybe I should go for help."

"No!" I still whispered but harshly this time. With the gate up, the leopards could get into the cage but it was my only way to escape them. I had to take the chance.

"I could go get Olga—"

"No, please!" I was afraid that, if she left their sight, the cats would turn on me. "Please."

She stood up straighter. "All right. I'm tying this off here, you can reach it when you get through the gate, release it to drop it." She bent over her knot. "I'll distract them down at the other end and you've got to be quick. Jump in and get the gate down. OK?" She was biting her lip. I hadn't raised my head, only moved it to watch.

"Right. Hurry…please!"

She moved to the other end of the cage, talking to the leopards, and getting them to follow her. There was one still in front of me, behind the others. I wondered if I could slip off the back of the couch but it was too high.

"Come here, you," Kathlyn said. "She won't come. Here, you."

I looked down and saw that she'd picked up one of the sticks and was waving it above their heads.

"Now!" she shouted as they jumped.

I bolted off the chaise and ran the few steps to the gate, looking for the rope end, but stumbled and fell into the smaller connecting cage before I could release the knot. The leopards howled. As I turned on my back to get up, one of them jumped up onto the chaise lounge and then leapt toward me. Her mouth was open in a fierce grin of sharp teeth and her claws were spread. There was no time to reach the rope. I curled into myself to protect my neck.

Bang! The gate dropped and the leopard smashed into it, roaring with frustration. Kathlyn was weeping. She'd managed to reach the rope and undo the knot just in time.

I turned over on the ground, shivering with the remains of my fear.

Thirty-Five

T he cats have never attacked anyone before coming here. Never. You can check all you want, you will never find another instance. And I had nothing to do with this," Olga Celeste said in her throaty voice. "Whoever says so lies. You can ask Otto. I was with him all the time. He can tell you that never before has such a thing happened. Never."

She glared furiously at Detective Whitbread. We were all in Col. Selig's office again, Kathlyn and I both seated in wingback chairs. Every time I shut my eyes, I saw that leopard, fangs bared, in a leap above me. Fitz put a glass half full of a golden liquid in my hands and urged me to sip it. It burned as it went down and I saw him give Kathlyn another glass, then pour one for himself. He looked as shaken as I felt.

"We will certainly question Mr. Breitkreutz," Whitbread said. Then he turned to Kathlyn. "Miss Williams, you said you went to the leopard cage looking for Miss Celeste and Mrs. Chapman?"

"Babe asked me to check on Mrs. Chapman. She said she hadn't been feeling well so Babe had one of the men carry her here, to the colonel's office. Babe couldn't leave the party herself but she said she was worried. She'd asked Olga to look in on Mrs. Chapman but she then hadn't reported back. So, when I didn't find anyone in the office, I went to look for Olga. Babe said she might have sent Mrs. Chapman home in a cab."

Babe Greer was brought in and the door shut firmly behind her by one of Whitbread's uniformed men. She ran to me. "Oh, Mrs. Chapman, I'm so glad to see you're all right. What happened? They're saying you were in the leopards' cage."

Whitbread motioned to me to be quiet and took Babe by the arm. "Did you tell Miss Williams that Miss Olga Celeste had taken Mrs. Chapman away?"

"What? Oh, no. I had Charles Clooney carry Mrs. Chapman down here to the office when she was feeling a little faint. We left her here. Then, when they finished filming, I came down to change out of my costume. I wanted to do it before everybody else thought of it because we had interviews with the press. But I didn't have time to look in on Mrs. Chapman so I asked Olga to do it when I went back upstairs. I was in a hurry. Then, when I didn't hear anything else, I asked Kathlyn if she could check and see if Mrs. Chapman was still here. But she never came back, either. I was in the office myself, looking for Mrs. Chapman, when I heard the commotion. It's so terrible. Did someone really lock you in with the cats? Who would do such a thing? It's lucky you didn't end up like Mr. Leeder. I'm so sorry, Mrs. Chapman."

Whitbread held up a hand to stop her. "Miss Celeste?" he asked.

Olga frowned. "She said something about Mrs. Chapman being ill but when I looked in the office she was gone. I assumed she had returned to her home. I went back to the party. I was with Otto, he'll tell you."

"I'll have to ask you to remain with one of my men while we find Mr. Breitkreutz," Whitbread said, leading her to the door. He gestured to Babe as well. "That's all for you, Miss Greer. Please." He shooed them out, then turned, saying, "Miss Williams, Mrs. Chapman, you remain here. I'll be back shortly," before he followed, closing the door behind him.

I looked at Kathlyn who was sipping her brandy. Some color was coming back to her cheeks. "I heard you call out for Olga," I said. "Did you see her?"

"No, I just assumed she was down there. I was looking for her to see if she'd sent you home in a cab. I thought that was what Babe said and, when there was no one in the office, I went down to look." She shivered. "But someone hit me." She fingered the back of her head and winced. "When I woke up, I realized you were in danger."

"Thank God you were there," I said. "Thank God you woke up. Did you see who put the sticks in the cage?"

"No, whoever it was, they were gone by the time I came to. I was just trying to remember what Olga taught me about keeping calm around the cats. I was terrified."

"Thank you for staying and not running away."

"You were right. There wasn't time."

"And then I fell." I ducked my head and took a swig of the brandy. It burnt a hole down my chest, at least it felt like that, but then I took a shaky breath.

"I reached the rope in time," Kathlyn said. "At least it's over."

I began to feel a warmth spreading over me. It was the brandy. "They can't think Alden's responsible this time. He's in jail," I said. "And they can't think it's you, because you saved me. If it *was* you, you would have let the leopards kill me." I shook myself.

"Emily, are you sure you're all right, my girl?" Fitz asked. He came and perched on the arm of my chair, his face filled with concern.

"Thanks to Kathlyn, I am. But who did this? Was it Olga? I thought perhaps she was being blackmailed about the leopards, but she claims they never attacked anyone before." I wondered if she'd done it for Col. Selig. She and Big Otto were completely in his debt. I didn't think Fitz or Kathlyn would even consider my suspicions, though. They were all bedazzled by him. "Someone *was* blackmailing people. Don't you see? It wasn't Hyde, he's dead." I hiccupped. My head was swimming a bit. "If it wasn't Hyde then someone must have been blackmailing *him*. Why else would he have been at the studios that night unless it was to meet the

190

blackmailer? Whoever it was, they made him censor Kathlyn's films, you see? Maybe he was working for Edison and someone found out." I clutched Fitz's jacket and he looked confused. "You've got to help us, Fitz. Whitbread won't listen to me. He's angry with me." I looked across to the closed door. Whitbread would be back soon. "You've got to help us find out who was blackmailing Hyde. We have to ask the mayor's wife. She must know something, even if she doesn't realize it. She's the only one who knows enough about him to know why Leeder or someone else would blackmail him." *Or, perhaps, why Col. Selig would have him killed*, I thought to myself. "We have to ask her again. You'll help, won't you, Fitz?"

He placed his hand on mine. "Emily, you must rest. You've had a horrible shock. I hate to think what those leopards might have done to you." He reached out and placed one of his big rough hands on my cheek. He looked bleak at the thought of what might have happened. With a big sigh, he pulled his hand back. "You're done in. I've got to get you back to your family."

"But you'll help, won't you, Fitz? Promise me."

"Aw, of course, darlin'. I'll help you. I'll see if Mrs. Busse can talk to you again tomorrow. But you come on, now. I've got the motorcar. Let me get you back to Hyde Park. Whitey'll see to it that Miss Williams gets home."

I realized then that Fitz was dressed in a morning suit. He must have been there the whole time, at the party. I looked down and saw I was still wearing the ivory gown that was ruined by dirt and tears. "My clothes," I said.

In an action that was unusual for him, Fitz strode over to pull open the door and yelled for Whitbread. When the solemn-looking detective appeared, he demanded that Whitbread release us and provide Kathlyn Williams with a ride home, while he took me.

"Enough of this, Whitey. Can't you see they're in shock?" When Whitbread frowned, Fitz stomped his foot. "I want Mrs. Chapman's clothes brought. Now!" he howled. I'd never seen him in such a mood.

Before the detective could reply, an officer behind him said, "I'll do it, sir," and hurried away. Whitbread stepped into the room, forcing Fitz to take a step back, but Fitz leaned forward, into the detective's long face. "No more questions," he said. "These women need to go home and rest after that scene in the leopards' cage. Are you mad, man? If you don't get me those clothes and let us out of here, I warn you, City Hall will have your badge."

"Don't threaten me," Whitbread said, but before they could come to blows the young officer rushed in with a bag of my clothes, which he thrust at Fitz.

"All right," Whitbread said. "You can go."

Fitz growled at him. Gratefully, I let the big Irishman guide me to his motorcar while he fended off everyone else. Whitbread followed silently. If I hoped for some sign of forgiveness or reconciliation on his part I was disappointed. He left us without another word.

As we drove to Hyde Park, I fell asleep on Fitz's shoulder but was wakened when we reached our apartment. I was home. Delia helped me upstairs and to bed while Fitz answered Stephen's questions as best he could.

I couldn't fall asleep until I felt Stephen climb in beside me and, when I turned to him, he told me Fitz had promised to take me to see the mayor's wife the next day. Only then could I fall asleep in his arms. I was convinced Mrs. Busse held the key to the mystery of why her cousin had been murdered.

Thirty-Six

I was weak the next day but insisted on dressing and going downstairs to wait for Fitz to fulfill his promise. I sat in the study mulling over the problem. Surely Alden would be released now. No matter how angry he was with me, Whitbread must see that someone else had locked me in with the leopards and that must be the person who'd done it to Leeder. That the tragedy could have been repeated, if Kathlyn Williams had not been there, was something that would give me nightmares for months, I was sure. But we were disappointed when we sent Jack to Clara's for news, only to learn that Alden had not been released and there was no change in his status.

I began to pace then, trying to understand what had happened. Was the man behind the curtain manipulating it all again? Stephen watched me gravely from behind his desk. He was also at a loss, and he knew the frustration would drive me to distraction. My only hope was that Fitz would be true to his word. If I could talk to Mrs. Busse at least I could feel I was doing something.

I went over the circumstances again and again in my mind, coming to the hazy conclusion that Col. Selig was somehow responsible for the whole mess, perhaps manipulating others from behind the scenes. Had he committed the murders himself or convinced others—perhaps Olga and Big Otto—to do his dirty work? I was still unclear about what motive could have driven him to kill both the censor and his own producer. But I must have been coming too close to the truth about what was behind it all, so he tried to get rid of me as well. I wracked my brain but couldn't remember what I'd said or done that might have alarmed him. I had a feeling that if I could only discover more about the dead censor, then I would see it all clearly.

Finally, we heard Delia open the door for Fitz. I stopped pacing and went to greet him. "Fitz, you've come. Have you arranged for us to see Mrs. Busse?"

He stood holding his hat in his hands. "Yes, she'll see us, but there's been a development. Col. Selig's returned and he's holding a meeting for the press in his Randolph Street offices this morning."

I tried to understand this. *What could he be up to?*

"Fitzgibbons, why haven't they released Alden?" Stephen asked. "Surely they can't think he had anything to do with the attack on Emily?"

Fitz's face whitened. "I'm afraid there have been some impediments."

"Impediments?" I said. "What do you mean? Someone tried to kill me in the same way Leeder was killed and it couldn't have been Alden. He was in jail. What does Whitbread mean by this?"

Fitz heaved a sigh and came into the room, taking a seat in the leather chair where Stephen sat when he wasn't at his desk.

"Sit down, Emily," Stephen told me. He took his seat at the desk while I lowered myself reluctantly to the sofa. "What is it?" he asked Fitz.

The big Irishman wiped his brow with a white handkerchief. "Apparently, some of the film people have been talking. It's that kind of a society, always talking behind each other's backs, I'm afraid. It got back to Whitbread that some of them were suggesting..." He looked at me warily, then at Stephen as if for protection. "Well, someone suggested that Emily and Kathlyn Williams might have acted out the scene with the leopards in order to try to prove her brother innocent. I know," he put up a hand as if to ward off my outburst, as I took a deep breath and shook with indignation. "I know, it's awful. In fact, Babe Greer went to Detective Whitbread and told him about the rumors in order to refute them. She absolutely denied them and suggested Olga Celeste and Otto Breitkreutz might be responsible. Whitbread can't believe such nonsense, but you can see, in the circumstances, he can't release Alden until he has the real culprit in custody."

He and Stephen looked at me, expecting an outburst. My blood was pounding at the spurious accusations, but I felt on the verge of tears. That Whitbread could entertain even the suspicion that I would plot with Kathlyn Williams to act out the leopard attack just proved how low his opinion of me had fallen. After all the years we'd worked together, that it would come to this...

My silence worried the men more than my expected outburst. I gathered my gloves and hat and wordlessly prepared to leave. Stephen and Fitz stood when I did.

"Fitzgibbons, you must promise me you won't take her back to that film studio. There have been too many incidents there. It's not safe," Stephen said, and Fitz nodded. "Emily, I wish you wouldn't pursue this. If Whitbread can be this unsympathetic, you can't rely on him."

I planted my straw hat on my head and stuck a pin in to keep it in place. "I won't sit around and do nothing. Whitbread thinks he can't rely on me. I'll admit, I've given him reason but, if we don't act, Alden will hang for something he didn't do. Fitz, please. We must go."

With a doubtful look at Stephen, Fitz stepped into the hallway. When I followed, Stephen grabbed my arm and pulled me toward him. Embracing me, he whispered in my ear, "The only reason I'm letting you do this is because it's Fitzgibbons." He held me away from him and looked into my eyes. "I know he'd sacrifice himself before he'd allow any harm to come to you. Remember that, and don't push him." He turned me around and ushered me to the door.

"I won't," I said, before hurrying down the steps and into the waiting motorcar.

We agreed to attend Col. Selig's meeting before the interview with Mrs. Busse. The Randolph Street offices were filled with newspapermen. If Alden were still at his job with the *Tribune* he would have been among them. It was hard for me to believe he would never again be one of that disheveled crowd that appeared like birds of prey at every new event in the city.

We were herded into a large office where Col. Selig was smiling behind a huge desk. Detective Whitbread stood woodenly behind him and I was surprised to see Broncho Billy Anderson nearby, grinning.

"Gentlemen of the press," Col. Selig said loudly, in an attempt to quiet the raucous group. "Welcome to the offices of the Selig Polyscope Company. I'm delighted to be joined by Mr. Anderson of the Essanay Film Manufacturing Company." He nodded to Anderson who stepped forward. "We're happy to announce the establishment of the Motion Picture Patents Company with an historic agreement signed yesterday in New York. The motion picture industry enters a new and exciting phase with this accord. The agreement joins the nine major film companies including Selig, Essanay, Edison, and others, with the leading distributor and the biggest supplier of film stock to standardize the manner in which films are distributed and exhibited in America."

There was a ripple of excitement through the room and murmurs of Edison's name. Everyone knew Edison had been exhausting the other companies with lawsuits. The agreement would bring those actions to an end. As Selig continued, it became clear that he and the others had given in to many of Edison's demands in order to protect those businesses that were already established and to discourage more competitors from entering the field.

As Selig described the "Trust," as it was called, and excited reporters asked questions, I realized this was an extremely important agreement for the filmmakers and that the negotiations had been carried on in the strictest secrecy. It explained both why Selig had disappeared and why Anderson had been in his office, the day of Babe and Alonzo's engagement, as well as his desperate attempts to contact the colonel afterwards. If Essanay missed being a part of the Trust, they would be ruined.

I wondered how important that secrecy had been. Was there something about the agreement that led to Selig or Anderson being blackmailed? Was the trust worth murdering a blackmailer to protect it? Had Hyde or Leeder found out something that would have prevented the agreement? Was that why they were murdered?

I saw Detective Whitbread across the room and wished I could tell him my suspicions. But he stood with a face of stone and I knew it would be useless.

I pulled on Fitz's sleeve to urge him to leave. Somehow, I knew Mrs. Busse would be able to tell us something about how her cousin could have been blackmailed, if we just pushed her a little more. And I hoped whatever it was could be traced back to one of these film people, so Alden could finally be cleared.

Thirty-Seven

I'm very sorry, my dear, but my cousin George led a blameless life. He suffered when his wife left him, but his most reprehensible act was to sit for hours in a nickelodeon." Mrs. Busse was so kind and helpful, I was fairly bursting to find an object for my anger and frustration.

Fitz watched me with apprehension from the other side of the drawing room table, where we'd spread out the contents of Mr. Hyde's box of belongings, which Mrs. Busse had brought back from the funeral in Indiana. I'd been pawing through them—mostly ledgers and correspondence—for almost an hour and I could tell that Fitz thought our time was up. I was still convinced there had to be something useful in the material, though.

"And you're certain you never heard him mention Mr. Edison?" I asked.

"No, never. I would have remembered that. I'm afraid he had no secrets to discover."

"I'm sure you're right," I said, surrendering with bad grace.

Mrs. Busse sympathized with my disappointment. "It's just that there wouldn't be anything he could have been blackmailed for. Poor George." Mrs. Busse turned over a picture in a flimsy frame. It was a wedding picture of a bride and groom. "His only fault was in loving a girl who was unfaithful. It's so sad, really."

I squinted, trying to see the picture, then asked, "May I look?"

With a little shake of her head expressing regret, she passed it to me. "I wasn't at the wedding, you know. George must have hidden that photo away. I've never seen it before." There was Hyde, in a morning suit with a striped ascot, his square face beaming, and a carnation in his lapel. Beside him, a slim girl smiled shyly, her face almost covered by a beautiful lace veil resting on her dark curls and falling close to her face, then down her shoulders to the floor. It was only when my eye traveled back up to the face that I felt a jolt of recognition. It was Babe Greer.

"I don't know how he'll react to your presence," Fitz told me, as his driver navigated through the crowded streets of the Loop. "Perhaps I should go in and bring him the news without you."

"No. I want to see his face," I said. I was holding the wedding photograph, which Mrs. Busse had reluctantly allowed us to take. She was as shocked as we were. She didn't know what to make of the fact that Babe Greer had been her cousin's bride. In the end, she let us leave with the picture.

I knew Fitz was very uncomfortable with the whole thing, but I was determined to show the picture to Detective Whitbread. Here at last was something he'd failed to find on his own. He would have to listen to me now, even if Fitz had doubts about the relevance of the connection. Of course there was something there! Babe Greer was Hyde's runaway bride. Why would she have concealed that fact, unless she had something to hide? Whitbread had missed this and I was going to confront him with it.

But we were forced to wait. We had to cool our heels for half an hour outside the same large interview room where Whitbread had informed Clara and me of Alden's arrest. Finally, a rather distressed-looking Alonzo Swift exited the room and we were invited in.

I ignored Whitbread's chilly reception and presented him with the bridal picture, demanding he get Babe to explain herself, *and* that he release my brother. I was still convinced that Col. Selig was at the root of all of this, although Whitbread and Fitz would never acknowledge that possibility. I was wary of making the accusation but sure that if they questioned Babe the truth would come out.

Whitbread listened to my rant for several minutes without speaking. When I ran out of breath he picked up the photograph and examined it closely. To my exasperation, he remained silent for some time. I was determined to force him to respond, so I kept my peace with some difficulty. Fitz looked back and forth between the two of us, obviously apprehensive that one of us would explode.

"We will question Miss Greer about it. May I keep the picture?" Whitbread asked Fitz, declining to look at me.

"Question her?" I burst out. "Of course you have to question her. But how can you keep my brother in custody, when you know about this and you know someone tried to have me killed?"

Whitbread continued to look at the picture in his hands. He was ignoring me and planning something. But he wasn't going to inform me of his plans. I knew it. He was still punishing me for my betrayal. It was too late to repair that, but there was no reason to punish Alden. I had to convince him to release my brother.

Fitz coughed. "The picture belongs to Mrs. Busse, the mayor's wife. It'll need to be returned to her…eventually," he said.

Whitbread frowned. "Fine. It will be returned to *the mayor's wife* when we're finished with it. Meanwhile, I must insist that you keep this matter to yourselves." He looked pointedly at me. "And you, Mrs. Chapman, stay away from Miss Greer…and all of the film people, for that matter. Go home and take care of your children."

"What will you do?" I asked. I didn't care what he insisted on, he couldn't ignore this matter. "Won't you even pursue this?"

He stood up. "Of course I'll pursue it. I'll visit Miss Greer today. But, even if what you suspect is true, if Miss Greer *was* married to Mr. Hyde, that does nothing to prove your brother innocent of the crime to which he *has confessed*." He put both hands on the table and leaned across it. "I tell you again, Mrs. Chapman, *go home*. If I find out that you have contacted Miss Greer or Mr. Swift, or any of the people connected to the Selig or Essanay film studios, I promise you I'll lock you in a jail cell myself."

He strode from the room. Fitz waved a hand at me to sit and wait as he hurried after Whitbread.

Of course, I was furious. Whitbread was blinded by his anger at me. How could he find out the truth if he went on like this? It was a sore thing to admit to myself, but I was truly afraid he could believe that I might have schemed with Kathlyn Williams to stage a fake leopard attack in order to free my brother. I didn't know how to disprove that accusation and I was frustrated to realize how little trust my former mentor had in me.

Fitz returned. He would go with Whitbread to confront Babe Greer with the photograph. He tried to convince me it was the best, and only, way for me to find out what occurred at that meeting. He begged me to return home and promised to report to me there. I wasn't sure if it was me or the film industry he wanted to protect, or if he just wanted to ensure the photograph was returned to Mrs. Busse, but I had no recourse in the matter. They would never allow me to accompany them.

But that didn't mean I couldn't follow them. Nothing could prevent me from going to the Bedford myself. I knew Babe Greer had her own suite, one floor below Alonzo Swift's apartment.

Thirty-Eight

I took a cab. It was an extravagance, but I was still shaky on my feet from the experience of the night before, and I was anxious to bring the suspense to an end. I had a pretty good idea who was behind it all now, but I had to prove my suspicions were true. I couldn't think or plan for anything else until I did that. I knew Stephen wouldn't approve, but I told myself I wasn't going to the studios, at least not yet, so I wasn't strictly going against his wishes. And I was confident there would be no wild animals allowed at the Bedford Hotel.

It was a comparatively staid older building in the Lincoln Park neighborhood. A bellman helped me climb down from the cab and I looked around before I entered the lobby, to be sure Detective Whitbread was not in sight. I suddenly realized that I only knew Babe had rooms on the floor below Alonzo Swift, but I didn't know the floor or the number. As I stood deciding how to get the information I needed, I thought I saw one of Whitbread's men enter. I took two steps back and put a pillar between us. He wasn't in uniform and disappeared toward the registration desk, which made me think I was mistaken. I was just scolding myself for such a display of nerves when I saw the tall figure of Whitbread himself stride across to the elevator. He was followed by Fitz, Col. Selig, and two uniformed officers.

I ducked back until they were safely in the elevator car, then darted out to watch the metal half-moon indicating the floors. It stopped on the fifth floor. I hurried away, looking for the stairs, and quickly found the door I wanted. As I climbed, I realized why I'd arrived before them. They must have gone to collect Col. Selig first. Why had they brought him? Had Fitz insisted? Was he still trying to protect the filmmaker on behalf of the mayor? *Oh, Fitz, how could you?* And why would Whitbread agree? What if, as I suspected, Selig *was* behind it all? And I'd become convinced that Babe herself might be another victim of the blackmailer. How could she tell them anything, when he was standing right there?

And I couldn't figure out if Mr. Hyde had been a blackmailer or if he'd been being blackmailed himself. Surely, he must have recognized his lost wife in the films during his screenings. If he did, had he still loved Babe enough to keep her secret? Perhaps, unlike Kathlyn Williams's husband, he was willing to sacrifice his love for her so she could have the acting career she wanted so badly. Had someone else threatened to divulge her secret?

On the other hand, perhaps Hyde had blackmailed her, threatening to reveal her past and forcing her to return to him. That would certainly cause problems for her career.

There was also the possibility that Hyde's death had no connection to his marriage to Babe. If he'd been working for Edison to destroy Selig, as I suspected, that was another motive to blackmail him...or kill him.

I was hoping that Babe would be able to fill in the gaps and shed more light on Mr. Hyde's background. When I reached the fifth floor, I hid in the stairwell with the door partially open, watching for Whitbread and the others to come out so I could see which door was Babe's. I needed to stay hidden from the detective and Fitz. I only hoped they wouldn't take Babe Greer away with them. If they did, I'd have to find another way to get the truth. I knew Stephen didn't want me to return to the studios, but there had to be something in Selig's office that could help me expose him. I'd have to be quick. I was sure

Fitz would come to see me in Hyde Park, as he'd promised, after the interview. When he found I wasn't there, the alarm would be raised.

I'd almost decided to give up on Babe, and to try reaching the studios before Col. Selig, when I heard the men leave. I peeked and saw it was a door halfway down the corridor. I watched Whitbread stomping toward the elevator before I shut the door tight and prayed no one had seen me. Finally, after waiting nervously, I looked out and they were gone. I hurried down to the room they'd left and knocked on the door.

"Mrs. Chapman, how are you? Come in, sit down. Are you sure you're recovered enough to be out?"

Babe's rooms had high ceilings and ivory-painted woodwork. There were French doors, open to a little balcony with black iron railings, along the far wall. A huge mirror in a gilt frame hung over a low fireplace. I sat on a pastel flowered armchair, across from a white silk loveseat where she sat.

She wore a high-necked gauzy white shirtwaist over a taffeta skirt in black and white checks that rustled when she moved. The large diamond engagement ring from Alonzo Swift was on her left hand and she wore tiny earrings to match. Her auburn hair was twisted up with a black velvet ribbon that left ringlets falling softly around her face.

"I'm fine," I said. "But my brother's still not been released."

"Oh, I'm so sorry. I told Detective Whitbread it was just mean gossip, that there wasn't a word of truth in the story going around. I think it was Olga who started it. She was telling people that Kathlyn had staged the attack in the leopards' cage to help your brother. It was just nasty of her. I don't trust that woman for a minute. You shouldn't believe a thing she says and that's what I told the detective."

"I know. Mr. Fitzgibbons told me. Thank you. But there's something else I must ask you about. I only do so because I believe Alden is innocent, but the police won't drop the charges." She frowned. I didn't want to give her a chance to think, so I plunged ahead. "Babe, you were married to Mr. Hyde, weren't you? In Indiana, before you came to the city."

Her face crumpled and I thought she was going to cry. "Oh, you know, too. The police found a wedding portrait. They were just here." She covered her face with her hands. "Oh, Mrs Chapman, I'm ruined."

"No, Babe. I know about the photograph...I saw it at Mrs. Busse's house and I recognized you. But I could see you were very young. You ran away, didn't you?"

She continued to hide her face in her hands. "I met a man," she said. "I was so foolish. When he left me, I couldn't go back. I couldn't face the gossips in that town. They'd never let me forget it...or George, either. I came to the city to start a new life. I changed my name." She let her hands fall away and sniffed. "It was so wonderful when I got to act in the pictures. I was so happy. I thought I'd left all that behind me."

"But then Mr. Hyde saw you in the films and he recognized you, didn't he?"

"Oh, I was so shocked. He came to see me, but I made him swear he'd never tell anyone. He wanted me back. I told him no, it couldn't happen. It was good of him to want to forgive me, but he knew we could never get over the disgrace. I asked him to let me keep being Babe Greer. He understood. He was such a gentleman. He deserved better than me. I told him that." She dug in a pocket and found a handkerchief. "I told the detective, but I don't know if he believed me."

"But someone found out, didn't they? When did he start to blackmail you, Babe?" I leaned forward. "Was it Col. Selig or Leeder? Tell me, Babe." She wouldn't have been able to admit it to Whitbread with Selig standing there, but I hoped I could get her to confide in me. She buried her face in the square of white linen to avoid answering. "I know he blackmailed other people, Babe. Kathlyn Williams got notes demanding money."

Her blue eyes stared at me over the handkerchief. "Kathlyn told you?"

"Yes, and Detective Whitbread has the notes."

Her mouth opened. Suddenly she stood up. "Notes," she said. "Yes, there were notes. Let me show you." She hurried to a bureau and pulled open a drawer. When she turned back to me she held a small pearl-handled revolver pointed at my heart.

Thirty-Nine

Babe, what are you doing?"

"Detective Whitbread warned me about you. He said he'd forbidden you to approach me but that, if you did, I should contact the police. He said you were dangerous."

I sat back in my seat, my hands wide in surrender. "I'm sorry, I just want to help my brother."

"Your brother! Your brother has been a pest and an obstruction for too long. Why is he always trying to cover for Kathlyn? She's the one who shot George. She met him at the studio and she shot him. She's the one who locked Leeder in with the leopards. He was blackmailing her about Vic and the Copper King. Her husband already suspected Vic wasn't his. He was jealous of the Copper King, even though she never let him make love to her. That's what she said, anyways. She told me. I was the only one she confided in. But she was desperate to keep her husband from knowing Mr. Clark was around again, and she was desperate to keep Selig from knowing she had a kid. Kathlyn Williams killed George and she would have been blamed, if *your brother* didn't keep trying to cover for her."

"No," I wanted to say, "it was Col. Selig." But I was staring down the muzzle of the wicked little gun, aware that it could do terrible damage. Babe held it in both hands, pointing it steadily at me, the big diamond gleaming on her finger. She didn't really believe I was that dangerous, she couldn't.

"Kathlyn didn't shoot your husband because he censored her films, and neither did Alden. You shot him because you wanted to marry Alonzo Swift." I was angry at myself for not seeing it before. I was so convinced Hyde was working for Edison, that Leeder blackmailed him, and Selig killed him, but I was wrong all along. What a vicious little viper. "What did you do, get him to censor Kathlyn's films? She's the one you've wanted to hurt all along, isn't she? Why?"

There was no way to pretend I didn't know. She was going to shoot me, then claim I'd attacked her. Somehow, she must have thought that would convince the police that I was capable of staging the leopard attack with Kathlyn, in order to save Alden. *They* would be portrayed as lovers who'd killed together to protect Kathlyn's career. That would not only destroy them but Clara and her children as well. And *I'd* be portrayed as the mad sister helping them. How was it that I hadn't seen all this before?

She laughed. It was a cackle. "Kathlyn got all the best parts. She was going to get Selig to send her to California because of those awful animal pictures."

"So you wanted to get rid of Kathlyn Williams so you could be the one to go to California?"

"I want to be the female lead. Alonzo will be the male. Whoever goes out there will be big, really big. Wait and see."

"How did your husband feel about that?"

"Poor George. He didn't understand. He thought that if he censored Kathlyn it would be enough to prove that he wanted to help me as a film star. But he still wanted me to come back to him. Of course, that couldn't be. Alonzo and I belong together." She smiled at the ring on her finger.

"So you got him to meet you at the studios and he let you get close enough to shoot him. But even that wasn't enough for you. You planned to make it look like Kathlyn had done it. You sent a blackmail note to Kathlyn to get her to the studios, didn't you?"

"Your brother tried to make it look like suicide but only managed to make them think *he* was the one who shot George."

"And Leeder saw him. Did Leeder see *you* the night you shot your husband? Is that why he had to be killed?"

She wrinkled her nose. "He was a lecher, just like everybody says. He suspected something and was threatening to tell the police he'd seen me at the studio the night George was shot. It was his own fault. He insisted I meet him at the cage. He was going to film there the next day and he wanted to show me what a big strong guy he was. I decided he needed to go."

"And you thought if you could get Kathlyn Williams to show up at the same time you could shift the blame to her...for whatever you decided to do to Leeder, didn't you? You slipped a note into her purse at the roadhouse, demanding so much money she'd have to show up to try to plead with her blackmailer for more time."

"Who would have thought she could get $10,000 that night?" Babe asked. "Your brother, again. If he hadn't interfered, he wouldn't have suffered. It's his own fault. He could have written scenarios for *me*."

"So what happened when you met with Leeder at the cage? Did you intend all along to lock him in and leave him there with the leopards?"

"At first I just thought I could sweet talk him into keeping quiet...string him along a bit. We were in the big part of the cage and the leopards were in the smaller part, with the gate down. He was taunting them, trying to impress me. But then he started pawing at me and grabbing at my skirt. That I couldn't tolerate. So I jumped out of the cage and locked him in...he'd stupidly left the key in the lock. He started to say truly disgusting things to me...so I grabbed the rope and lifted the gate up. I left before the leopards got to him. I'd had enough."

I was horrified that she'd admitted so casually to causing Leeder's death. Her face remained perfectly calm and she patted her hair as she gazed at herself in the mirror.

"But that wasn't enough for you, was it? You still wanted to make the police think someone else was responsible. So you tried again at the party. You locked me in the cage and sent Kathlyn Williams down. You put something into my drink, didn't you?" She grinned. "Then you hit Kathlyn on the head so she'd be found there." I remembered those terrifying minutes in the leopards' cage. "And you teased the leopards with sticks to rile them. What kind of a monster are you?"

"I'm a film star," she said. "You're worse than your brother. You wouldn't see what was right in front of you...that Kathlyn Williams was the guilty one. You kept interfering." She took one hand off the gun to pull at her hair. Tresses fell to her shoulder, then she ripped the sash of her dress. "You and Kathlyn acted out the scene in the cage to try to save your brother and, when that didn't work, you came after me, just like the detective warned me you would."

"No," I said, holding still, afraid that any movement would provoke her to shoot. "Don't!"

She smiled. Suddenly, I heard a noise behind me. Her hand wavered and I dropped to the floor. I saw Whitbread's long arm reach out to grab the gun. They struggled. She shot, and I felt a huge mass fall on top of me. I screamed. Fitz groaned and rolled off me. He'd been hit.

Forty

H e's hit in the arm. Help me get him up," Whitbread said. He'd handcuffed Babe Greer, and handed her to one of the uniformed men, before kneeling over Fitz.

I got out of the way, as Whitbread and the other officer struggled to get Fitz onto the loveseat.

"Help me get his jacket off, then get me some towels," Whitbread said to his officer.

I moved in beside Fitz to prop him up while they pulled off his jacket and Whitbread ripped off his shirt sleeve.

Fitz groaned. His big head slipped onto my shoulder, as Whitbread and his man wrapped his arm tightly to stop the bleeding. The white silk of the loveseat was now stained with blood.

"She got me," Fitz said.

"You'll be all right," Whitbread replied. He took Fitz's unharmed left hand and placed it on the improvised bandage. "Hold that tight. It'll stop the bleeding. The bullet went straight through. You'll live."

Fitz closed his eyes as he squeezed his arm.

When Whitbread went off to order one of his men to find a doctor, I remembered what Stephen had said that morning. No wonder he'd warned me to look out for Fitz. Fitz opened his eyes.

"How did you come to be here?" I asked. "She would have killed me. You saved my life."

He smiled, then winced at the pain in his arm. Babe was weeping crocodile tears when Whitbread returned and directed that she be taken down to the waiting police van.

"It was Whitey," Fitz said. "He knew if he told you *not* to see Babe Greer, it would make you more determined to do exactly that." He sighed deeply and insisted on sitting up. I helped him.

Whitbread had purposely forbidden me to talk to Babe Greer, knowing I'd disobey him. I felt the roots of my hair tingle as a blush rose up my face. "Why?" I asked.

"Because, of course, Miss Greer would claim that she was also a victim of the blackmailer," Whitbread said.

A spectacled man carrying a leather satchel arrived, then pulled up a chair and began to unwrap the towel around Fitz's arm.

"This is Dr. Church. He'll patch you up," Whitbread explained.

"Oww," was Fitz's reply.

Whitbread frowned at him. "Relax, man, you'll be fine."

As the doctor worked on Fitz, the big Irishman got grumpy. Looking at the detective, he said, "You could have got her killed, Whitbread."

"She should have been safe enough. I had her followed, but my man lost her in the lobby. Nonetheless, we were back in the adjoining room, as planned, before anything happened."

"You said we'd have to wait," Fitz said.

"I had no idea she was already in the building."

"We could have been too late."

I looked up at Whitbread, who stood with his legs wide and his hands on his hips. "Why did you think she'd attack me?" I asked. I was glad Whitbread had expected it. I never would have been able to prove Babe Greer's guilt, even after I figured her story out. And I hadn't expected an attack. I'd been on the wrong track altogether, thinking Col. Selig was responsible. "How did you know *she* was the blackmailer?"

"Tell her about Alonzo Swift," Fitz said, then he set his teeth in a grimace as the doctor worked on him, cleaning the wound.

"Mr. Swift admitted to us that Babe Greer threatened to both expose the existence of his family back in Maryland and to get his films censored, if he didn't find a way to divorce his wife and become engaged to her."

"You knew that, before we brought you the photograph," I said. I remembered that we'd seen Alonzo Swift leaving the interview room at the police station when we arrived to present the photograph to Whitbread.

"Swift had seen her with the censor. He thought she was using Hyde to ruin the career of Miss Williams. He had no idea the man was actually her husband. If he'd known that, he could have resisted her threats by exposing her own marriage. She told him he would get the same treatment from the censor as Miss Williams if he didn't go along with their supposed romance...the romance that was designed to boost her career."

Fitz turned away from the doctor to look at me. His big face was unusually white. "Whitbread whipped her up when we came to show her the wedding picture. He knew how to get under her skin. He got her worried about what you might know and do, then he warned her that you might attack her. He put the idea in her head that she could get away with shooting you and say it was self-defense."

"Perhaps," Whitbread said. "But Mrs. Chapman was *not* shot and Alden can be released now. That *is* what you wanted, isn't it, Mrs. Chapman?"

Fitz looked up at the tall detective then winced again as the doctor began to stitch his wound.

I looked at Whitbread. He was standing with his arms folded across his chest. It was a cold stare he turned on me, not a friendly one, but I realized he'd staged this scene as the only way to clear my brother. "Thank you," I said.

"And now, Mrs. Chapman, you and your family are free to leave for the summer. I believe you planned to spend time at Woods Hole? I suggest, I very strongly suggest, that both you and Alden take your families and leave the city as soon as he's released. There are multiple witnesses to Miss Greer's confession. I assure you, you're not needed."

With that, he turned on his heel and left the room. I felt a vacuum when he was gone, as if he'd taken all the air with him and I had to struggle to breathe. Still, there was a lightness in my heart when I turned back to comfort Fitz. Whitbread was right. We could leave now and he was doing me a favor by letting me go. I was sad because I suspected it was more to get me out of his sight than as a favor that he'd released me, but I was relieved, nonetheless.

Forty-One

I was able to bring Alden back with me when I returned to Hyde Park, finally fulfilling the expectations of my family. I insisted on going to the police station myself to get him released. Fitz accompanied me, despite his wound and my protestations, going so far as to offer his motorcar to take us home after the driver dropped him at his town house.

"Thank you, Fitz. Are you sure you'll be all right?" I asked when we reached his door.

Alden helped him out of the car. His arm was in a sling. "You're very welcome. I'll be fine. Mrs. Murphy, my housekeeper, will rejoice in an excuse to fuss over me, believe me. I'm glad it's all worked out. You tell your husband I said we'll all be very happy when you're safely out of town. There's been quite enough excitement." He glanced up at the door of his house where an older lady in an apron was waiting. Then he bent to speak to me inside the motorcar. "Take care, Emily, and take care of that family of yours. We'll be wanting to see all of you when you're back in the fall." He straightened up. "When we've all had a chance to recover."

Wordlessly, he and Alden shook hands. Then he sighed and trudged to his door where the housekeeper immediately began clucking over him.

As we pulled away, Alden settled into the seat beside me. The atmosphere was strained. During the car ride from the station, Fitz and I had explained how Babe Greer's guilt was discovered.

Alden had hardly spoken during our tale. Even now, he seemed tense, as if he either didn't want to speak at all or had a dammed-up lake full of explanations he was waiting to pour out. I wasn't sure when I'd have another opportunity to talk to him alone, so I felt compelled to speak.

"Alden, we're all so relieved. Everyone was so worried about you." I looked out the window. "It'll be so good for everything to get back to normal." Everything had been so disrupted. We'd had to put off so many plans and it had been such a strain. I felt suddenly so much lighter. Spring blossoms left on the trees we passed looked lovely again, even more so than before. It was such a relief to have the worry lifted, like a dark veil that had been dropped over everything and was finally being raised.

Alden shifted in his seat. "Thank you for your help, Emily. I *am* grateful. Whitbread told me how you were locked in with the leopards. Babe Greer must be quite mad to do what she's done. But I must tell you there is no normal for me to go back to." After all of this, he was going to be difficult again.

"I don't know what you mean," I lied. I was ready to sulk.

"I'm not going back to newspapers. I'm going to California."

"Alden, after all you've put Clara through, you're still going to leave her?"

He was very pale. He must have been thinking about all this while he was alone in jail. "Emily, I know what I've done to Clara, but it's for her own good, and for the children, too. There's nothing for me here, don't you see that? I have a chance to do something, to *be* something, to do real work, even if *you* don't think it's real. Yes, it's a risk. I'm taking a chance by following Selig out to California but…can't you see? I'm dying here. I'm smothered. I can't live like this. I'm a failure."

I shrank back from the anger he was radiating. At least he was talking about following Col. Selig, not Kathlyn Williams. "What about Kathlyn Williams?" I asked. It slipped out. I didn't want to ask but I did.

He turned to stare at me with his big icy-blue eyes. "Emily, I told you. It's not Kathlyn Williams, it's *The Adventures of Kathlyn* I care about. Clara's the only woman I've ever loved but I've failed her. Don't you see? I can't bear to face her like this. I can't go on this way."

The motorcar reached Alden and Clara's house, and I could feel Alden's emotion as he looked up at his shiny black front door. I put a hand on his arm. "You have to talk to Clara," I said. "She loves you, Alden. You know that."

He nodded and climbed out of the car. I looked back as we drove away, unsure of what would happen to their family.

Forty-Two

Summer sunlight streamed through the high windows of Dearborn Station. Whistles, and the clacking of wheels, provided background noise to the hurrying crowds coming and going around us. Clara and I stood still, like a rock formation with people streaming by like water. Stephen and the boys had followed the truckload of Clara's luggage to the baggage car to see it properly stowed. Lizzie and Penny stood a few feet away, chattering happily. Unexpectedly enough, the children were excited about the move despite the fact that they'd be separated. Jack, Lizzie, and Tommy had already begun to nag us about planning a visit. Clara herself looked calm and regal in a cherry traveling suit with black velvet trim. She wore a new hat with a white plume that fluttered in the busy air of the train station.

I was the only one who was heartbroken. "Clara, I'll miss you so much!"

"I know, Emily, but I know you'll write and I promise I'll tell you all about California."

"Are you sure this is what you want?" I asked. I'd asked that question over and over again in the past week. Even during the family dinner held before Alden departed for California with Col. Selig and Kathlyn Williams, I couldn't help but express my doubts. The film people had packed up and disappeared like gypsies in the night. They were still making films in Chicago, but all the hubbub and interest was being drained away to Los

Angeles. Now, seeing Clara and her children off at the station, I resented the fact that Alden was not there to help them. I couldn't understand why she didn't.

It was true that Alden had been incredibly happy with Clara's decision to follow him to Los Angeles. He and the children had whooped for joy. But I was sad to see Clara sacrifice so much—her work, her studies, her house, the life they'd created in Chicago—she was leaving all of it behind. We'd seen each other nearly every day since I'd come to Chicago so many years before. Our children had played together and attended school together. I couldn't imagine the years that would pass now without our seeing each other.

Clara reached a gloved hand across to mine. "Emily, I can see this is hard for you. But you know things can't always stay the same." When I pouted, she shook her head. "Emily, as a scientist, I know that living organisms have to change to grow. Even us." She nodded in the direction of our daughters. "If we don't grow, we die. Think of it this way, in the spring I'm always having to dig up the hostas that have grown too big. I have to pull them up and divide them to replant them separately, otherwise they couldn't continue to grow. That's what we're doing now. It'll be painful but, in the end, it'll be good. You'll see. Growth and change are necessary to life."

"But, Clara, what about your work? You're going to California for Alden to do what he wants to do, but what about you? Isn't your work important, too? How can you give it up so easily?" I knew when I asked that, I was thinking for myself, as well as for Clara. I always had doubts about the time I spent away from my children. Was I wrong to pursue a career, instead of devoting myself completely to raising my children? Certainly, there were many people who thought so, but I'd always assumed Clara wasn't one of them. I thought she believed, as I did, that my work at Hull House and the university was every bit as necessary as my husband's. Was Clara ready to deny that now?

She pulled her hand away to reach into her pocket and bring out a letter. Smiling at me, she pressed it into my hand. "Do you remember Sarah Monks?"

"She was at Woods Hole that first summer," I said. I remembered a woman who was older than us and had devoted her life to biological study, even though she was not employed by a university and had not done a formal degree.

"I wrote to her. That's her response. It just came a few days ago. I haven't had a chance to tell you about it in all the frenzy. She's got a cottage on Terminal Island in Los Angeles Harbor. There's a field station there connected to the University of California. It's not as big as the laboratory at Woods Hole, but they're in summer session now. The children and I will stay with her, on the island, until we find a house near the Selig studios. Or, we may have a new house built."

The letter was full of enthusiastic plans for collecting specimens, laboratory work, lectures, and even picnics. Miss Monks obviously wanted to repay the hospitality she'd experienced at the Marine Biological Laboratory in Woods Hole so many years ago. I read it silently.

"I'm not giving up my work, Emily, it's just changing. I'm sure we'll want to consult with the scholars at Woods Hole. I'll be writing to you and Stephen about the work as soon as we get there. And, in the fall, we'll find schools for the children and work for me. I'm not giving up anything, Emily, and neither should you. What's a little distance to us in this age of rail travel and telephones?" A whistle blew close by. Clara embraced me. "Goodbye, my dear Emily, but not for so very long. We'll let you know how we're doing. At the very least, we'll be back for Christmas."

She strode away, down to where Stephen was helping Ollie into their carriage. Penny and Lizzie followed, but I stood there bereft. No matter how Clara tried to console me, I was sad to see them go.

Suddenly, Lizzie was by my side again. "Don't worry, Mama," she said. "We'll go out to see them. Col. Selig took the elephant and all the other animals. Besides, I'm going to be a film actress." Lizzie had been very impressed by the young actress she'd seen playing Dorothy in the *Wizard of Oz*. Ever since then, she'd declared her theatrical ambitions. Of course, that wasn't the first occupation she'd claimed to aspire to, and I wondered how many more there would be. The expression on my face must have alarmed her. "Oh, but not for a long time," she assured me. "Not till I'm sixteen, at least." She hugged me.

That made me laugh, despite the tears filling my eyes. Looking at Stephen and my sons still talking to Clara through the carriage window, I remembered the year my mother died. Alden and I returned to Boston and, along with our sister, Rose, we stayed at our mother's bedside for her last days. I remembered thinking, then, that it was as if a kaleidoscope was turning. Everything changed when our mother passed away. The entire beautiful pattern that had been our lives was gone in a second. It was true that a new pattern formed in its place. It was a pattern that included Stephen, and my children, and my life in Chicago. But the old pattern was gone forever, existing only in my memory.

The kaleidoscope was turning again. The days when the lives of Clara, Alden, and their children had intertwined with ours were gone. I knew from experience that a new pattern would emerge. But the one that was disappearing with the departure of that train would be gone forever. I watched the last car move out of the station and I cried. In the end, I allowed myself to be comforted by Stephen and the children, knowing our train for Woods Hole would leave the following morning.

Afterword

The idea for *Death at the Selig Studios* came to me when I attended the 2013 Chicago Book Expo, which was held at St. Augustine College in the Rogers Park neighborhood of Chicago. I was surprised to learn that the building we were in had once been a film studio for Essanay. At the Expo, Michael Corcoran and Arnie Bernstein, the authors of *Hollywood on Lake Michigan: 100+ Years of Chicago and the Movies* (2013), gave a presentation. Another recent book, *Flickering Empire: How Chicago Invented the U.S. Film Industry* (2015), by Michael Glover Smith and Adam Selzer, also describes the early Chicago filmmakers.

What captured my interest was the fact that silent films were being made in Chicago around the time the Emily Cabot mysteries are set, just before the industry moved out to California. One of the reasons this series is set at the turn of the nineteenth to the twentieth century is that was a time when the seeds were planted for many things that grew, and were later of huge importance, in the twentieth century. I hadn't realized that Chicago was the place where two of the earliest silent film producers made movies. Like the fields of social work and the sciences, which I portrayed in the earlier books of the series, the film industry continued to grow and become extremely influential over the course of the next century. It seemed like a perfect setting for Emily—and her friends and family—to confront another new technology.

When I began to do research, I found that both the Essanay and Selig Polyscope studios were active at the time. Eventually, I settled on the date of 1909, and I chose Selig as the setting, with Essanay in the background. The fact that Broncho Billy Anderson started at Selig, and then formed the competitive studio, was useful. The fact that Edison was feuding and litigating patent rights with other film companies at the time became a good conflict for the plot. I've taken some license with the timeline for the Motion Picture Patents Company agreement, which was actually signed a little earlier in the year than I portray it in this book. That 'trust' lasted until 1918. The fact that it restricted films to a single reel was one reason it was eventually abandoned. The Chicago studios were just about to move their operations to California, largely for the sunlight necessary to filming, and that circumstance was also quite useful to the plot.

Two books that were helpful in researching Col. Selig were *Col. William N. Selig: The Man Who Invented Hollywood* (Andrew Erish, 2013) and *Motion Picture Pioneer: The Selig Polyscope Company* (Kalton C. Lahue, 1973). In 1910, Selig moved to Los Angeles and took with him all the animals he'd purchased from the defunct circus. When the film company went under, he ran an animal park that was open to the public until it finally closed during the Great Depression.

Olga Celeste, the Leopard Lady, was a real person who worked in the film industry for many years, even working on the 1938 Katherine Hepburn film, *Bringing Up Baby*. Big Otto, Tom Mix, Otis Turner, and Tom Nash were actual people who worked for Selig. Mix went on to have a major Hollywood career, starring in over two hundred films for Selig.

I've taken some literary license with the timeline for Kathlyn Williams, whose main career at the Selig studios did not develop until after the time period of this novel. She did indeed star in *The Adventures of Kathlyn*, a thirteen-part serial filmed by the Selig studios, which was released in 1913. The scenario for the film was written by Gilson Willets.

Very few Selig Polyscope films remain from that time period. However, there are a few available on YouTube. *The Cowboy Millionaire* (starring Tom Mix, directed by Otis Turner, and released in 1909) is available at: https://www.youtube.com/watch?v=xKL1otPY_LY.

Selig's version of *The Wonderful World of Oz* can be seen here: https://www.youtube.com/watch?v=IB1D3MQTLY0. This production came about because L. Frank Baum had used the Selig studios to create films that were part of his presentation of *The Fairylogue and Radio Plays*, in which he presented a sort of travelogue of Oz using films, slides, and live actors. Those productions were not a financial success, and Baum couldn't pay Selig what he owed him, so Selig made a deal with him to produce the first *Wizard of Oz* film, which was released in 1910.

A much longer film, *The Spoilers*, was filmed by the Selig studios after their move to Los Angeles and released in 1914. It is a multi-reel film based on a novel by Rex Beach and stars Kathlyn Williams. It can be viewed at: https://www.youtube.com/watch?v=pojdDGvAaxE

Hunting Big Game in Africa was indeed produced by Selig in 1909, but no prints exist. The studio filmed it, waited for news that Roosevelt had shot a lion, then released it. They never claimed it was really Roosevelt in the film, but the artful depiction was far more popular than the more boring actual film clips from the real trip, which were released later.

Fred Busse was really the mayor of Chicago in 1909, but it was Edith Ogden Harrison, the wife of Chicago's five-term mayor, Carter H. Harrison, Jr., who had her novel *The Lady of the Snows* made into a film by Essanay in 1915. There was indeed a board for film censorship and Selig supported it, as he had a vision of film entertainment extending beyond the nickelodeons to a wider, more general audience. He wanted families to be able to watch the films, and he was a visionary in that, as in many things. George Hyde, Babe Greer, and Alonzo Swift are all fictional characters invented for this novel. Babe and Alonzo are loosely based on real people like Gloria Swanson and Francis X. Bushman, who were getting a start in Chicago films at the time this novel is set. Arnold Leeder is also fictional. What we would today call a "director" seems to have been referred to as a "producer" during the early days of the film industry. Also, the term "movies" was used to refer to people involved in the industry. It is interesting to discover how many of the procedures that are still prevalent in filmmaking were there right at the beginning. They would film a scene three times, then look at the negatives, before allowing the actors to go for the day, in case they had to re-shoot the scenes—much like what are now referred to as "rushes."

You can still see parts of three of the buildings mentioned in this book. The Selig building, minus the glass-walled studio on the top and the backlot, is at 3900 N. Claremont (near the intersection of Western and Irving Park). It now houses condo apartments. The Essanay building, at 1345 W. Argyle, is now the home of St. Augustine College. Just a few blocks away, the Green Mill Cocktail Lounge stands at the corner of Broadway and Lawrence, in what remains of Pop Morse's roadhouse.

Acknowledgments

As usual, many thanks to Emily Victorson, outstanding editor and publisher of Allium Press of Chicago. Also to the Boston Athenaeum, which once again helped me to obtain some of the books I used for research. Thanks to Sophie Powell and the participants in her Novel in Progress workshops at Grub Street in Boston, where I received useful reviews by my fellow authors. And thanks again to Nancy Braun and Anne Sharfman for being beta readers. I miss our old writing group.

The topic of this book is a little out of the way for my socially progressive character, Emily, but I hope it portrays one of the many powerful forces that were just beginning to make an impact on the world, which eventually became the one we live in now. I plan to continue with more stories of Emily and her family and friends in the new century, and I hope readers will continue to follow her adventures.

Notes from the Designer

The font used for the title of this book (including the chapter heads) is Good Bad Man, which was created in 2014 by the type designer Chank Diesel for use in the restoration of the 1916 silent film *The Good Bad Man* starring Douglas Fairbanks. For more information see: https://www.theatlantic.com/entertainment/archive/2014/07/a-font-that-speaks-for-silent-film/374197/

The text is set in Garamond.

The image of the Selig Polyscope studios at the front of this book was found here: https://www.atlasobscura.com/places/former-site-of-selig-polyscope-film-studios, although the citation given for it appears to be incorrect. No alternative source was determined.

ALSO PUBLISHED BY ALLIUM PRESS OF CHICAGO

Visit our website for more information:
www.alliumpress.com

THE EMILY CABOT MYSTERIES
Frances McNamara

Death at the Fair

The 1893 World's Columbian Exposition provides a vibrant backdrop for the first book in the series. Emily Cabot, one of the first women graduate students at the University of Chicago, is eager to prove herself in the emerging field of sociology. While she is busy exploring the Exposition with her family and friends, her colleague, Dr. Stephen Chapman, is accused of murder. Emily sets out to search for the truth behind the crime, but is thwarted by the gamblers, thieves, and corrupt politicians who are ever-present in Chicago. A lynching that occurred in the dead man's past leads Emily to seek the assistance of the black activist Ida B. Wells.

Death at Hull House

After Emily Cabot is expelled from the University of Chicago, she finds work at Hull House, the famous settlement established by Jane Addams. There she quickly becomes involved in the political and social problems of the immigrant community. But when a man who works for a sweatshop owner is murdered in the Hull House parlor, Emily must determine whether one of her colleagues is responsible, or whether the real reason for the murder is revenge for a past tragedy in her own family. As a smallpox epidemic spreads through the impoverished west side of Chicago, the very existence of the settlement is threatened and Emily finds herself in jeopardy from both the deadly disease and a killer.

Death at Pullman

A model town at war with itself…George Pullman created an ideal community for his railroad car workers, complete with every amenity they could want or need. But when hard economic times hit in 1894, lay-offs follow and the workers can no longer pay their rent or buy food at the company store. Starving and desperate, they turn against their once benevolent employer. Emily Cabot and her friend Dr. Stephen Chapman bring much needed food and medical supplies to the town, hoping they can meet the immediate needs of the workers and keep them from resorting to violence. But when one young worker—suspected of being a spy—is murdered, and a bomb plot comes to light, Emily must race to discover the truth behind a tangled web of family and company alliances.

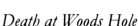

Death at Woods Hole

Exhausted after the tumult of the Pullman Strike of 1894, Emily Cabot is looking forward to a restful summer visit to Cape Cod. She has plans to collect "beasties" for the Marine Biological Laboratory, alongside other visiting scientists from the University of Chicago. She also hopes to enjoy romantic clambakes with Dr. Stephen Chapman, although they must keep an important secret from their friends. But her summer takes a dramatic turn when she finds a dead man floating in a fish tank. In order to solve his murder she must first deal with dueling scientists, a testy local sheriff, the theft of a fortune, and uncooperative weather.

Death at Chinatown

In the summer of 1896, amateur sleuth Emily Cabot meets two young Chinese women who have recently received medical degrees. She is inspired to make an important decision about her own life when she learns about the difficult choices they have made in order to pursue their careers. When one of the women is accused of poisoning a Chinese herbalist, Emily once again finds herself in the midst of a murder investigation. But, before the case can be solved, she must first settle a serious quarrel with her husband, help quell a political uprising, and overcome threats against her family. Timeless issues, such as restrictions on immigration, the conflict between Western and Eastern medicine, and women's struggle to balance family and work, are woven seamlessly throughout this mystery set in Chicago's original Chinatown.

Death at the Paris Exposition

In the sixth Emily Cabot Mystery, the intrepid amateur sleuth's journey once again takes her to a world's fair—the Paris Exposition of 1900. Chicago socialite Bertha Palmer has been named the only female U. S. commissioner to the Exposition and she enlists Emily's services as her social secretary. Their visit to the House of Worth for the fitting of a couture gown is interrupted by the theft of Mrs. Palmer's famous pearl necklace. Before that crime can be solved, several young women meet untimely deaths and a member of the Palmers' inner circle is accused of the crimes. As Emily races to clear the family name she encounters jealous society ladies, American heiresses seeking titled European husbands, and more luscious gowns and priceless jewels. Along the way, she takes refuge from the tumult at the country estate of Impressionist painter Mary Cassatt. In between her work and sleuthing, she is able to share the Art Nouveau delights of the Exposition, and the enduring pleasures of the City of Light, with her husband and their young children.

THE HANLEY & RIVKA MYSTERIES
D. M. Pirrone

Shall We Not Revenge

In the harsh early winter months of 1872, while Chicago is still smoldering from the Great Fire, Irish Catholic detective Frank Hanley is assigned the case of a murdered Orthodox Jewish rabbi. His investigation proves difficult when the neighborhood's Yiddish-speaking residents, wary of outsiders, are reluctant to talk. But when the rabbi's headstrong daughter, Rivka, unexpectedly offers to help Hanley find her father's killer, the detective receives much more than the break he was looking for. Their pursuit of the truth draws Rivka and Hanley closer together and leads them to a relief organization run by the city's wealthy movers and shakers. Along the way, they uncover a web of political corruption, crooked cops, and well-buried ties to two notorious Irish thugs from Hanley's checkered past. Even after he is kicked off the case, stripped of his badge, and thrown in jail, Hanley refuses to quit. With a personal vendetta to settle for an innocent life lost, he is determined to expose a complicated criminal scheme, not only for his own sake, but for Rivka's as well.

For You Were Strangers

On a spring morning in 1872, former Civil War officer Ben Champion is discovered dead in his Chicago bedroom—a bayonet protruding from his back. What starts as a routine case for Detective Frank Hanley soon becomes anything but, as his investigation into Champion's life turns up hidden truths best left buried. Meanwhile, Rivka Kelmansky's long-lost brother, Aaron, arrives on her doorstep, along with his mulatto wife and son. Fugitives from an attack by night riders, Aaron and his family know too much about past actions that still threaten powerful men—defective guns provided to Union soldiers, and an 1864 conspiracy to establish Chicago as the capital of a Northwest Confederacy. Champion had his own connection to that conspiracy, along with ties to a former slave now passing as white and an escaped Confederate guerrilla bent on vengeance, any of which might have led to his death. Hanley and Rivka must untangle this web of circumstances, amid simmering hostilities still present seven years after the end of the Civil War, as they race against time to solve the murder, before the secrets of bygone days claim more victims.

Honor Above All
J. Bard-Collins

Pinkerton agent Garrett Lyons arrives in Chicago in 1882, close on the trail of the person who murdered his partner. He encounters a vibrant city that is striving ever upwards, full of plans to construct new buildings that will "scrape the sky." In his quest for the truth Garrett stumbles across a complex plot involving counterfeit government bonds, fierce architectural competition, and painful reminders of his military past. Along the way he seeks the support and companionship of his friends— elegant Charlotte, who runs an upscale poker game for the city's elite, and up-and-coming architect Louis Sullivan. Rich with historical details that bring early 1880s Chicago to life, this novel will appeal equally to mystery fans, history buffs, and architecture enthusiasts.

◆

The Reason for Time
Mary Burns

On a hot, humid Monday afternoon in July 1919, Maeve Curragh watches as a blimp plunges from the sky and smashes into a downtown Chicago bank building. It is the first of ten extraordinary days in Chicago history that will forever change the course of her life. Racial tensions mount as soldiers return from the battlefields of Europe and the Great Migration brings new faces to the city, culminating in violent race riots. Each day the young Irish immigrant, a catalogue order clerk for the Chicago Magic Company, devours the news of a metropolis where cultural pressures are every bit as febrile as the weather. But her interest in the headlines wanes when she catches the eye of a charming streetcar conductor. Maeve's singular voice captures the spirit of a young woman living through one of Chicago's most turbulent periods. Seamlessly blending fact with fiction, Mary Burns weaves an evocative tale of how an ordinary life can become inextricably linked with history.

Set the Night on Fire
Libby Fischer Hellmann

Someone is trying to kill Lila Hilliard. During the Christmas holidays she returns from running errands to find her family home in flames, her father and brother trapped inside. Later, she is attacked by a mysterious man on a motorcycle...and the threats don't end there. As Lila desperately tries to piece together who is after her and why, she uncovers information about her father's past in Chicago during the volatile days of the late 1960s...information he never shared with her, but now threatens to destroy her. Part thriller, part historical novel, and part love story, *Set the Night on Fire* paints an unforgettable portrait of Chicago during a turbulent time: the riots at the Democratic Convention...the struggle for power between the Black Panthers and SDS...and a group of young idealists who tried to change the world.

A Bitter Veil
Libby Fischer Hellmann

It all began with a line of Persian poetry . . . Anna and Nouri, both studying in Chicago, fall in love despite their very different backgrounds. Anna, who has never been close to her parents, is more than happy to return with Nouri to his native Iran, to be embraced by his wealthy family. Beginning their married life together in 1978, their world is abruptly turned upside down by the overthrow of the Shah and the rise of the Islamic Republic. Under the Ayatollah Khomeini and the Republican Guard, life becomes increasingly restricted and Anna must learn to exist in a transformed world, where none of the familiar Western rules apply. Random arrests and torture become the norm, women are required to wear hijab, and Anna discovers that she is no longer free to leave the country. As events reach a fevered pitch, Anna realizes that nothing is as she thought, and no one can be trusted... not even her husband.

Where My Body Ends and the World Begins
Tony Romano

On December 1, 1958, a devastating blaze at Our Lady of the Angels School in Chicago took the lives of ninety-two children, shattering a close-knit Italian neighborhood. In this eloquent novel, set nearly a decade later, twenty-year-old Anthony Lazzeri struggles with survivor's guilt, which is manifested through conflicted feelings about his own body. Complicating his life is a retired detective's dogged belief that Anthony was involved in the setting of the fire. Tony Romano's delicate handling of Anthony's journey is deeply moving, exploring the complex psychological toll such an event has on those involved, including families...and an entire community. This multi-faceted tale follows Anthony's struggles to come to terms with how the events of that day continue to affect him and those around him. Aided by a sometime girlfriend, a former teacher, and later his parents—after long buried family secrets are brought into the open—he attempts to piece together a life for himself as an adult.

FOR YOUNGER READERS

Her Mother's Secret
Barbara Garland Polikoff

Fifteen-year-old Sarah, the daughter of Jewish immigrants, wants nothing more than to become an artist. But as she spreads her wings she must come to terms with the secrets that her family is only beginning to share with her. Replete with historical details that vividly evoke the Chicago of the 1890s, this moving coming-of-age story is set against the backdrop of a vibrant, turbulent city. Sarah moves between two very different worlds—the colorful immigrant neighborhood surrounding Hull House and the sophisticated, elegant World's Columbian Exposition. This novel eloquently captures the struggles of a young girl as she experiences the timeless emotions of friendship, family turmoil, loss…and first love.

A companion guide to *Her Mother's Secret*
is available at www.alliumpress.com. In the guide you will find
resources for further exploration of Sarah's time and place.

City of Grit and Gold
Maud Macrory Powell

The streets of Chicago in 1886 are full of turmoil. Striking workers clash with police…illness and injury lurk around every corner…and twelve-year-old Addie must find her way through it all. Torn between her gruff Papa—who owns a hat shop and thinks the workers should be content with their American lives—and her beloved Uncle Chaim—who is active in the protests for the eight-hour day—Addie struggles to understand her topsy-turvy world, while keeping her family intact. Set in a Jewish neighborhood of Chicago during the days surrounding the Haymarket Affair, this novel vividly portrays one immigrant family's experience, while also eloquently depicting the timeless conflict between the haves and the have-nots.

A companion guide to *City of Grit and Gold*
is available at www.alliumpress.com. In the guide you will find
resources for further exploration of Addie's time and place.

CPSIA information can be obtained
at www.ICGtesting.com
Printed in the USA
FFOW03n0906210518
46706187-48832FF